Lee Jackson lives in London with his partner joanne. His first book, *London Dust*, was nominated for the Ellis Peters Historical Dagger Award. He is fascinated by the social history of Victorian London and spends much of his time on the ongoing development of his website www.victorianlondon.org

Praise for *A Metropolitan Murder*

'Once again Mr Jackson has succeeded in creating the atmosphere of nineteenth-century London'
Sunday Telegraph

'[Lee Jackson] demonstrates quite brilliantly what the genre can do. This is a rare and succulent piece of work. It's a sure thing that he'll go on to do better.'
Literary Review

'The smoky, foggy, horse-dung laden atmosphere of the London streets steams off the page'
Spectator

'*A Metropolitan Murder* is stuffed full of authentic details of London in the mid-nineteenth century, with special reference to the criminal underworld. The numerous sights, sounds and smells all help to recreate an atmospheric snapshot of Victorian life. Lee Jackson then skillfully blends these minutiae into his racy and pacy plot.'
Historical Novels Review

Praise for *London Dust*

'Full of power and substance, *London Dust* is an assured debut . . . a compelling and evocative novel that brings the past, and its dead, to life again'
Guardian

'This is a novel to read and savour. *London Dust* is a remarkable achievement and, for a first novel, a quite staggering one'
Birmingham Post

'Victorian London is vividly brought to life in this short novel . . . for an atmospheric picture of the period it's hard to beat'
Sunday Telegraph

Also by Lee Jackson

London Dust

A
METROPOLITAN
MURDER

by

Lee Jackson

arrow books

Published by Arrow Books in 2004

3 5 7 9 10 8 6 4 2

First published in the United Kingdom in 2004 by William Heinemann

Arrow Books
The Random House Group Limited
20 Vauxhall Bridge Road, London, SW1V 2SA

Random House Australia (Pty) Limited
20 Alfred Street, Milsons Point, Sydney,
New South Wales 2061, Australia

Random House New Zealand Limited
18 Poland Road, Glenfield,
Auckland 10, New Zealand

Random House (Pty) Limited
Endulini, 5a Jubilee Road, Parktown 2193, South Africa

The Random House Group Limited Reg. No. 954009

www.randomhouse.co.uk

A CIP catalogue record for this book
is available from the British Library

Papers used by Random House are natural, recyclable products made
from wood grown in sustainable forests. The manufacturing processes
conform to the environmental regulations of the country of origin

ISBN 0 09 944022 4

Typeset by Palimpsest Book Production Limited,
Polmont, Stirlingshire
Printed and bound in the United Kingdom by
Bookmarque Ltd, Croydon, Surrey

PART ONE

PART ONE

CHAPTER ONE

THE METROPOLITAN THUNDERS headlong through the tunnel, spewing smoke and churning up dust. Roaring towards King's Cross, it passes a series of peculiar alcoves lit by solitary yellow lamps, the haunt of subterranean railwaymen who loiter in their man-made hollows. They are waiting for the last train, these slouching shadows with flashing white eyes, waiting until they can begin their nightly work upon the tracks.

'Almost on time, Bill?' remarks one to another.

'I reckon,' says his comrade, dourly.

The Metropolitan hurtles onwards, station to station, burrowing beneath the New Road, under-mining the trade of the humble hackney carriage and omnibus, quite oblivious to the slow and weary tread of pedestrians who tramp the street above. For some of them, the price of a return ticket is simply unat-tainable; for others, the Underground Railway retains a daemonic aspect, and many swear that they would rather brave the worst of London's winter than descend into a man-made pit. No matter, says the rail-wayman at work below their feet. He *never pays no heed* to such ignorance from the surface-dwellers, though he readily admits the train goes like the devil, vomiting smoke from the throat of its funnel, spewing burning ash that rises like bile and sparks against smoke-blackened bricks. At least, he says, the Railway pays good wages, and it keeps you warm and dry, and goes double-quick to where it must go. In point of fact, he says, the Metropolitan goes as fast as a man may safely travel without endangering his health. True, he finds that no-one nowadays is much impressed by the facts or figures, and new lines are being planned to here, there and everywhere. But this line will remain the oldest and, therefore, the most famous by far. This is the Metropolitan Line. And this is the last train of the day.

Who takes the last train? Let us take a look at the rear compartment, designated *second class*. Scattered upon cloth-covered benches (a thin, uncompromising layer of cloth, mind you) sit half a dozen private persons, whose means or inclination do not encourage them to pay a sixpence for the well-padded privileges of *first*. In one corner there is a young girl, a pretty but rather shabby creature, with red hair tied up clumsily with a single ribbon; she lies slumped asleep, her head against the wall. In truth she is rather too shabby, her shawl too threadbare and frayed, even for *second*. All the same, some of her fellow passengers quite envy her. At the very least, she need not affect to read the advertisements that have been pasted to the walls of the carriage, whereas, for most railway travellers, there is a positive obligation to cultivate such distractions.

On the other side of the aisle, for instance, a fresh-faced maid-servant finds herself obliged to make a point of straightening her sleeves and ignoring the gaze of the handsome guardsman who sits opposite, smoking his pipe and absent-mindedly stroking his whiskers. Admittedly, the guardsman is not in uniform, but she would know a soldier anywhere; she

4

is quite familiar with that breed of men, and does not wish to fall in love with another. In any case, sitting next to the maid-servant is her mistress, which, fortunately, prevents any unhappy dalliance. Indeed, the good lady needs constant attention; she is a poor traveller, given to raising her eyes heavenwards (or, at least, up to the ground) with every chance reverberation that rattles the compartment, her hands firmly clasped together in silent prayer. So great, in fact, is her anxiety that her unfashionably large crinoline seems to tremble quite of its own accord. She too affects to take no notice of her fellow passengers, but she cannot resist the occasional glance. She is particularly struck by a peculiar young man, who is seated opposite the sleeping girl; he wears a grubby winter great-coat, and pencils notes in a little leather-bound book as the train rolls along. But then he looks up at her, and nods a polite acknowledgement, thus deflecting her interest back to the heavens. When a decent space of time has elapsed, she looks back in his general direction. She observes the sleeping girl, who lolls this way and that, her face half-hidden by her shawl; the girl, she realises, smells of gin.

Tut tut, she mutters, raising her eyebrows and silently encouraging her maid into making similar expressions of heartfelt opprobrium; she willingly obliges.

But, stop! A roar of steam and the brakes do their work as the train approaches Baker Street, as the track splits, past the glimpse of another train, another tunnel, then juddering to a stop amongst what seems like a thousand gas-lamps. And here is the gloomy face of a booking-office boy in his navy uniform, deputised to stand duty upon the platform and to check the contents of each compartment. He begins, once the train is quite stopped, by opening the doors one by one, regardless of whether there are passengers inside the carriage.

'Terminating here, ladies and gents, as there is works at Paddington. This way, ladies and gentlemen, if you please.'

'Disgraceful!' says one. 'Short-changed!' says another. Muted complaints all round.

The booking-office clerk looks sheepish, and shrugs his shoulders. 'A letter,' he says, 'a letter to the station-master is best, if you are dissatisfied.' He says it once, twice, half a dozen times. And, in the end, it proves sufficient. Gradually, the train is emptied of passengers: top-hatted, lop-sided clerks, drunk and sober, merry and miserable; a troup of fine ladies, fresh from the Temperance Hall; theatre-goers; music-hallers; men, women and children, first class, second class, all mixed together. In short, anyone who has paid their fare.

But what is this? It seems that the rear compartment takes a little longer to empty than the rest. True, the guardsman departs briskly enough. Indeed, he is too quick for the liking of the young maid-servant, who promptly decides she did not like him at all. And then comes her be-crinolined mistress, a perfect pantomime of confusion as her circumference is squeezed through the passenger door, pushed by the maid, pulled by the guard. But, even then, two remain: the drunken woman and bookish young man.

'Sir, end of the line, if you please? Last train terminates at Baker Street tonight. There's works at Paddington.'

'Oh, I am sorry, I lost track of myself.'

He looks around, as if woken from a dream. The young woman with the ribbon in her hair lies fast asleep.

'Shall I wake my, ah, fellow traveller here?' he offers.

'If you wouldn't mind, sir, much appreciated.'

'Of course.'

The young man puts away his notebook in his great-coat, and leans over to the slumbering girl, tugging gently at her sleeve. She makes no movement, and so he smiles apologetically at the booking-hall clerk, and he tugs a little harder. She leans a little forward, then topples to the side, falling down from her seat, landing head first on to the dusty wooden floor of the carriage. There she lies, without a murmur, her neck askew, her features quite lifeless and dead, staring blankly at the man who pushed her over.

'Lor!' exclaims the clerk, unsure whether to get inside the carriage or stay well clear. In the end, he adopts the latter option. 'Lor! You've killed her.'

The young man, meanwhile, shakes his head, though it is impossible to tell whether in denial or simple disbelief. He kneels down and touches her face. Cold.

'Murder!' cries the clerk. And the cry goes out, along the platform, echoing down the mouths of dark and dingy tunnels; but, by now, there is hardly a soul to hear him. A couple of the last passengers turn and look, but hurry on up the steps to finish their journey home. The young man in the carriage, meanwhile, stands for a moment quite frozen. Then he darts forward, his notebook falling from his pocket as he does so. He runs through the open carriage door, pushing past the boy, who dares to offer no resistance, and up the steps that lead to the ticket hall.

The clerk stares at the lifeless body.

'Murder!' he exclaims rather weakly, his voice giving way.

CHAPTER TWO

MIDNIGHT.

Let us put Baker Street behind us, for now, and travel eastwards a mile or two, to the venerable square of Lincoln's Inn Fields. In an unassuming house in a side street near that ancient enclosure, sits a woman working by lamp-light. Her name is Miss Philomena Sparrow, and she is bent over a ledger marked 'February Accounts'. Dockets and invoices lie scattered around her writing desk, and her face is a picture of intense concentration. Indeed, it is only when a clock strikes twelve – the grandfather clock that sits in the hallway adjoining her study – that she looks up from her task, quite astonished by the lateness of the hour. Reluctantly she removes her reading glasses and rubs her eyes. She appears a little anxious, but any private thoughts she may possess are interrupted by raised voices beyond her door, echoing from an upstairs landing. She frowns, massaging her brow with the tips of her fingers. After a moment or two she takes a deep breath, then, straightening her back, gets up to walk to the door.

'Jenny?' she calls, standing in the hallway.

'Ma'am?' replies a girl in nurse's uniform, who swiftly descends the stairs to meet her.

'What's that noise?'

'Agnes White, ma'am. She's very restless. Says she wants her medicine again.'

'More? Please remind her of the fifth Rule of the House: Temperance In All Things. I swear, it was her daughter that did it; she has quite unsettled her. I have remarked upon it before. She is always the worse for seeing people.'

'Yes, ma'am.'

'Tell Agnes White that we are a refuge, not a druggist's. She will have no medicine until tomorrow, at the appointed time. And you may tell her that if she gives any more trouble we shall review her letter of recommendation.'

'Yes, ma'am. Will you really, ma'am?'

'No, no, I suppose that I will not, but tell her that, all the same. And there is no sign of Sally Bowker, I suppose?'

'No, ma'am, no sign. Not since after tea.'

'I had hopes of Bowker, Jenny. Why would she break the curfew?'

'Sorry, ma'am. Don't know, ma'am.'

Miss Philomena Sparrow sighs to herself, dismisses the nurse, and walks wearily to her bedroom at the rear of the house. Above the door is a motto, a piece of intricate Gothic needlework, mounted behind glass in a wooden frame, the proud achievement of a previous resident, or perhaps of a previous Lady Superintendent, like herself:-

Home Sweet Home.
Holborn Refuge for Penitent Women.

———

Agnes White sits upon the edge of her bed. She is not an old woman; her age is no more than forty years, but she does not wear it well. Her face, in particular, is gaunt and lined, her complexion sallow, which gives her a wan appearance that is only heightened by her long jet-black hair that falls loose over the dirty white nightgown provided by her nurses. Her eyes, morever, seem almost vacant.

What time is it? Who's that?

'Hulloa, ma.'

'Lizzie?'

It is a twelvemonth since she last saw her daughter, but she would know her own flesh and blood anywhere. And how she has grown!

But what time is it? This is quite wrong. Lizzie cannot be here. Not now.

'Hulloa, ma. I've come back to see you.'

Was it before? She cannot recall.

'Ma? Can you hear me? What's this? Is it your medicine? You're confused, ain't you? Is that what they're feeding you?'

It helps me rest up, she says. No, wait a moment, does she speak? Perhaps she only thinks she is speaking. It is hard to say.

'Ma? You're asleep, ain't you?'

What time is it?

Ah, she thinks, that is all right. I am already asleep.

❧

'Agnes?'

What time is it?

Tea-time? No, that was earlier as well. This afternoon.

❧

Tea-time. Twenty girls saying their prayers.

'Our Father who art a Heathen,' whispers Agnes White.

There, that's done.

'Pardon me, Aggie, dear.'

Agnes watches Sally Bowker excuse herself and leave the table. Miss Sparrow's little pet, they call her, the other girls. Pretty little Silly Sally. Agnes dislikes her intensely; she puts on airs and graces, even though everyone knows she would snap open her legs wider than the Thames Tunnel for a kiss and a kind word. Pardon me, indeed!

Sally curtsies to Miss Sparrow, and makes her way upstairs. Agnes leaves it a moment, then gets up and follows her.

Odd. It is a different house from what she had expected; the stairs seem quite out of place. No matter.

'Goin' out?'

Sally has on her best cotton print, and her red hair tied up loosely with an old maroon ribbon, fraying at both ends. She wraps her shawl around her shoulders; it is a dirty old rag, thinks Agnes White, and it suits her. Dirt cheap.

'Mind your own,' replies the girl, turning on her heels and going into the street, closing the door behind her.

Agnes follows her, traipsing down the steps on to the pavement.

But it is the wrong street entirely; it is not Serle Street, the well-ordered terrace upon the corner of Lincoln's Inn Fields, that daily rebukes the Refuge for Penitent Women with its polished front steps and brass name-plates. It is entirely different: it is not quite like any street in particular, and something like several streets in general. In fact it is narrow and cramped, more of an alley, the sort of place Agnes White used to take the men and boys, or they took her, between the warehouses by Wapping High Street.

Familiar enough.

She walks along nervously, stumbling a little over

the muddy and uneven cobbles, wondering how she has come to be so far from home. There is no gas here, of course, nor any light from any of the warehouses, and there is a mist rising from the river.

Wait. A noise.

Tap, tap, tap, tap. The sound of boots on the stones behind her. It cannot be Sally; she doesn't even have a decent pair of boots. She cannot see anyone. Best to keep walking.

Tap, tap, tap, tap.

Closer now, feet walking briskly, catching up, hot breath on her neck. A cold hand around her throat.

Then falling, falling, falling.

———

'Agnes?'

'Agnes? Are you awake?'

Agnes White wakes up coughing, her throat so tight she cannot find the strength to sit up. Her skin is cold and clammy, her sheets damp with sweat. The girl helps her up, raising her pillow.

'Lizzie?' she says, spluttering the word.

'No, Aggie, it's me, Jenny. You know me, don't you?'

She nods, looking blearily at the nurse.

'You were dreaming. I'd only just got you off, then you woke me up. You'll wake the Missus and all, if you're not careful.'

Agnes coughs again, a rackety chest-heaving cough, hunching her shoulders so tight they are visible through her gown, like knives embedded in her skin.

'Don't talk, you'll do yourself an injury. Look, here, I brought some of your medicine. The Missus said I shouldn't, but . . . well, anyhow. Shall I pour it for you?'

Agnes White nods, and so the girl carefully measures the liquid from the bottle and presents a spoonful to her charge. Agnes leans forward, and willingly swallows the thick brown treacle, like an eager child. It tastes of burnt sugar, and it slips down her throat so easily that she immediately wants more, nudging the girl's arm, urging her to dole out another helping. The nurse shakes her head, putting the bottle aside.

'Steady now. Half of it's gone already.'

Agnes says nothing. She can feel the dollop of glutinous liquid travelling through her body, falling into the pond of her stomach, and rippling outwards. The soporific effect of the laudanum mixture spreads through her like the warmth of a fire on a cold day; it cossets her, drags her limbs down into the bed, and closes her eyes.

'There,' says Jenny, 'that's better, my dear, ain't it? The Missus said your gal upset you, coming here like that. That right, is it?'

Agnes nods, exhausted, falling asleep once more, though her throat is still awfully sore.

CHAPTER THREE

'MURDER!'

Outside Baker Street railway station, a young man named Henry Cotton runs as fast as he has ever run. It is fortunate for him that he is young and fit. He darts with impunity between the cabs that stand in the gas-lit rank outside Baker Street, and then out across the Marylebone Road. He does not pay any heed to the passing traffic, and looks neither left nor right in his headlong progress. Likewise, he does not turn back, not even for an instant, to listen to the distant shouts that echo inside the station. He merely dashes onwards, his coat flapping around him, as if driven by some primitive instinct for survival, faltering only when he slips in the viscous mud that lines the road. His arms flail wildly in the air, but he does not fall; instead, he rushes onwards, breathless and frantic, into the shadows.

Of course, his flight does not go unnoticed, but his figure soon disappears from the view of those in pursuit. Moreover, if no-one is quite certain of the direction that he takes, it is not surprising; he himself has no inkling of the name of the road down which he turns, nor why he then chooses another turning, and then another again. In fact, he barely possesses any true impression of the world about him for several minutes until a terrible shortness of breath finally brings him to a halt.

When he has finally gathered his senses he finds himself to be in a well-kept mews, a sloping cobbled side street where the horses and carriages of neighbouring properties are safely stabled under lock and key. He leans forward against a wall, his lungs bursting, and braces himself against the overpowering dizziness that suddenly sweeps over him. It is impossible to say quite how long he stands there, stock-still, listening to the pounding of his heart.

A horse snorts loudly in one of the stables, no doubt woken from its sleep. Henry Cotton starts at the sound and stumbles on, along the length of the mews, half tripping, here and there, on the uneven stones. He comes to the opposite entrance of the secluded passage, which opens out on to another thoroughfare. A single jet of gas from a nearbly street-lamp illuminates the scene, and the light shows up the thick mud that clings to his trousers.

He takes a breath, then sets off briskly along the way. After a few yards realises he has turned on to Marylebone High Street.

━━

'Murder?'
  'Aye – look at that, won't you?'
  'Lor! And he ran clear off?'
  'Like a regular devil.'

━━

Henry Cotton keeps up his pace, walking with a determined gait. There is a chill wind, and he pulls the collar of his great-coat tight around his neck, keeping his head down, staring at the pavement.

He finds that Marylebone High Street, a bustling

place by day, possesses none of its diurnal vigour during the hours of darkness. Even the gas-lights seem gloomy, and Cotton passes a mere handful of pedestrians, representatives of the ragged and homeless tribe that wander the streets in the small hours. Their very presence seems almost oppressive. A squat dark-haired fellow, leaning against a wall, an Irishman by his appearance, eyes him with suspicion as he goes past. Two others, hunched in conversation, beetle past, crossing to the other side of the street; he wonders, for a moment, whether they do so in order to avoid him. None of them ventures to ask him for money; he is too dishevelled for that. He tries to brush some of the muck from his trouser legs, but the effort only smears the filth about and dirties his hands.

Turning up his collar once more, he keeps walking, fast as he is able. It is not long before he turns off the street, into the roads that lead through to the Regent's Circus. Here and there, in a handful of the houses, a light still burns in the parlour or bedroom, a hint of warmth behind firmly closed shutters or curtains. But the night air is cold as ice, and, as he walks, he notices the waning moon that hangs in the sky. Time and again, it vanishes behind the rooftops then reappears; but something in its cold grey pallor reminds him of the girl's face, lying upon the floor of the train, and its light seems horribly unwelcome.

——

'Has someone gone for the peelers?'
   A nod.
   'He won't get far.'

——

A black cab, smart and polished, hurtles along Portland Place towards the park at top speed, the sound of the horse's hooves beating a swift clipping rhythm. Henry Cotton waits for it to pass. Only once it has gone by does he spy the police constable standing opposite. The policeman is preoccupied in talking to a girl, a demi-mondaine in a garish emerald dress, who loiters at his side. She touches the constable's cheek coquettishly, and holds on to his arm as if they were stepping out together. None the less, the constable is sensible enough to the world around him to spare Henry Cotton a quick glance, leaving Cotton no option but to proceed across the road.

'Evening, sir,' says the constable, examining him with a more leisurely gaze.

'Good evening, officer.'

'You need any assistance, sir?' he replies, looking down at Henry Cotton's mud-spattered trousers, and raising an enquiring eyebrow.

'Only a change of clothes when I get home. I slipped crossing the road. Foolish of me.'

The policeman smiles. 'Well, you be careful, sir. Never worth hurrying to your death, is it?'

'Yes, well, indeed. Good night to you.'

The constable nods, satisfied with the progress of his enquiries. He has already returned to his conversation with the woman, even as Henry Cotton turns to take leave of him.

In five minutes more, walking at a good pace, Cotton stands at the door of his lodgings, a terrace in Castle Street. He surveys the road on both sides, making sure there is no-one watching. Once he is satisfied, he scrapes his boots, turns his key in the lock to let himself in, then quietly ascends the stairs.

The room itself is a small one, situated on the top floor, furnished in the Spartan style that suits many London landlords, if not their tenants. Cotton sits himself down upon the bed. The only light is from the flaring of the gas in the street below, which emits a residual luminescence that filters through the sash window. Even so, he can still make out that there is mud on the rug, which he will have to clean away; on the stairs outside too, no doubt. Instinctively, he reaches to remove his hat, and he realises he is not wearing it.

His memory stabs at him, his stomach turning, at the thought of the dead girl.

He left his hat upon the train.

Along with his notebook.

Chapter Four

By day, the station at Baker Street is warmed by the constant human traffic that streams through the concourse, down to the platforms, and back up again. If the weather is dismal, and the clever arrangement of skylights set into the vaulted roof of the station affords no daylight, then the gas will be turned on, and the traveller may be cheered by the bright glowing globes that hang like baubles above his head. There is even some warmth to be had, on frost-bitten mornings, from the furnace of a train at a standstill, or in the steam that belches out as the train departs, and condenses in rivulets on the damp brickwork. By night, however, Baker Street becomes less temperate; there is often no gas in the pipes, even if it were wanted, and the few men who work on the track carry oil-lamps, and wear the thickest of winter coats. To the station's night-watchman who, on occasion, sees them in the distance, they seem like fleeting yellow spectres, ghostly fire-flies that come and go in the tunnels, though he will readily admit he possesses a fanciful imagination. Tonight, however, the watchman has no opportunity to indulge his fancies. Rather he finds that the platform has not been cleared, and the last train has not moved on to its nocturnal rest. Instead, there is a tall, burly policeman, grave and sullen, at the station entrance, and a gang of half a dozen or more of his uniformed comrades, each bearing a bull's-eye lantern, standing upon the platform, either peering into the nearby railway carriage, or engaged in casual conversation. The watchman walks down and mingles amongst them.

'They'll get an inspector down here, won't they, sergeant?' asks a young constable, addressing an older man who stands beside him as he shuffles his feet in a vain attempt to keep out the cold.

'Oh, yes, my boy,' replies the sergeant, 'they'll send for someone, all right. They won't leave a mess like this to the man what found her, who was just doing his duty, will they? Too simple.'

'Did you find her, sir?'

'I happened to be first here, yes. But, you've got to understand,' he adds, sarcastically, 'the likes of us ain't suitable for brain work, you see?'

Such talk goes on for an hour or more; nothing much is done, nothing of great significance is truly said. It is perhaps two o'clock in the morning before a shout goes out to the men upon the platform, who, after interrogating the watchman, have long since found a stove, and each acquired a steaming cup of coffee.

'Look lively, someone's coming,' exclaims a voice from the ticket hall.

'Who is it, then?'

'Hmph! Can't you hear it? I don't bleedin' believe it.'

'Hear what?'

'That! It's Webb, ain't it? They've gone and got Webb. What odds do you give us, eh?'

At the mention of this name, a couple of the older policemen laugh and exchange knowing looks; a couple more give vent to choice expletives. The young constable, who spoke earlier to the sergeant, puts down his coffee and hurries up the steps to the ticket hall.

It is undoubtedly an odd noise, coming along the empty road: a tinny rattling sound, the sound of thin, iron-shod wheels, unlike any normal cart or carriage. The young constable pushes forward to see the source of excitement: a man balancing precariously on a two-wheeled crank-driven velocipede, peddling at full tilt towards the station. Indeed, the constable cannot help but smile; he has seen one or two similar contraptions in the parks, but generally ridden by young men far too eager to show off their agility, or bruises, to promenading young ladies. The rider in this case, however, bicycling along the surface of the Marylebone Road, jostled up and down with every rotation of the wheels, is a stout policeman in his late forties.

'God help us, it's Webb all right,' whispers the sergeant, sardonically. 'The Boneshaker Bobby.'

'He's a bleedin' inspector,' says another man, 'and he'll hear you.'

'Hush.'

Decimus Webb leans deftly on the front wheel of the velocipede and rounds towards the station. He is not a handsome man by any means, but has a mop of brown curly hair, which peeks uncontrollably from under his helmet, a fulsome bearded face, and large heavily lidded eyes. The latter, in particular, seem to possess a rather mournful quality, quite suited to his work, and in his expression he resembles nothing so much as a jowly old hunting dog. Yet, despite his progress on the bicycle being rather comical, his red-faced physical exertion in odd contrast with his rather languid features, in all fairness he still manages to swing the vehicle over towards the station in a graceful arc.

It is a feat that is marred only by the slight look of nerves as he alights, swinging his left leg over the frame, and dropping on to the pavement. Somewhat breathless, he does not say a word until he has parked his conveyance up against the station wall and dusted himself down.

He looks round at the assembly of men in blue, and frowns.

'You'll be issued one of these soon enough,' he says, gesturing at the bicycle, 'mark my words. Excellent machine. Monsieur Michaux, of Paris.'

'I ain't riding that Frog contraption,' mutters the sergeant.

Webb hears the comment, but ignores it. 'Sergeant Watkins, is it?'

'Yes, sir,' answers the reluctant sergeant.

'Well, Sergeant Watkins,' Webb says, speaking slowly and mordantly, looking over the men standing before him, 'I can only assume that we are anticipating a riot?' He pauses for effect. 'Some uprising of subterranean socialists, perhaps?'

'A riot, sir? I don't take your meaning.'

'Why else should I find half of D and X Division defending Baker Street railway station? Tell me, sergeant, if you will, how many men have you here?'

A couple of the men behind the sergeant sheepishly put down their coffee mugs. Watkins himself blushes a little.

'Well, sir, on a serious matter like this, naturally a couple of lads came when I whistled and . . .'

Webb sighs, a deep exhalation of breath, shaking his head. The sergeant falls silent.

'Organise it properly, sergeant, will you? So that it does not resemble a tea-party?'

'Very good, sir.'

'And perhaps,' continues Decimus Webb, in an exaggerated tone of exasperation, 'when you are quite done, I may look at this body. And you, constable . . .'

'Sir?' says the young man eagerly.

'Do keep your eye on my "boneshaker", won't you?'

'This is how she was found, is it?'

Decimus Webb stands over the woman's body.

'Yes, sir, exactly,' says the booking clerk, standing behind him. 'Well, at least, when he pushed her over . . .'

'Hush, my good man, hush. We have not reached that juncture,' says Webb. 'At least she has not been moved, that is something. Now, what time did the train leave Farringdon Street?'

'It would be half-past eleven, sir.'

'And stopping at all stations in between, no doubt.' The man nods. 'Every one, sir.'

'There were others in this carriage when it arrived, besides the fellow who ran? It is second class, is it not?'

'Yes, sir, it is. I saw a few others, I saw a man, a couple of women . . .'

'And, of course, you let them simply depart?'

'They were gone before I knew, sir, really, I had no time to collect my wits. They had already left the station, and this fellow just pushed past me so hard he sent me flying.'

'Well, I see we must return to this "fellow". We have a description of this man, do we, sergeant?'

'Yes, sir, he was—'

'No need, sergeant, not yet. It is sufficient that we have it.'

Webb sits down on the bench, still looking at the body. 'I am more interested in the woman. What do we know of her?'

'She was strangled, sir,' says the sergeant, following him. 'Obvious. Marks on the neck. And the limbs ain't that stiff as yet, so it weren't too long ago.'

Webb bends down, and gently peels back the woollen shawl from the girl's neck. In the light of the sergeant's lantern, dark bruised shadows are visible around her throat.

Webb frowns. 'It was not a ligature; it was done by hand.'

The booking clerk steps back, his face quite white. 'By hand?' he echoes.

'Now, about the man what legged it, sir,' interjects Sergeant Watkins, 'he left his hat . . .'

'And what have we learnt from our study of the hat, sergeant?' asks Webb, glancing at the article and raising his eyebrow ironically. The hat is an undistinguished black item, which lies upon the seat of the carriage, opposite the woman's body. 'Did he perhaps have a big head? Then he is our man, of course! Really, sergeant, do you imagine he is our culprit? Why would he linger on the train, after all? We must find him, naturally, but I really suggest that you keep an open mind.'

'I was also going to say, sir, that he also left a notebook.'

'Does it contain something of use?' asks Webb absent-mindedly, paying Watkins little attention as he walks round to the other side of the body. 'His address perhaps?'

The sergeant shakes his head.

'I can only make out some of it, sir. I think much of it's in some kind of shorthand. But from what I can make out . . .'

His voice trails off as he watches Webb bring his face close to that of the dead woman, examining her features in minute detail.

'Do you think she was a street-walker, sergeant? I believe that she is wearing rouge, and no hat or bonnet to speak of. She rather looks the part, eh? She could pass for a whore, could she not?'

'Possibly sir. There is nothing to identify her that we can find. Now, about this here notebook—'

'Really, sergeant, what about it? I will look at it in good time.'

'I merely think that it may change your opinion of him.'

'Who?' asks Webb, still intent on the body, bending over it from a variety of angles.

'The man who ran off.'

Webb turns round and faces his truculent colleague. Standing in the carriage, above the woman's corpse, he looks him in the eye.

'Change my opinion? Really?'

There is perhaps a hint of irony in his question. He pauses for a moment, as if the possibility that such a thing might happen truly confounds him.

'Now, sergeant, I must confess, I am rather intrigued.'

CHAPTER FIVE

MORNING.

A girl of twenty years of age stands outside the Holborn Refuge for Penitent Women. Indeed, she loiters upon the corner of Serle Street, just as the sun struggles to surmount the ornate chimneys of nearby Lincoln's Inn, and throw some light on the dusty labours of legal minds who scratch a living within that red-brick fortress. The girl's name is Clara White, and she looks quite out of place, wearing her plain cotton dress and shawl. For it is the time of day when, like iron filings, a black-suited mass of clerks, laden with bundles of papers tied in red ribbon, are drawn from their offices in the Inn, to the magnet of the law courts.

'Mind there, Miss!'

It takes her a moment to realise she is the object of this gruff admonition. It is a man holding a dozen or more paper folders clutched to his chest, a precarious arrangement at the best of times. By taking a single step backwards, she realises that she has almost sent him toppling into the road. She turns to offer a few shy words of apology, but the man has already darted past, not even turning his head; he has no time for such sentiments. And yet, it is so cold, in the shadow of Lincoln's Inn's high walls, that Clara has to shuffle about to keep warm, this only makes her more hazardous to the over-laden law clerks. She stands, therefore, a little closer to the railings of the refuge.

The Holborn Refuge itself is a plain soot-choked three-storey house, the last in a terraced row. Most of the adjacent premises are, in fact, affiliated to the legal profession, whether by providing lodgings, or a place of work. In consequence, the existence of the refuge in Serle Street is something of an anomaly, the result of an idiosyncratic, if not vexatious, bequest from a long-dead benefactor; and the peculiar comings and goings to which such an establishment is inevitably subject are more tolerated than welcomed by its neighbours. Clara White is well aware of this, and looks anything but comfortable.

Finally, nine o'clock comes. The bells of St Dunstan-in-the-West chime out in Fleet Street, and carry across the rooftops. Clara pauses for a moment, then hesitantly approaches the familiar steps that lead to the front door of the refuge. It is painted black, and has a large iron-work knocker, no doubt intended to represent the features of some impressive animal. The breed, however, is quite unintelligible, the iron's original character having been quite worn away by the demands of its daily existence. In this, the knocker bears some slight sympathetic relation to the house's inhabitants.

Clara tries striking lightly upon the door.

No reply.

She tries the knocker again.

The door swings open just as she raps upon it for a second time. The woman who stands before her is the lady superintendent herself, Miss Sparrow, in her day uniform of dark blue cloth, a colour not dissimilar to that worn by the Metropolitan Police.

'Ah, Miss White,' she says, 'you realise you are early? The visiting period is from five minutes past nine to half-past, precisely. We place a high price upon punctuality here; I am sure you can recall?'

'I am sorry, ma'am, but it is rather cold outside, and I thought there would be no harm.'

'That is all very well, but you know we must all set an example to the girls. Still,' she says, 'I suppose you had better come in, now you are here.'

'Thank you.'

Clara White follows her into the hall but Miss Sparrow comes to a halt even before there is a chance to shut the door behind them.

'Miss White, before we proceed any further, I am afraid your mother is still rather unwell, or, at least, that is how it appears. And, I am sorry to impart to you that I also have certain suspicions about her conduct.'

'Suspicions, ma'am?' Clara's heart sinks.

'You will recall our third Golden Rule, no doubt? I fear your mother does not abide by it.'

Clara struggles to recall the particulars of the guidance offered by the refuge. Her answer is not intended to be humorous, and, in truth, she colours slightly as she says it.

'Chastity?'

Miss Sparrow herself blushes.

'Really, Miss White! Temperance, Miss White. Temperance is the Third Rule. I entered her room yesterday, whilst she was doing her chores, and believe I smelt gin.'

She waits for the full weight of this statement to impact upon the girl, but there is little sign of shock. Indeed, though there is undoubtedly disquiet in Clara's face, it is tempered by a long-standing familiarity with her mother's transgressions.

'You cannot be sure, ma'am?' says Clara, hesitantly. 'Might it be one of the other women?'

Miss Sparrow wavers. 'At present, I have no proof,

that is true. But you recall the view we take of intoxicating liquors, Miss White?'

'I do. But, perhaps, ma'am, if that is all, I might see her now?'

'Yes, I suppose you may,' replies Miss Sparrow, somewhat grudgingly. 'You are fortunate to be allowed such frequent visits by your employers.'

Clara nods.

'Very well. Follow me,' the superintendent continues, imperiously striding up the stairs, though her guest might easily find her way unaided. At the top of the landing she comes to a halt. 'Ten minutes and no more, Miss White,' she says sternly, leaving the visitor by the door and stalking off back down the stairs. 'We do not want to tire her, do we?'

Clara White watches Philomena Sparrow return to her study, then peers into the room. Agnes White sits upon the side of the bed; she looks small and shrunken, and shudders with each cough, her shoulders tense and her cheeks bulging. The room, no doubt once a library or something similar, when the house was a private residence, now merely contains two iron beds for its residents, and a plain washstand. At first, her mother does not notice her, and Clara merely observes her in silence. Finally, however, Agnes sees her visitor.

'Clarrie,' she says, greeting her daughter quite flatly, as if she were merely continuing an existing conversation, 'I'm awful sick. Did you get it?'

'What?'

'The medicine what the doctor said. Did you get it?'

'Medicine?'

'Sorry, I think she means this,' says a nurse, who appears in the hallway from the adjoining room. 'I was up with her last night. Carried on something awful, didn't you, Aggie?'

29

Clara looks round at the nurse. The girl, not much older than Clara herself, holds out a brown medicine bottle: '*Balley's Patent Quietener, The Finest Extract of Laudanum*'.

'She's been downing it like there's no tomorrow, ain't you, Aggie? I thought we had a little bottle or two put by, but she's had it all.'

'Does it do her good?' asks Clara.

'It stops the coughing, helps her sleep, but we can't get no more this month. Miss Sparrow says we can't afford it.'

Agnes White coughs again.

'Is there anything I can do?' asks Clara, glancing pityingly at her mother. 'Do you think I could get some for her myself?'

'Of this? If you like, if you can afford it. I don't see how the Missus could say no. Anyhow, I'll leave you be,' says the nurse, smiling sympathetically, and then turning back down the corridor, 'I must see to the others, but I think she'll be all right. You're a tough'un, ain't you Aggie?'

Clara thanks her, and turns to look at her mother once more.

'Little madam,' says Agnes White, watching the nurse depart. 'She'll have it herself, that one.'

'Your medicine? I do not think so.'

'Mark my words. It's too late for me, anyhow. It's my time. I'll be the next to go.'

She gestures at the empty bed opposite her own. Anyone who did not know the room would not recognise her meaning, but it is clear enough to her daughter. The bed is freshly made, and the odd little ornaments that belonged to her room-mate, and once sat neatly arranged on the wooden table, have been tidied away. Clara frowns at her mother's morbid thoughts.

'I had better go,' she says. 'They will be missing me. I just came to see that you are all right.'

'Will you come again tomorrow?'

'I suppose so, if I can get away.'

'I'll be gone by then, anyhow.'

'Ma, don't be ridiculous. The doctor said it ain't anything.'

'Doctors don't know nothing. I'm dying.'

'I really must go.'

'Well, Lizzie knows I'm right. She knows it. She agreed with me.'

'Lizzie?' says Clara, perplexed.

'I says, "I'm dying, ain't I?" and she says, "Yes, poor dear, I fear you is."'

'Don't fret, I'll be back tomorrow, ma. You will rest up, won't you?'

Agnes mutters something in reply, but her daughter does not stay to question her further. Instead, she goes directly downstairs and knocks on Miss Sparrow's study.

'Come in.'

Clara goes into the room, and finds Miss Sparrow at her desk.

'Ah, Miss White? How do you find your mother?'

'May I ask something of you, ma'am?'

'If you wish. If you can be brief. I have work to finish.'

'It is just something she said, my ma. I know she will talk nonsense, but has she had another visitor?'

'Yes, indeed. I think your sister came and saw her yesterday.'

'Lizzie?'

Philomena Sparrow looks in her notebook, and peers back at her. 'Yes, Elizabeth. I have a note of it here. Is there something wrong?'

'It's just that we . . . I have not seen her for a year or more.'

'Well, I am sure your domestic affairs are very pressing, Miss White, but I must get on myself. Send my regards to Dr. Harris, if you please.' She looks at Clara pointedly, pushing her spectacles up her nose.

'I will,' replies Clara. 'I am sorry to disturb you.'

Clara curtsies, and retreats back into the hall, where she finds the same nurse standing there who spoke to her outside her mother's room.

'Don't mind her,' the woman whispers, relishing the sharing of a confidence, 'she's upset about Sally.'

'Sally?'

'You know, Miss, the girl what was sharing with your mother.'

'The red-haired girl? I never saw that much of her. When did she die? Was it sudden? It ain't catching, is it?'

'Oh Lord, bless you, she's not dead. She just didn't come back last night, skipped the curfew. She's as likely laid up in some gin-shop in the Dials as anything, if I know Sally Bowker.'

'My mother thinks she's dead.'

'Really? Lor! Whatever gave her that idea?'

CHAPTER SIX

IT IS NEARLY half-past the hour when Clara White takes leave of the Holborn Refuge for Penitent Women, and makes her way past frost-bitten Lincoln's Inn Fields. She skirts the square, and then walks along the refuse-laden alley that links it with High Holborn. It is not, however, a simple matter to cross this great thoroughfare. The only persons who brave the traffic, and seem to move about with casual impunity, are a gang of street Arabs – half a dozen ragged boys and girls who dart with apparent ease between passing carriages. She stands and watches them for a moment, as one child performs cartwheels, in the hope that a penny may be discarded in her direction, an ambition that appears destined to remain unrealised. Then, a bus pulls up sharply by the side of the road, obstructing her view. The horses snort in exhaustion, and twenty men or more alight, streaming past her on both sides. They are the typical suburban clerks, in neat suits, some in silk hats, and several spring down from the top deck in merely two or three steps, like trained acrobats. They do not even catch their breath. Instead they turn around, this way and that, like human spinning-tops, finding their bearings, then plunge straight into the crowd. There is no 'good morning' or 'how d'ye do' to be heard; no chance acquaintance can hope to interrupt their progress. Indeed, Clara herself cannot hope to stand still for long, and so falls in with the foot-traffic, jostled along until she comes to the corner of Gray's Inn Lane. There she finally manages to cross at the junction, dodging the mud as best she can, until she stands before a small, old-fashioned shop, Pickering & Co. Druggists and Chemists &c.

The shop window looks particularly ancient, comprised of two dozen or more small panes of green-tinged bullion glass. It contains, moreover, shelves bearing translucent bottles of green and blue hues, guaranteed to attract the attention of passers-by, a particular favourite of local children. Indeed, a couple of street boys linger by the door, but Clara quietly brushes past their entreaties and goes inside. Within she finds an old gentleman, the aforementioned Pickering, sitting behind the counter. He stands up and nods in a business-like manner as Clara enters.

'Morning, Miss. Nice to see you again.'

'Good morning.'

'And to what do we owe the honour, Miss?'

'The usual mixture for Mrs. Harris, if you please, and also,' she continues, struggling to recall the name, 'do you have a bottle of Balley's Mixture?'

'Balley's Quietener?'

'Yes, that is the one.'

'Why, yes, Miss,' he says, surprised, 'I do. Now, the mixture for Mrs. Harris, I've some prepared; but, how much of the Balley's would you be requiring? Bottle or half-bottle? Mrs. Harris feeling nervy, is she, bless her?'

Clara merely nods. Perhaps she reasons that an unspoken deception is better than an all-out lie. At all events, she does not contradict him.

'A bottle would be fine, thank you.'

'Very well, Miss, you wait there. I'll just be a moment.'

The old man disappears beneath the mahogany-topped counter, and can be heard to open several drawers and cupboards. When he finally rises again, he holds a blue-green jar for the benefit of Mrs. Harris, and a clear glass bottle of the patent drug, labelled 'Balley's' in bold black type. He takes a smaller, empty bottle, and measures out the viscous dark brown liquid.

'Strong stuff this, Miss,' he says, squeezing a stopper into the bottle, and placing both containers in a paper bag, padding it with a wrap or two of crushed news-paper. 'You tell Mrs. H. to be careful – not more than a few drops after a meal.'

'I will tell her,' Clara says.

'And I'll put it on the account?'

Clara pauses for a moment. 'Yes, that's fine,' she says at last.

'Good day then, Miss. Perhaps you could remind Mrs. Harris, the account is due next week?'

'I will,' she replies nervously, as she takes the little parcel. 'Good day.'

Clara opens the shop door and steps once more into the busy street. On the corner of Gray's Inn Lane there is now a boy selling penny sheets, with a little crowd gathered about him, the newsprint dirtying their eager hands. Their talk is of 'murder' and 'the Underground Railway', but she does not take it in as she passes by. Rather, she makes her dash across Gray's Inn Lane, hoisting her skirts as high as decency allows, running as fast as she can.

—

It is not five minutes more before Clara White stands outside a house on Doughty Street, just north of Gray's Inn. It is not a large house, and not too dissimilar to the refuge, with the principal exception that it is finished with stucco painted a smart white, and its front steps are much better polished. She takes a moment to ensure her mother's medication is concealed in her apron, and Mrs. Harris's clearly on display, then descends the area steps, and opens the kitchen door.

'Where've you been?' asks a voice, even before her face can be seen.

'I've got Mrs. H.'s medicine, Cook,' she says gingerly, displaying the paper bag to her interlocutor.

Cook, a fulsome-bodied creature with the muscular arms and ruddy complexion of so many of the women in her trade, scowls. 'And look at the state of you,' she exclaims, gesturing in exasperation at Clara's muddied skirts.

'Well? What do you want? I can't fly, can I?'

'Hmph!' says Cook. Her snort of derision fills the room like a little explosion. 'Don't you cheek me, girl. Clean yourself up, that's all.'

'Did they miss us?' asks Clara, as she hunts for the clothes brush kept for such contingencies.

'I reckon not. Alice took 'em breakfast and said you were sick. I ain't telling no lies, mind you. Not if they asks me, personal like.'

'They won't ask, will they?'

Cook snorts again and shrugs her large shoulders. 'If they didn't have their heads so high in the clouds, they would. And this house would be a darn sight better for it. That's my pennyworth, anyhow.'

'Yes, well . . .'

As she speaks there are footsteps on the stairs, and another person appears, a small girl in a plain kitchen-maid's outfit, carrying a silver tray. She is a couple of years younger than Clara, and smiles when she sees her.

'About time,' she says, as she descends the steps.

'You scared us. I thought you were Mrs. H.,' says Clara.

'Come on, when did you last see her down here? Tell us, how's your ma, then?'

'Awful, Ally. But then she always were.'

It is not a very funny joke, but they both allow themselves a smile. Cook's face merely looks deep into a pan of porridge simmering on the range, which she removes from the hob. The new arrival, whose full name is Alice Meynell, walks over to Clara, and leans close to her.

'Have you heard?' she says, whispering.

'What's that?' interrupts Cook. 'Speak up!'

'There's only been a murder,' the girl continues, still whispering, 'on the Underground Railway. There was a girl strangled, right in the railway carriage, right before everyone's eyes. Throttled till she was dead.'

'Really?' says Clara, still busy with her skirts. She seems less interested by this information than Alice Meynell might have reasonably expected.

'What's the matter with you, anyhow?' asks the girl.

'Sorry, I was thinking of something else. Something my ma told me.'

'Well, what was this, then? Tell all.'

'Said she'd seen my sister. And I didn't even think she was in London.'

Cook thumps her fist on the kitchen table.

'There'll be murder here if you don't do some work, girl. That goes for both of you.'

Alice pulls a face at her, and continues talking. 'You've never said much about her, your sister.'

'No. I just wish I knew where she was.'

CHAPTER SEVEN

'BEG YOUR PARDON, sir? What's that? A shilling? A shilling for the Remarkable Compound? No, sir. Not a shilling, though it would be a regular bargain even at that price. Come closer, sir, lend me your nose, as the Bard of Avon would have it. "Ear", you say? No, I can do precious little with that! Come a little closer, and let the scent of the Remarkable Compound elevate your nostrils! Don't be fearful now! How does it smell? Sweet? Of course it does. That, sir, is the smell of Vi-tality.'

It is mid-morning and a crowd of two dozen or more persons move a little closer into the corner of Clare Market, a maze of little streets that trail off from Lincoln's Inn Fields towards the Strand. The object of everyone's attention is a man standing upon a wooden crate, waving in the air an unstoppered bulbous bottle made of dark green glass. He is of middling height and, though he wears a dark suit of cheap fustian, it conceals a striking green silk waist-coat, and the hint of a gold chain, which may or may not be affixed to a pocket-watch. His features, more-over, are quite handsome, and his fair hair sleek with macassar oil. He looks, in common parlance, some-thing of a 'cheap swell'. A good proportion of those watching him are women.

His voice booms through the marketplace.

'You, ma'am! Yes, you! Won't you take a sip, gratis? Really? Is that so? No, ma'am, rest assured, I would not hazard to bother, befuddle, nor bamboozle a lady such as you! As my old father said to me, "You can bring an horse to the trough, but you can't make him drink." Really? No, ma'am, I did not compare you to an equine, you misunderstands me. I has a great deal of respect for horses . . .'

The crowd laugh and the man smiles; he is no more than twenty-eight years of age, but he has the booming voice and assurance of someone much older. He puts his hand out, asking them for silence.

'We may have a jolly time of it, my friends, but I might ask of you to stop and think. How many of you is suffering from a sickness? How many of you would likely benefit from the remedy of the Remarkable Compound? How many, aye, more's the point, has been on bended knee to the blasted relieving officer, and taken his blessed chit to the doctor, but has found no relief? Aye, a good number, ain't it? Of course, I cannot promise you long life and health, nor can any fellow on God's green earth. But there is steps a man may take, good long strides, which sets you on the right road. What's that? Proof, you say? The Compound is its own proof positive, ma'am, rest assured. Really? Well, let us put it to the test. Now, what do I see here? You, Miss? Yes, you at the back. I ain't a gentleman for saying it, but you are suffering from an infirmity, are you not? Do come forward, if you will?'

A girl of about fifteen or sixteen years of age steps forward from the back of the crowd; she wears a striped cotton dress, and her face is barely visible under a tangled web of chestnut-brown hair that falls loose about her shoulders. As she walks to the front she visibly limps, and a few of those nearby notice that she cradles her left hand under her shawl, supporting it with her other arm. The street doctor beckons her forward and puts his arm around her, though she looks uncomfortable to be the focus of everyone's attention.

'Now, Miss, I ain't so green that I can't see something is amiss with that peg of yours, and your hand there. Now show us your arm, will you? No need to be ashamed of a natural infirmity, Miss. Go on.'

The girl blushes, but brings out her arm, showing her hand to be crooked and arthritic in appearance, and blistered about the knuckles. A couple of women in the crowd mutter in sympathy.

'Now, I don't know what your hospital man would say of it, but that is what we commonly called "withered", ain't it, my friends? That is an awful burden for a young gal, ain't it? Now, here you go, my beauty, you try a sip of this.'

He hands her a bottle from his tray, laid out beside the box, and the girl hesitantly takes a couple of sips.

'Now,' says the man, gravely, 'tell us how you find the effect, if you will?'

'A little better,' says the girl, shyly, still hiding her face beneath her hair.

'It make you feel a little better? And that is just two sips, ladies and gentlemen. Now, Miss, I do not want to supply you with false hopes, but may I make a suggestion?'

The girl looks puzzled and nods.

'Apply a couple of drops of the Compound to your hand, Miss.'

'My hand?'

'Yes, to your hand. And rub it in. Rub it in good.'

The girl looks shocked, but takes up the bottle again and drips a couple of drops of the liquid on to her crooked wrist. She gives back the bottle, then massages

40

the liquid along the length of her hand, rubbing her fingers vigorously. As she does so, a delighted smile gradually spreads across her lips and, when she is done, her hand is suddenly not half as crooked as it was, and the blisters have all but vanished. The street doctor looks triumphant, and motions to everyone to gather closer.

'There, Miss, now how is that? Not bad for a free sample, is it?'

'I can move my fingers!'

'Do you hear that, ladies and gentlemen? Her fingers! Now, that is what we might call Remarkable, is it not? Now, I cannot bring myself to name the full price for this Remarkable Compound, not when we have witnessed this here child's happiness. I will not say it is elevenpence, nor tenpence, but I must say ninepence unless I am bent upon starving my own poor family. Miss, would you care to buy an actual bottleful? You would? Yes? Anyone else?'

And several hands fumble in pockets and purses, all of them willing to give the doctor's elixir a try. One, however, is a short gentleman in a decent suit of clothes, who swiftly pays his money, and immediately raises a bottle of the liquid to his lips. He swills it around his mouth thoughtfully, then stretches out his arms in an attempt to prevent further transactions.

'This, sir,' he exclaims, 'is a mockery of the medical science. It is nothing more than sugared water!'

The street doctor frowns, weighs up his antagonist, and attempts a rebuttal.

'That, sir, as I just said, is the taste of Vi-tality. Would it not taste sweet to any man?'

'I, sir, am not *any* man. I am an assistant-surgeon at St. Bartholomew's. And I tell you that this concoction is nothing more than coloured water, pure and simple, except perhaps that I doubt it is very pure. It is utter fakery! And as for this girl's hand . . .'

The street doctor blanches a little, but is seemingly about to make a reply, whilst attempting to continue the transactions he has already begun, when he spots the distinctive uniform of a police officer appearing abruptly around a nearby corner. At this sighting, the doctor simply turns and runs, making no pretence of doing anything else. He leaves a clatter of medicine bottles behind him. The girl, meanwhile, suddenly loses all semblance of infirmity and follows in his wake as fast as any trained sprinter. The crowd is quite stunned, not least the half-dozen or so already having exchanged their money for goods, unsure whether there is any advantage in taking an abandoned bottle, regardless. The policeman, meanwhile, merely shouts out, 'Stop! Stop, thief!' and pursues both man and girl at full speed.

Clare Market is a dangerous region for anyone wishing to make hasty progress, its back alleys littered with the detritus of nearby houses and the market trade, encompassing both abandoned animal and vegetable matter, carpeted with cabbage leaves and herring bones. The man and girl are undoubtedly sure-footed, but the blue-coated policeman seemingly makes better time, and catches up with them just in sight of St. Clement's church, adjoining the Strand. Any one of the prospective purchasers of the Remarkable Compound who were to observe the scene, however, would think it a strange apprehension. For all parties suddenly draw to a halt, without any scuffle. But what does it matter? There is no person present to form such a conclusion, and that is precisely why the chase stops.

'All right, Charlie,' says the street doctor, smiling at his pursuer, and cheerfully slapping him on the back. 'Perfect. He was trouble, that little fellow.'

'Lor, you needn't have run quite so far, eh?' says the policeman, a little flushed and breathless.

'Better safe than sorry. I didn't take much, though.'

'You never do. Well, call it three bob, Tom, and have done.'

'You're a hard man,' says the street doctor, reluctantly ceding part of his takings.

'And you're a lucky one. Now don't let me see you here again for a day or two, eh? Or I'll have to take you in.'

The street doctor nods, and smiles, watching the policeman depart. His smile disappears when the man is gone. He pulls the girl over to the church wall.

'Well, Lizzie, my darlin',' says Tom Hunt, 'we'll have to come up with something else, won't we now?'

'I never liked that fake anyhow. My hand hurts, keeping it cramped up like that.'

'Liking ain't important. Just do as you are told, and we'll do all right.'

Lizzie grimaces as her husband pinches her arm. 'Where will we go now, then?' she asks.

'Bill will put us up tonight, I reckon. It's been a week or two, ain't it? A bit of a rest, and I can have a think.'

Lizzie Hunt, née White, scowls.

'We never get a decent lodgings,' she says.

CHAPTER EIGHT

'QUITE A SENSATION, ain't it?'

Sergeant Watkins and Inspector Decimus Webb sit facing each other in Bates' Coffee Room adjoining the Marylebone Tavern, overlooking Marylebone High Street. The former scrutinises several crumpled sheets of paper that he holds in his hand, whilst the latter sips from a cup of dark coffee, fresh from the urn.

'Here's one,' continues the sergeant. '"Dreadful Railway murder! Man escaped into tunnels!" Who'd have thought, eh? It's news to me, I must say.'

'If you will read these penny sheets,' says Webb, 'you can expect no better. When is a murder not "dreadful"?'

'I'd say it depends on the circumstances, sir. In any case, you have to admire them, getting it printed up so quick. I've seen them on every corner this morning. The girl's barely cold.'

'It is not a matter of admiration,' says Webb, 'though at least it may help us in finding a name for our woman, assuming she possesses a family or, at least, some acquaintance of one sort or other.'

'And assuming it weren't them that did for her, sir.'

'Hmm. Do they mention her hair?'

'Her hair?'

'Red hair, sergeant. Think, man. It is distinctive, is it not? It may alert someone who knows her.'

'I believe some do, sir. "Flame-haired", one says here.'

'Ha! Well, that is a little grandiose. Still, we have other reading matter to consider.'

'You've taken a good look at that notebook, then, sir?'

'Yes, and you were quite right,' replies Webb, though there is no hint of gratitude in his tone. He picks up the book and opens it at random, flicking through the pages. 'It is, in the least, rather interesting. Let us pick a choice piece,' he says, somewhat theatrically selecting a paragraph with his finger, and reading out loud, 'seventeenth January.

'Left C— St, and walked to Clare Market. It is no more than a mile or so on foot, and I was not disappointed; the place is a truly remarkable spectacle at night, though only to be fully witnessed when the gas has been extinguished in the butchers' shops, and everything is shuttered up. Clare Market! How odd that any gentleman who wishes to acquaint himself with the *demi-monde* is directed to visit the glittering delights of the Haymarket, to take in Mott's or Miss Hamilton's; how odd that he will be advised to seek out the *habituées* of the *pavé* on *that* famous thoroughfare. Let a man come to these "market" streets! for there can be few other areas of the metropolis where one may become so easily acquainted with the temptations of the flesh. And it is human flesh, of course, offered up on every street corner, by some of the most wretched vestiges of womanhood a man might encounter. And yet, if the truth be told, the readiness with which this human tribute is tendered, and accepted, is as much a sorry testimony to the bestial nature of *man*kind, as it is a disgrace to the *woman*. Poor sinning creatures, one and all!

'But enough moralising! In short, from the vantage of my "lodgings" (the dreadful room, rented Thursday last) I was well-placed to observe the little group of doves flocking below.

'I made, therefore, the following observations between the hours of ten o'clock and midnight:

'No. of women: 6

No. of men: 26

Longest interval between transactions: *18 minutes*

Shortest interval between transactions: *2 minutes*

Duration of transactions: *between 1 and 4 minutes; an average of 2.5 minutes*

Money exchanged: *always upon completion of transaction*

'Of the women themselves, one was forty years or older, one between thirty and forty, two between twenty and thirty, and two under twenty years; indeed, one of the latter appeared little more than a child of twelve or thirteen. None was dressed in particular finery; all, however, were bare-headed, eschewing a winter bonnet or cap.

'Of the men, rough-looking costers predominated, dressed in the corduroys and the high, laced boots that distinguish their class.

'Most remarkable that, in all instances, the business I observed would have been clearly visible to any passer-by, man, woman or child

46

(and it is *not* unknown to see young children alone upon these streets, even at such a late hour), a consideration which seemed to trouble neither party!'

'Regular Paul Pry, ain't he?'

'Hmm. I cannot read the rest – ' says Webb, scanning the page – 'more of his blasted scribbling. Ah, wait, a final paragraph.

'I became puzzled by the activities of a particular girl, who walked down the street, then left in the company of a man, on three separate occasions; did she have a room? I resolved to test this, and struck up a conversation. She was a pretty girl, of very slender figure, barely on the verge of womanhood. She led me through narrow passageways to, as I had suspected, a barely furnished room, above a cook-shop.

'I gave her three shillings and quizzed her. Made two pages of notes. She thought my enquiries highly amusing, and said she preferred the "regular business".

'I did not oblige her on that score!'

The sergeant laughs scornfully. 'Did he not?'

'That is what he says. As much as I can make out. You know, I believe it is a type of shorthand, though I do not know it. We must have someone more expert in these matters take a look. Do you know someone who might fit the bill, Watkins? I confess I do not.'

'I'll see what can be done, sir.'

'Good. And what do you make of our author? Are you "baffled?" We are obliged to be baffled at this stage in proceedings, are we not? That is what the papers will say, if they are not saying it already.'

'I think you read too many newspapers yourself, sir, if I may say so. It is quite plain, is it not? He is a deviant. He stalks these women, under some pretext of making this study of them, and now he has plucked up the courage to do for one.'

Webb takes a leisurely sip on his coffee, then wipes his moustache.

'On a train? A peculiar choice, is it not?'

'People get up to all sorts on trains, sir, rest assured.'

'Really, sergeant? You speak from experience? I thought you were a married man?'

'No need to twist my meaning, sir.'

Webb smiles at the sergeant's discomfort.

'And what of the witnesses? We have at least three, do we not, who boarded the carriage at Gower Street, and who saw him already there? And one, is there not, who thinks he was there at King's Cross?'

'So it seems. I've put some of the lads at each station, asking questions. We'll have a better idea in a day or two, I reckon.'

'And yet these witnesses, they saw nothing peculiar? And so he did it between Farringdon Street and King's Cross. Think on it. How long is that? Five minutes? A little more? Ten minutes to Gower Street?'

'Why not? She was full of gin.'

'And so, they are alone, and he takes his chance?'

The sergeant nods. 'He probably followed her, picked his moment.'

'And then wrote notes in his little diary the rest of the way? Although I cannot find the entry, if he did so. And he set her carefully upon the seat, hiding her neck with the shawl. Why did he not get off the train? Why did he wait?'

'Well, I can't answer that. A man can't answer for the actions of a lunatic, can he?'

'You might at least try, my dear sergeant. Still, never

mind. I think we must find him, whatever is the case, although I fear he has gone to ground. Agreed?'

'Agreed, sir.'

'Good. Now, get me another coffee, will you?'

Chapter Nine

'Mr. Phibbs?'

Henry Cotton stirs in his bed. He has slept fitfully, in his clothes, and his head aches; it takes him a few moments to realise that the noise is someone banging upon his door.

'Mr. Phibbs? I know you is in there!'

'Yes?' says Cotton.

'Is it you, tramping mud in my hall? My Susan has been on her hands and knees cleaning up all morning.'

'Leave me be, Mrs. Samson. I am unwell.'

'That's as maybe, ain't it? But Susan ain't nobody's slave. She may fetch and carry, but she has a natural pride, sir. She is not to be done down.'

'I will recompense her when I see her. Please, Mrs. Samson, please let me alone.'

'Well, that is something. But think on, sir, next time you go mud-larking, if you will.'

The woman walks noisely down the stairs. Henry Cotton, meanwhile, pulls the covers up to his neck, and attempts to fall back to sleep.

—

'Mr. Phibbs?'

A voice from the landing again. A younger voice this time.

'Mr. Phibbs?'

'Yes?'

'Mrs. Samson says don't you want a fire got up, if you're stopping in?'

'What time is it, Susan?'

'Two o'clock, sir.'

'I must have been asleep. I'll be going out soon.'

'As you like, sir.'

Henry Cotton listens to the girl's footsteps descending the stairs and takes a deep breath, then sits up upon the bed, looking around the simple furnishings of his lodgings.

There is a jug of water on the washstand, left for him the previous evening; he walks over and plunges his hands inside the porcelain, then splashes his face. Once done, he walks to the window and peers out into the street.

He must make preparations.

He must leave.

It does not take long for Henry Cotton to change his clothes. Divesting himself of the scruffy great-coat and cheap fustian suit of the previous night, he folds them away into an ageing but capacious carpet-bag. Next he takes off his dirty cotton shirt, but replaces it with one of fine Irish linen, together with a pristine white collar and cuffs. Then, from his wardrobe, he retrieves a different suit entirely: not fustian, but shiny black cloth of the finest cut. He puts it on, together with a cravat of red silk, fixing it with a silver pin. All this is done in record time, and, glancing in the mirror, he mentally congratulates himself at the speed of his transformation.

The remainder of his clothes follow into the bag. Next, he makes a meticulous search of the room itself, though it boasts few personal possessions. A pen, a razor, several notebooks, all proceed in the same direction, together with a Bible and three-volume novel. Then he walks over to the writing desk, which sits by the window, and opens and closes each drawer, checking that they are empty. At last, the only remaining trace of his presence in Castle Street is the glass inkwell, which sits atop the desk; he takes it and empties the viscous blue liquid on to the hearth, watching it soak into the cinders of yesterday's fire. He then wraps the inkwell in a piece of cloth, and that too he puts in his bag. There is nothing left. The room, hardly replete with home comforts at the best of times, appears quite barren. Cotton takes a final look, then walks over to the door, and listens. There is no-one upon the landing, as best as he can tell. Consequently, he opens the door, softly closes it behind him, then walks down the stairs as casually as possible; or, at least, as casual as any man may be, when absconding from his lodgings with a week's rent owing.

Outside there is daylight. To Cotton, it seems bright and unexpected after the gloom of Mrs. Samson's residence. Indeed, the sun is so strong that even the accumulating smoke of the city's countless chimneys has done nothing to obscure its harsh winter light.

Henry Cotton lowers his head and hurries through the side streets towards Soho.

———

It is not twelve hours since Henry Cotton ran blindly through the backstreets of Marylebone in the pitch-darkness; and yet, in bright daylight, his progress through the narrow lanes that lie between Oxford Street and Leicester Square leaves just as indistinct an impression upon his senses. Assuredly, his feet proceed one in front of the other in measured steps; he avoids every obstruction of persons and goods upon the pavements, and the menace of traffic upon the roads; but his mind is fixed upon other things entirely.

And yet, for all that, he is forced to stop when he reaches St. Martin's Lane. It is, even in quiet moments, a road that no man could cross without his wits about him. Indeed, as Cotton stands upon the kerb, he has a fancy that there is something about the lane that resembles a poorly constructed Roman circus, as a succession of black cabs struggle uphill, and, to all appearances, race immediately back down at a breakneck speed. In truth, in his distracted state of mind, it seems to him that he may stand there for ever; it seems quite possible that the London traffic is wholly impassable and that he is quite trapped by it. Then he notices a newsboy standing nearby, a clutch of penny broadsheets under his arm.

'Metropolitan Murder! Murder on Underground Railway!'

Henry Cotton steels his nerve, then gives the boy a penny. Taking a copy of the broadsheet, he hurries onwards between a gap in the traffic, towards Covent Garden and Clare Market. It is somewhere between those two locations that he finally pauses to read the sheet he has bought. He finds, with some astonishment, that his own name is not mentioned, nor is there much of a description given of the young man who fled the scene of the crime.

He cannot help but smile, and several passers-by wonder at the peculiar look of relief and joy that plays upon his face.

CHAPTER TEN

'WHAT DO YOU make of it, sergeant?'

'This, sir? I don't know what to make of it, sir.'

'It is not mutton, nor pork, nor, I think, would I dare to call it beef.'

Two policemen stand before a butcher's shop in the narrow lanes of Clare Market. In the daylight, it is a district principally devoted to the livelihoods of butchers and costermongers. One of the establishments belonging to the former class of business-men has caught their eye, a place where the day's best meat has been laid out upon dirty wooden blocks, for the public gaze. Every piece is a little discoloured and unwholesome in appearance, either in its entirety or in part.

'I'd say it's the finest scrag-end,' continues Webb. 'None better than Clare Market meat, is there, sergeant?'

The sergeant says nothing, but the butcher, a burly, aproned fellow, looks daggers at the pair of uniformed men; he has had no customers since the police took an interest in his merchandise. Webb addresses him jovially.

'What do you call it, my good man?'

'That, sir, is beef.'

'Well, I will not bother to enquire from which part of the animal. But perhaps you may help me?'

'If I can,' says the proprietor, more than eager to remove the obstruction to his trade.

'I am looking for a "Mrs. H.". I believe she runs a lodging-house hereabouts.'

'You don't know her proper name, then?' asks the butcher.

'If I knew that, I would, most likely, not need to ask.'

The butcher shrugs, as if to indicate the depth of his disinterest in Webb's motivation. 'There's a Mrs. Hodgkiss two doors down, she's the deputy there, far as I know.'

'An old woman?'

'She is.'

'Now, that is good news. Perhaps, Watkins, whilst we are here, you would care to purchase a choice cut for your good lady wife?'

'I have some nice bacon,' says the butcher in a conspiratorial tone, 'what we keep back.'

'I will give it a miss, if you don't mind,' replies the sergeant drily.

'Well then,' says Webb, pulling Cotton's leather-bound notebook out of his pocket. 'What are we waiting for? We have our little guide-book, after all.'

━

Walked to Clare Market. A good deal of fog about; the roads particularly muddy and danger-ous.

On reaching the lanes, I immediately went to the house which I singled out yesterday. The entrance in common usage not upon the main thoroughfare, but reached by an alley down the side. I swiftly found a door, bearing its promise of 'Dry Lodgings', and it was through this narrow and derelict-looking portal that I entered.

The room inside contained ten souls, or there-abouts, sitting around a small deal table; they were men and women of the lowest type, and though the chatter between them was lively enough, there was a definite want of vitality in their pale coun-tenances. True, there was a fire burning in the hearth, but not a large one, and it gave out little warmth, producing a dim light which only served to illuminate the poor condition of the walls, which were badly afflicted with mould. Several of this ragged convocation turned to look at me, but they soon decided that I did not merit their full atten-tion. I cannot say whether my shabby disguise was wholly successful, or if it was merely sufficient that I was neither landlord nor the police. At all events, I summoned my courage and asked after the woman whom I had ascertained was the deputy of the place, a certain Mrs. H—

'Mrs. Hodgkiss?'

Webb and Watkins step into the back kitchen of the house. The old woman lolls by the hearth upon a wooden bench, tending a small stove, wrapped in a dirty red shawl. There is no-one else to be seen.

'Mrs. Hodgkiss, is it?'

The old woman looks up, peering at the sergeant and Decimus Webb.

'Who's asking?'

'Can't you see who's asking?' asks Watkins impa-tiently. 'Her Majesty's Police.'

'How should I know? My eyes ain't what they was.'

'You're the deputy here, then, are you?'

'I am.'

'Your eyes can't be that bad, then, can they? Perhaps you could show us around.'

'Oh, I don't know about that,' she replies, looking into the fireplace, 'some of 'em upstairs might cut up something dreadful, being disturbed, like. Won't take kindly to it.'

'Madam,' says Webb, leaning down close to her face, 'we'll do more than disturb 'em, if you don't lend a hand. Besides, I do not think I shall need to see the whole place. I have something particular in mind.'

The woman scowls, but stands up with a surprising agility.

'Follow me,' she mutters grudgingly, whispering something to herself, about the iniquity of 'pestering an old woman.' The two men follow her, into the hallway, then up bare wooden stairs on to the first-floor landing. A couple of lodgers peer out of half-open doorways, and then hastily close them. Webb gestures for the old woman to stop, and tries to open one of the doors, but finds it locked.

'Is that the front room?' asks Webb.

'It is,' says the old woman.

'Who has the key, then?'

'Party what is renting it.'

'I wager he has paid well in advance?'

The woman nods, though her face betrays a certain anxiety that the policeman might know such a thing. 'A month ahead, as it happens.'

'That is unusual for a place like this, is it not?'

'What do you mean "place like this"?' asks the woman, indignation in her voice. 'This is decent lodgings, this is.'

'I'd say it's unusual, sir,' suggests Watkins.

'And how much did he pay?'

The old woman looks reluctant to disclose such confidential arrangements. Webb merely stares at her.

'Half-sovereign, if you must know.'

'A good amount. No doubt the room is furnished?'

'After a fashion. But I ain't taken anything under pretences.'

'I am sure not. Tell me, was he a smart-looking man?'

'Not so much. Talked quite fancy, though.'

'So he was a gentleman?'

'Maybe,' she says. 'Queer sort, if he was.'

Webb smiles. 'I agree. Perhaps you could let us in.'

'I told you, it's the party what has the keys.'

'Well, I do not think he will return. There is no spare?'

The woman shrugs.

'Please don't take me for a fool, Madam. Just let us in.'

———

When she was finally located, I found Mrs. H— to be a most obliging and conniving elderly creature, squatting like some wintering toad in an alcove by the fire. Yes, she said, she had the room vacant, though she informed me, most seriously, that she was 'most particular' about tenants. This was mere humbug, of course; a full month's rent quickly served to make her more agreeable. I quickly found myself the tenant of the first-floor parlour.

I had been pleased to learn that the room was let furnished. However, my joy diminished when I discovered that the sole piece of furniture was a plain iron bedstead and soiled mattress. Furthermore, I found that the boards were quite bare, the walls alive with mould, and even the mantel was cracked. None of this, however, seemed to diminish the proprietorial pride of Mrs. H—. I did not, therefore, enquire as to the condition of 'unfurnished!'

———

Decimus Webb waits until the old woman has gone downstairs before he examines the room. It is a short procedure, however, since it contains little of interest; indeed, it contains very little of anything at all.

'Nothing.'

'Indeed, sergeant, nothing. No furniture barring the bed, no clothing. Dust everywhere. No-one has lived here, have they? It is just as our man writes in his book. He merely came here to observe the street below. "Seeing everything but unseen." But we know a little more at least.'

'Do we?'

'I think so. He dresses shabbily, deliberately; he hopes to blend in; a disguise. But he writes like a well-educated man; and we know he has money, enough to pay a month's rent.'

'It ain't much, sir, is it? We don't even know his name.'

'Now, Watkins, that is an excellent idea. Be so good as to go and ask Mrs. Hodgkiss if she caught his name?'

'Right now, sir?'

'If you please.'

Watkins goes downstairs, shaking his head, whilst Decimus Webb stays in the room, and walks over to the window, looking at the bustle of the market street. A few moments later the sergeant returns.

'Phibbs, she says,' says the sergeant.

'Phibbs?' Webb turns away from the window. 'How droll. I wonder if he intended it as a joke?'

'Sir?'

'A pun, sergeant. Most likely, anyhow. Not a particularly clever one, I admit. Don't worry. We will find Mr. Phibbs, one way or the other.'

'Perhaps if we kept an eye on this place, sir? We don't have much else to go on, do we?'

'I doubt he will return here, sergeant. If he wishes to avoid us, at least, he will not be so foolish.'

Outside in the street a solitary man lingers for a moment on the corner, looking at the figure with his back to him, in the window of the first-floor room of Mrs. Hodgkiss's lodging-house.

Henry Cotton curses his luck, picks up his carpet-bag and hurriedly walks on.

CHAPTER ELEVEN

A HINT OF THE dim late afternoon light shines through the parlour window at Doughty Street. Clara White rubs away at the glass, stepping back off the footstool to observe the results of her labours. There is a thick layer of dirt upon her cloth, but, though the interior is improved, the exterior of the window is so badly smutted by the London smoke that she cannot, in all honesty, discern any difference. As she peers out on to Doughty Street itself, however, she sees a boy approaching the house, a scruffy lad dressed in a dirty corduroy suit and wearing scuffed brown boots, who stops, checks the building's address, and descends the area steps, pulling his leather satchel from around his neck.

'Done already, White?'

Clara jumps in surprise at the voice behind her, blushing as she turns to address the mistress of the house.

'No, ma'am. Nearly, though, ma'am.'

Mrs. Harris stands behind her, observing the window with a look of mild disdain. She is a short, stocky woman in her fifties, wearing an elaborate moiré day dress, intricately patterned. The fabric is a colour that might be described in fashionable pages as 'Bismarck', but it is identified in her housemaid's mind merely as 'nutmeg'. Moreover, the outfit incorporates a large and unwieldly bustle. In consequence of this appendage, when Mrs. Harris walks into a room, Clara cannot help but think of a duck emerging on to dry land. It is not an insight, however, which she vouchsafes to her employer.

'Then why have you stopped?'

'There's a boy, ma'am, delivering something. Just gone down the steps.'

At that moment, a bell rings in the kitchen.

'Is Cook not there?' asks Mrs. Harris.

'I believe she is out marketing, ma'am. And Alice is upstairs.'

'Then you had better hurry. But be sure to come back and finish. I cannot abide work half done.'

'Yes, ma'am.'

Clara curtsies and hurries, as swiftly as decency permits, down to the 'tradesman's entrance'. This is the name bestowed upon it by Mrs. Harris, though it normally suffices with being, simply put, the kitchen door. The boy is standing there and rings the bell again just as Clara appears.

''Arris?' he asks, without any preliminary.

'This is the Harris household,' replies Clara White, in her best housemaid's voice, though it is a voice with a strong hint of the Thames about it.

'Package for 'Arris, darlin', says the boy, brandishing a large brown paper parcel retrieved from his satchel. He cannot be much more than twelve years old.

'Don't darlin' me . . . give it here,' replies Clara, taking it from him. 'Who should I say it's from?'

'Babbingtons, there's a card inside.'

'Well, thank you. You can leave it with me, then.'

'No, thank *you* . . . darlin',' says the boy, grinning and running back up the steps before she can reply.

Clara toys with the idea of pursuing him, but thinks better of it, picturing her mistress's face if she were to see her boxing the boy's ears. Instead, she shuts the door and takes the parcel inside. The name of the shop is not unfamiliar, and by the weight and dimensions it is easy enough to guess that it is one of her master's regular deliveries of books.

She is about to take it upstairs, when she pauses upon the kitchen steps, looking at the string and wrapping.

She turns back, still holding the package, and opens the door to the scullery. Once inside, with the door ajar, she glances at the old washtub she put there earlier in the day; raising it up a little, she checks that her bottle of Balley's Quietener lies concealed beneath it.

Looking over her shoulder, she takes the parcel, and carefully unwraps the string.

———

'Oh dear, no. No, this is not the thing at all.'

'Sir?'

Dr. Arthur Harris, Clara's employer, sits at his desk with the parcel unwrapped, reading the spines of the half-dozen items supplied. He is a comfortable cherubic-faced man; indeed, his wife has often been heard to remark that if it was not for the whisps of grey hair atop his head, it would be hard to judge whether he was six or sixty. In truth, however, he falls into the latter category; and yet, as he examines his new acquisitions, the look of sheer disappointment present upon his face is one perhaps more commonly associated with more junior members of society.

'Where is Johnstone's 'History of the Parish Pump'? Really, Clara, I specifically asked for it.'

'I can't say, sir.'

'Quite. Quite. Neither can I. I expressly asked for it to be delivered; I was told it was "in stock" and whatever that may be taken to mean, I now am quite unable to say.'

'Perhaps it was forgotten.'

'I suppose that may be. But what am I to do?'

Clara frowns and looks suitably thoughtful. 'I could fetch it for you, sir. If you tell me where it's from.'

'Could you? Could you, Clara, my dear?' He reaches out and clasps her hand in gratitude.

'Yes, sir. Where should I go?'

'Babbingtons, my dear girl; on the corner of Newcastle Street, not far from the church. Do you know it?'

'Yes, of course, I know that street.'

'Well, yes, I suppose you do. How easily we forget your past life, eh, Clara? It is a testament to your character.'

He touches her hand again, his fingers lingering on hers. She blushes but says nothing.

'Well,' he says, turning away and looking at his watch, 'what are you waiting for? Off you go! Tell them that if they keep this up I may consider taking my custom elsewhere.'

Clara curtsies, and leaves the room, suppressing a smile. She composes herself as she descends the stairs at a trot, and, having ensured that no-one has monitored her progress, she returns to the small scullery under the kitchen steps. There, once ensconced inside, she retrieves two objects from beneath the washtub: a small pamphlet entitled 'History of the Parish Pump', and the bottle of Balley's Patent Quietener. She hides them both in her apron pocket, then opens the scullery door to go back into the kitchen. As she does so, however, she hears the voice of Mrs. Harris, suddenly booming from upstairs.

'White! What on earth are you doing down there?'

'Got to go out, ma'am. Dr. Harris asked me to.'

'"Got to go out!" I never heard the like. Where to, for pity's sake?'

'Bookseller's, ma'am.'

There is a noise upon the landing, something between a sigh and a 'huff'. It is a noise familiar to Clara White and quite unique to Mrs. Harris, signalling a generalised contempt for the world, for the untidy and thoughtless behaviour of all its inhabitants, and for her husband in particular.

'Well, I am sorry, but that is quite out of the question. There is too much to do here, without you being sent on fool's errands.'

'But Dr. Harris told me . . .'

'My husband,' says Mrs. Harris, with stately superiority, 'is a clever gentleman and a scholar. I expect to find *him* in bookseller's; that is natural and proper, and to be expected. You, on the other hand, I expect to find here, going about your chores. Finding you in other places . . . well, that will only cause confusion. And now, look, you have me shouting down the stairs like some fishwife!'

'Sorry, ma'am. It was just a book that weren't delivered and . . .'

'Really! Whatever it is, it can wait until tomorrow, I am sure. Doubtless Dr. Harris will agree with me.'

'Tomorrow? Yes, ma'am.'

'Good. Now, back to your duties, if you please. That window is quite revolting. It practically turns my stomach to look at it.'

Mrs. Harris does not wait for a response and disappears from view. Clara, meanwhile, reluctantly turns around, intending to return her secrets to their hiding place; she finds Alice Meynell standing quietly behind her.

'Where were you off to in such a hurry?' she asks.

'Did you snitch on me?' replies Clara, surprised.

'To the missus?'

'Sorry. Of course, you didn't. It was just an errand.'

'Anyone might think you've got a gentleman friend. Sneaking out at all hours . . .'

'It's just ma again. I told them at the refuge I'd get her some medicine, that's all. She's in a bad way.'

'And how're you going to pay for that? On tick? I thought you were flat out.'

Clara nervously touches her apron. 'I'll find a way. She was awful bad, Ally. You'd do exactly the same if you saw her.'

'She ain't my mother, though.'

'Count yourself lucky.'

CHAPTER TWELVE

Evening falls on Lincoln's Inn Fields, as the lady superintendent of the Holborn Refuge acknowledges a knock at her door, and calls in one of her nurses.

'Agnes White again?' asks Miss Sparrow, wearily.

'She moans in her sleep something terrible, ma'am. And if she's awake, she coughs.'

'Well, I fear we must let it take its course. She is bent on being ill; I am sure of it.'

'Should we not . . . ?' asks Jenny hesitantly. 'I mean, should we not call the doctor? The other gals are saying it's a brain fever, that it might be catching.'

'Well, I am, at least, quite sure it is no such thing. Indeed, I can find nothing much wrong with her, except her nerves and drink. Besides,' says Miss Sparrow, looking up from her books with a look of frustration, 'where should I find the money for a doctor?'

'I just thought . . .'

'And your compassion does you credit, my dear,' says Miss Sparrow, sighing. 'But we must set limits. And needs must.'

'Her daughter said she might buy her another bottle of the Balley's, ma'am.'

Miss Sparrow smiles. 'Now, nothing would suit me more. Still, in the meantime, I suppose we must see if we can calm her. You may go and do your best, Jenny. Remind her that this is the Quiet Hour. Remind her of that.'

'Yes, ma'am.'

The girl stands there, nervously.

'Well, was there something else?'

'You'll think I'm foolish, ma'am,' says the nurse, unfolding a piece of paper she has been holding behind her back. 'It's just something silly that Aggie said, about Sally. It's just, I was reading about this murder last night at Baker Street – you've heard about it, ain't you? And I was thinking about Sally and . . .'

'And what?'

'Well, it couldn't be her, could it, ma'am? I mean, it says here "flame-haired". I mean, that was the girl that were killed.'

'Really, Jenny, you must do something about these awful fancies of yours. What would Sally Bowker be doing upon a train? Show me that,' says Miss Sparrow, her face quite composed.

Jenny steps forward and hands her the broadsheet. Her employer scans it briefly before looking up at her.

'You'd do better to read nothing at all, Jenny, rather than read such nonsense.'

'Sorry, ma'am,' says Jenny, a little abashed.

'Yes, well, go and see what can be done for White, will you? At least keep her quiet.'

❧

In her mind's eye, Agnes White sits upon a wooden stool, in the tap-room of the Black Boy. There is noise, and bustle, and jollity. She is suddenly a pretty young woman again, nineteen years of age.

But then she looks down and sees that she is carrying a child. She touches her face and finds it slightly fattened and flushed. And, whilst with one hand she cradles her balloon belly, with the other she holds a glass of gin. She places it upon the table, and tops it up from a half-bottle of Cream of the Valley, then takes another deep swig. The burning liquor slips easily down her throat, but she still feels the tightness in her back, iron fingers tugging at her womb.

She downs another measure, then gets up. It seems a dizzying, tumble-down kind of place but she staggers to the looking-glass and examines her face properly. Something is wrong with it, she can see that, but she cannot place it; but she has not trusted her reflection for twenty years or more.

How old? she wonders, looking at herself. How old are you?

Really? That old. Lord spare us.

—

'Aggie,' says the nurse, gently stroking her face as she turns this way and that upon the mattress, 'Aggie, come on now. You'll be choking yourself again . . . That's better, you just sleep nice and quiet. I'll get you up later, when supper's ready.'

—

'Take her to the workhouse!'

'Whorehouse, more like.'

'You take her!'

Aggie White crouches by the hearth of the Jolly Anchor. They are arguing about her, she can hear that much; they want her to go to Wapping Workhouse; and there is a fiddle playing in the background, the same melody again and again. She gets up, unsteady, holding on to a chair. It topples over and she falls back into the dust.

'If she drops it here, there'll be hell to pay.'

But, too late, here it is; there should be pain, but

perhaps she has forgotten that part. It is a baby, a girl, blood-blue and screaming as a woman finally cuts the cord with a penknife.

She cannot remember if it was Clara or Lizzie. Lizzie?

— ❦ —

'I want to see her. Tell her, I want to see her.'

'Who, Aggie?'

'Lizzie!'

'Don't get upset, dear. Your daughter? She was a nice girl. She'll be back, I'm sure,' says Jenny, re-arranging her pillow. 'You just rest now.'

'I want to see her, tell her I'm sorry.'

'There, you just rest now, dear. I'll tell her.'

— ❦ —

Philomena Sparrow stops writing, and looks outside. Serle Street is quiet at this time of day, and there is little to be seen except for the occasional carriage leaving Lincoln's Inn. She picks up the crumpled sheet of print that Jenny left her, and reads it again.

> . . . made the awful discovery of the body of a flame-haired woman, who is believed to have approximated twenty years of age, her neck broken and her body quite horribly contorted. The woman's identity remains a mystery to the Metropolitan police. Her assailant, who, in a touch of the grotesque, sat calmly by her corpse throughout the journey, upon being detected, ran from the station towards Marylebone . . .

She sits in silent contemplation for a few moments, then gets up and retrieves her bonnet and mantle from a hook by the door. She shouts upstairs.

'Jenny, I am going out. I leave you in charge. Do make sure that everyone is punctual for supper.'

'Yes, ma'am,' returns the nurse, appearing on the landing.

'And how is White?'

'She seems better settled now, ma'am.'

'Well, we have others to tend to, do we not?'

'Yes, ma'am.'

'I'll be back shortly.'

Miss Sparrow opens the front door, the crumpled sheet of paper in her hand, wondering what is the best route to Marylebone police station.

—

Agnes White opens her eyes. She is alone in the room, and it is getting dark outside. She gets up and looks out of the window, and sees the figure of Philomena Sparrow walking towards Lincoln's Inn Fields in the fading light. She looks for her boots, which lie beside the bed, and hurriedly puts them on.

No-one notices as she descends the stairs, and lets herself out into the street.

CHAPTER THIRTEEN

A HALF-MILE DISTANT from Lincoln's Inn, Decimus Webb stands in the ticket hall of Farringdon Street railway station. The station itself is only a temporary wooden structure, beset on all sides by works and protective hoardings, part of the extensive excavations required for its rebuilding in stone, and the extension of the railway eastwards. None the less, temporary or not, with the station clock having chimed five o'clock, the public are already entering the building in large numbers, processing down the stairway on to the platform.

'How long?' says Decimus Webb incredulously, continuing a conversation with an off-duty ticket clerk, a small balding man with a white moustache, who stands nervously beside him.

'Three minutes, sir, that's God's honest truth, I assure you.'

Decimus Webb shakes his head in disbelief.

'And it would have been three minutes last night, would it? From here to King's Cross?'

'Ah, well, last night there was works at Paddington, that might have held her up.'

'A-ha! How long then, last night?'

'Oh, I should reckon four minutes.'

'Four minutes' delay?'

'Oh no, sir, four minutes to King's Cross in total. That would be my guess.'

'Not long to kill someone, is it? Four minutes?'

'Well,' says the clerk, a little flustered, 'I couldn't say, sir. But I was here all the time. There's two men who can vouch for it.'

Webb snorts in laughter, and claps the man on the shoulders. 'Do not worry, Mr. Jones. I did not have you in mind.'

The man nods, but does not seem to find it quite so amusing.

'And you were on the ticket desk yourself, all last night?' continues Webb, watching the people as they walk into the station, but still addressing the man at his side.

'I was. From five o'clock till finish.'

'And you did not see the woman in question? She had red hair – quite striking, I would have thought.'

'Not that I recollect, sir, no. But she may have had a return ticket from Paddington or Baker Street. She would not need seeing, if you understand me.'

'Quite,' says Webb, nodding. Abruptly he then turns his head to the clerk. 'A return ticket, did you say?'

'Yes, sir. That is the common thing, on the evening trains. Folk rarely travel just the one way, do they?'

'Yes, I know that, my good man . . . Watkins!'

Webb shouts the man's name in the same way another man might shout 'Fire!' or 'Murder!' A good number of persons nearby jump in astonishment, not least Mr. Jones the ticket clerk; Webb, however, stands there unconcerned, offering a polite nod to anyone who stops and stares at the source of the uproar. Sergeant Watkins, meanwhile, appears from the plat-form, gently pushing his way through the mêlée of passengers heading in the opposite direction, and making gradual progress to the side of his superior.

'With respect, I am not a dog, sir.'

'Watkins, if you were a dog I could merely whistle. Tell me something, did our mystery woman have a ticket on her person?'

Watkins pauses for thought. 'No, sir. Not that I recollect.'

'Now why would that be?'

'She might have lost it in the scuffle.'

'Scuffle?'

'When he strangled her.'

Webb looks disbelieving. 'She might. There were discarded tickets upon the floor, were there not? I seem to recall seeing them.'

'Oh, they will insist on doing that, sir,' interjects Jones the ticket clerk, 'though we tell 'em to keep 'em, even after inspection.'

'But I believe you said there was no guard last night?'

'On the train, sir? No, not the last train. It was them works at Paddington, playing havoc with our rota, you see?'

'And so the girl could have caught it without a ticket?'

'Oh no,' says the clerk, frowning at this slur on the efficiency of the Metropolitan Railway, 'we had a man on the gate here.'

'I've spoken to him, sir,' says the sergeant. 'He recollects nothing.'

'He did not see the girl?'

'He doesn't say that. Says he can't remember one way or the other.'

'Really? What remarkable vigilance,' says Webb, looking thoughtful for a moment, then extending his hand to shake that of Mr. Jones. 'We are done here, I believe. Thank you for your assistance.'

Mr. Jones nods, and is about to make his way out,

when sergeant Watkins addresses Webb.

'Sir? I've also got the men who were working the track last night; they're ready for you at Baker Street. I can telegraph and get them down here if you like.'

'No need; we shall take the train. Perhaps it will provide some insight.'

Watkins agrees, and the two men begin to walk down to the platform. A small voice, however, calls out from behind them.

'One moment, gentlemen,' says Mr. Jones. 'You'll be wanting a ticket.'

———

The train containing Decimus Webb and sergeant Watkins pulls slowly out of Farringdon station. It is watched by a workman who stands idly by the signals, wearing a thick oilskin coat, the kind favoured by many of those who work on the tracks. The platform is now all but cleared of people, for a short while at least, and, looking at the station clock, he makes his way along, up the steps and out towards the ticket hall.

'Night, Bill. You off?'

'There'll be another man through the tunnel soon, he can pick up.'

'You in the Three Cups tonight, Billy?'

'Maybe.'

He is a burly man, Bill Hunt, with the hard square face and broad shoulders typical of a body accustomed to physical labour. He does not speak much, and his colleague does not press any further questions upon him, though talk of murder is upon everyone's lips; they soon separate. Hunt makes his way into Farringdon Street itself, against the tide of travellers bound in the opposite direction. They are largely city clerks, and the large man in dirty oilskins appears an oddity amongst them. He keeps his eyes fixed upon the ground, however, amongst this sea of silk-hatted strangers, and manoeuvres gradually to Victoria Street, and then across the busy road, up the slope that leads to Hatton Garden. His path is quite predetermined and he soon turns off into a side street, at one end of which hangs a sign of three golden goblets, signifying the Three Cups public house. It is a small establishment, and would be all but invisible from the street were it not illuminated by a large iron gas-lamp, its brilliance somehow quite ill-suited to the narrow passage in which it is set.

The inside of the place, however, with which Bill Hunt is rather familiar, is not so bright. Indeed, it is not untypical of the shabbier sort of little gin palace that apes its larger rivals on Drury Lane. Like them, it boasts a mahogany bar, though the wood is chipped and stained; like them it is illuminated by gas, though it has only two lamps. Naturally, there is also the tobacco smoke, which hangs in the air like a fog, and the pervasive smell of spilt liquor. All in all, it is precisely what a Clerkenwell man expects of his local public and, however much there may be mud upon the floor and peculiarities in the ale, and however much the air may choke him, it seems cosy enough to the likes of Bill Hunt. Indeed, Hunt knows well many of the folk that drink there, and a few of them greet him as he walks in. He is surprised, however, to be hailed by one voice in particular.

'Bill! This is a treat!'

'What?'

He looks around and sees Tom Hunt seated in one corner of the room; he has a smile on his face, unlike his young wife, who sits sullenly beside him.

'I didn't expect to see you in a hurry, Tom Hunt,' says Bill, wearily.

'Didn't you? Your own cousin? Your own flesh and blood?'

'It's only been two weeks. And there's a matter of a half-crown between us, ain't there?'

'Let me stand you a drink, eh?' persists Tom, ignoring the question. 'Let me get you a drop of purl? That's still your favourite tipple, ain't it?'

Bill Hunt groans. He is not a quick-witted man, and though he feels irritation at his cousin's banter, he is resigned to it, in much the same way as a weary ox suffers the stings of a gadfly.

'Come on, Bill, sit and have a drink.'

He sits down, reluctantly, stealing a glance at Lizzie Hunt as he does so.

'How are things with you, old man?' asks Tom.

'The police have been crawling about,' he says, 'asking questions down the railway.'

'Really? Why's that? You been a bad boy, Bill?'

'I ain't done nothing,' he says hastily.

'Tom,' interjects Lizzie, 'don't tease him. You know what it'll be. You was only just talking of it.'

Tom Hunt grins. 'Aye, that poor girl, eh? Strangled. Weren't you, were it, Bill? Eh? That's a good'un, ain't it? Always the quiet ones, they say, Liz.'

'No, it weren't,' replies Bill Hunt, scowling.

'Don't take on, old man,' replies Hunt, laughing at his cousin's expense. 'Just my little joke, that's all. Now, let me get you that drink.'

'What do you want, Tom?'

'Well, let's just say me and Liz are having difficulties with our accommodation.'

CHAPTER FOURTEEN

DECIMUS WEBB'S TRAIN pulls in at Baker Street. He lets his sergeant go on ahead, and, in a couple of minutes, he finds himself standing by the track, past the end of the platform, next to a small wooden shed that serves as a repository for the workmen's tools. Beside him are sergeant Watkins and a dozen or so men in soot-blackened clothing – cloth or oilskins that afford no protection to their faces, which are as dirty as that of any miner. They all stand either hunched over their picks and shovels, or slouching with hands in pockets; they do not so much avoid the policeman's gaze as simply ignore it.

'Gentlemen,' says Webb, 'as you know, sergeant Watkins has assembled you here so I may ask you a few questions.'

A couple of the men spare him a glance, but none of them speaks. Webb, however, is unperturbed and continues to address them.

'Firstly, how many of you saw the train last night?'

'The last train, was it?' asks one man.

'Yes, the last train.'

Most of the men nod, or mutter some acknowledgement. The man who spoke adds, 'We all would have seen it. We all is ready to work, once it's gone by.'

'And what is your work?'

'Repairs and that. And there's the new station buildings at Farringdon, and the new line. All needs looking after, night and day.'

'And, tell me, did you see or hear anything peculiar or unusual in relation to that last train?'

'How do you mean?' says the same man.

'Well, perhaps a scream or shout, or something you saw in the carriage.'

A couple of the men smile. Most of them shake their heads.

'And what's so funny?' asks Watkins sharply.

'No offence,' says one of the men, 'but you ain't been in the tunnels, have you? You don't see much of anything when the train goes by, excepting dust and steam. And you wouldn't hear nothing but the wheels neither. Not if there was a brass band playing, you wouldn't hear it.'

Webb pauses, fixing his gaze on the man who spoke.

'I see. Well then, thank you, gentlemen. If you think of anything more, please let me know. I believe that will be all for now.'

The men look surprised at the brevity of the interview, but relieved at its termination. Webb climbs the steps back on to the platform. Watkins follows him.

'Well, that was hardly worth it,' says Watkins.

'I had nothing more to ask them. And, besides, none seemed keen to talk.'

'You can tell he planned it, eh?'

'Planned?'

'He gets the girl alone in the carriage. No-one can see a thing, no-one can hear her screaming.'

'And what about someone in the next carriage? Would they not have heard her?'

'Not with the noise of the train, surely?'

'Maybe. Tell me, is my velocipede still here, sergeant?'

'We had it taken back to the station house last night,

sir, for safety. We thought that would be best.'

'Hmph. I had thought to ride it directly home.'

'Home already, sir?'

'I do not think there is much more I can do today. I need to think on it. We are missing something, I know it. Hold on, what's this?'

As he speaks, a boy rushes down the steps from the ticket hall and makes directly for the policemen.

'Message for Inspector Webb, if you please, sir.'

'I am he,' replies Webb.

'Sergeant Tibbs says can you come to the station house directly, sir. Says it's urgent.'

'How curious,' says Webb. 'Tell me, young man, do you know what this is about?'

'That was the message, sir,' says the boy.

'But do you know what it pertains to, young man?'

'There's a lady, sir. That's all I know.'

'A lady? Well, run on and tell sergeant Tibbs that I shall be there directly; and tell him that had he not taken my velocipede into his custody, I should be there all the quicker.'

'Sir?'

'Never mind, here's a penny for you. Just tell him I will be there shortly.'

The boy eagerly takes the penny, and runs at full pelt past the crowd of passengers waiting on the platform.

'So much,' says Webb, 'for an early finish.'

A half-hour later, and Decimus Webb enters his office in Marylebone Lane.

'Inspector?' Philomena Sparrow turns her head and rises from her chair.

'Indeed, but please seat yourself, ma'am,' says the inspector.

Miss Sparrow complies, watching the inspector manoeuvre round his desk to take the seat behind it; he is impeded by heaps of paper and notebooks, which lie both on its surface and scattered upon the floor around its boundaries.

'I am afraid that I have been sitting a full hour, Inspector,' says Miss Sparrow.

'Well,' says Webb, finally lowering himself into his chair, 'we will keep you no longer than necessary, now that I am here. Now, I understand our good sergeant Tibbs has shown you the . . . ah . . . deceased?'

'Really, you may say "body" Inspector. It is all the same to me.'

'Indeed? May I? You show remarkable composure, ma'am.'

'I am quite accustomed to death, Inspector, in my profession.'

'You are, I understand, lady superintendent of the Holborn Refuge, is that correct?'

'Of course it is. That is precisely what I told your sergeant two hours ago. Must I repeat everything?'

'It is quite likely,' replies Webb, smiling. 'And so, tell me, you believe you recognise the body?'

'There is no question, Inspector. It is Sally Bowker, one of our girls.'

'I see. Has she been with you long?'

'A month or so.'

'And has she any family? They should be told, if so.'

'Not to my knowledge. I would need to check our records, but I believe she said she was an orphan. It is not a simple matter to check, of course. The girls have a habit of, shall we say, fabrication.'

Webb picks up a pencil from the desk and twirls it between his fingers as he talks.

'That is a shame. And, forgive my bluntness, ma'am, but she was a *magdalene*, yes?'

'There is no need to spare my blushes, Inspector. Yes, she was on the streets before she was reformed.'

'Ah,' says Webb, raising his eyebrows a little, 'you consider that she was quite reformed?'

'She was one of our best, Inspector. You do not know, I am sure, how much a woman may be changed in a month by prayer and hard work. I cannot believe that she would have fallen from the path.'

'But, I suppose, you cannot account for her presence on the Metropolitan Railway? One certainly might wonder what business a young girl, any young girl, might have there, if one saw her travelling so late at night. Or perhaps she was on some errand for yourself?'

'No,' replies Miss Sparrow, hanging her head a little, 'she broke our curfew. I regret that I cannot account for it.'

Webb smiles indulgently. 'Nor would I ask you to, ma'am. Tell me, did, ah, Sally have any particular acquaintances who might have wished her harm?'

'Acquaintances, Inspector? I could not say. She did not keep company with anyone outside the refuge, not to my knowledge.'

Webb does not reply to this point. 'And there is no-one at your establishment to whom she was particularly close?'

'No-one that I know of,' replies Miss Sparrow.

'And you cannot tell me why anyone would want to . . . ah . . . do away with the girl?'

'I cannot. Surely that is your job, Inspector, and to catch this lunatic, whoever he may be.'

'Oh, indeed, ma'am. It is indeed. I am merely not convinced that it is a "lunatic", as you put it.'

'What other explanation is there?'

'Oh, my dear Madam, if I knew that already the matter would be done with, and we both could be somewhere else entirely. Perhaps, I wonder, might we visit you tomorrow, *in situ*, as it were, and discuss the matter in more detail then?'

'Is that necessary? It will disturb my girls.'

'I am afraid it is very necessary, ma'am.'

'I see. If you wish. Well, if that is all for the moment, do you think I might go now? I have been away long enough already.'

'Indeed. One moment, and I will find a constable to escort you.'

'That would be good of you,' replies Miss Sparrow, curtly, without much hint of gratitude.

Webb gets up and makes for the door, stumbling over a stack of books as he does so.

'I won't be a second,' he says, as he dusts down his trousers.

———

'Well, sir, what do you make of that?' says Watkins, a few minutes later, when Miss Sparrow has left the building.

'Of Miss Sparrow? An intelligent woman. She cared for the girl, I think.'

'Tibbs said she seemed a queer old fish, sir. Prickly, he said.'

'Have you met sergeant Tibbs' wife, Watkins?'

'Not to speak of.'

'Well, rest assured sergeant Tibbs is in no position to pass judgement.'

'If you say so, sir.'

'I do. Now, where is my blasted velocipede?'

'Off home, sir?'

'If I have your permission, sergeant, yes. We have had this conversation already, have we not?'

'Take care, sir. Them roads is terribly dangerous at night, you know.'

CHAPTER FIFTEEN

As Inspector Webb readies himself for his journey home, another figure makes a slow and solitary progress through an altogether different part of the metropolis – Agnes White.

For two hours or more she has wandered this way and that, and even the acutest observer would be hard-pressed to find a method to her meandering. None the less, as night falls and a thick river-fog begins to creep from the Thames, she appears to be drawn eastwards. True, she does not take a direct route; rather her journey is characterised by a preference for ill-lit streets and alleys over the regular thoroughfares, and it is only when the fog has settled into a dense brown pall upon the City that she hazards the open roads. Indeed, the mist is black as coal-dust, and soon makes every route seem impenetrable. In fact, as she comes to St. Paul's Churchyard, it seems that even the gas struggles against the darkness, and the proud lamps that line the road, designed to illuminate the great cathedral, are muted and dim. But she presses on past the great church, past the shops of the booksellers and publishers for which the district is famous, their doors long since closed for the night. All the time she keeps her eyes fixed firmly upon the road, though she can see only a few yards ahead, and continues along the pavement of Cheapside, and into the nocturnal heart of the City.

At last, she reaches the Royal Exchange, passing the stately Mansion House, its interior half visible through tall windows, and by some chance catches a glimpse of draped velvet and chandeliers. She shivers a little, instinctively wrapping her shawl tighter around her head and shoulders, concealing her face and arms. A policeman watches her go by. In truth, it would be easy to mistake Agnes White for an apparition; seeing her in the distance, one might imagine a wisp of life had been breathed into a set of old clothes, with nothing inside.

But the policeman thinks nothing of it; he sees many such sights.

—

In Doughty Street, Clara White takes a solitary candle and ascends the stairs to her bedroom. She shares the room with Alice Meynell, but the kitchen-maid is still busy downstairs, attacking the pots and pans, which form the residue of the Harrises' dinner. In truth, Clara is not that fond of the white-washed little attic; it is perpetually cold, and she finds the slanting roof strangely oppressive. But she has no other place to go.

She puts her candle down, sits upon the covers, and takes up the needle and thread that she has by her bed. But it is a half-hearted effort; the thread seems reluctant to approach the needle and, once it is finally pulled through the eye, she repeatedly pricks her fingers in the half-light. She had hoped to repair a frayed chemise, a garment that, if truth can be told, warrants replacing in its entirety. Instead, she reluctantly puts it down upon the bed and shifts herself so that she sits by the window. Outside she can dimly make out the rooftops of Doughty Street and beyond, a forest of brick and sloping tiles, half-hidden by the fog that forms a dense sooty canopy about the houses. She presses her face against the glass to see how cold it is, and feels the draught of chill air on her cheek.

In a matter of moments she is asleep.

Agnes White walks for an hour or two more before she crosses the canal bridge between the East London and London Docks. In the pitch-darkness, she can smell the pungent river, the dirty tidal flood that washes past Wapping Reach, and she smiles to herself.

She takes a brief rest; her feet are sore. Then, after a few minutes, she carries on, hobbling past the warehouses on Old Gravel Lane, then on to the High Street. Here, a dozen or more publics and gin-shops vie for the trade of the innumerable river workers, dockers and sailors who make Wapping their temporary home. Here, too, as in every neighbourhood of the capital, each of these merry establishments appears to be in competition as to the size of the gas-light projecting above the door. She passes one familiar place after another; the raucous shouts and the smell of porter remind her of a time, not long ago, when she would have readily stepped inside.

'How much?' says a German-accented man, a sailor who splits from a gang of men coming in the opposite direction, putting his arm around her waist as she walks. 'How much?'

It must be two months or more since she has heard such words. It used to be a simple business, she thinks to herself, picking up the trade on Wapping High Street. A quick fumbling down the nearest alley, or by the shore when the tide was out; it was all done in a minute or two, and a good shilling or maybe two, depending how drunk the man.

But something has changed. She feels uncomfortable, though she cannot say why. Perhaps, she thinks to herself, she has grown too old. Or was it something her daughter said?

She looks round. The German has gone back to his friends, cursing her in guttural eruptions of a language that she cannot fathom.

It does not matter, she thinks. She must keep going.

What was it Lizzie said?

———

'I want to go home.'

Lizzie Hunt lies beside her husband on a rough woollen sheet, laid out neatly on the floor of Bill Hunt's little room. The latter is sound asleep, still in his work clothes, lying upon the bed in the corner. Her husband, upon the other hand, buttons his flies and sits up, leaning against the wall; she straightens her skirt and sits beside him, resting against his arm.

'We ain't got no home, remember? Not since they chucked us out. That's why we're here.'

'And it's shaming, with him 'ere,' she says, looking at the prone figure of her husband's cousin.

Tom Hunt smiles. 'He's dead to the world. Where's the harm?'

Lizzie says nothing but curls up next to him, nuzzling against his chest for warmth.

'You should wash,' he says.

'He ain't got any water.'

Tom looks around to confirm this suspicion, and grunts acknowledgement of the fact.

'You'd better be going then,' he continues, touching her cheek lightly.

She starts a little, sitting up straight. 'Do I have to, Tom? Not tonight?'

'In particular tonight, after this morning. We need the bloody money. Go on.'

He pushes her away, not too hard, but enough to dislodge her from his side. 'And don't come back after five minutes neither.'

Lizzie nods, a look of resignation on her face; she gets up, finds her boots and puts them on.

'Here,' says Tom, beckoning her back to him.

'What?' she replies wearily.

'You do think about me when you do it with them, don't you? Like I said.'

'Yes,' she replies.

He smiles, and gets up to kiss her on the cheek.

'Good girl. That's the best way.'

CHAPTER SIXTEEN

A CONVERSATION:

'Born? I was born in Wapping, sir. A place by the river. The Black Boy.'

'In a public house?'

'Yes, sir.'

'A curious place.'

'It were my mother's doing, sir. She was drinking there.'

'I see. What is your mother's name?'

'Agnes, sir.'

'Agnes White, is it not?'

'You know her?'

'I have met her. Tell me, what does your mother do?'

'I don't like to say.'

'Come, speak up. You may be frank with me.'

'Well, she's always been a sloop, sir.'

'What? Ah, that is the river slang, is it not? Sloop of War?'

'Yes, sir.'

'And your father?'

'He was most likely sailing on an East Indiaman that was moored at St. Kats. That's what my ma reckoned. I only know that much, sir, nothing more.'

'A sailor? I see. And have you any brothers or sisters?'

'Only one that lived more than a twelvemonth. Lizzie.'

'A sister? And she is still alive? How old is she?'

'Fourteen now.'

'And your mother raised both of you, relying on her own devices?'

'And my gran'ma – she had a big house by the river, near Wapping Stairs. Gravehunger Court. She took in lodgers, and we stayed with her, on and off.'

'And tell me, Clara, do you like this life that you have now? Do you take to it?'

'No, sir. I don't like it much.'

'And would you change, if you had the opportunity?'

'I would change, sir, quick as you liked, if there was something better for me. But there ain't.'

'You are a good girl. It is a good thing I chanced upon meeting you, my dear. A very good thing for you, rest assured. Now, my name is Harris.'

—

Alice Meynell tiptoes into the Doughty Street attic bedroom, and sees her room-mate slumped by the window, an exhausted candle sitting upon the bedside table. She puts down her own light and she gently persuades Clara's semi-conscious form to lie properly upon the bed, teasing out the blankets from beneath her, so that she can then cover her body and get in beside her. She herself then unties her boots, removes her own dress, corset and petticoat, and, in her chemise, climbs into the bed, which they are obliged to share.

In the darkness, she looks for a moment at Clara's face, and wonders what she might be dreaming about.

—

Clara frowns.

The questioner has melted away and, as often happens in the unconscious hours after midnight, she finds herself standing outside a house by the river, upon the first floor, her grandmother's house in Wapping. It is an old dilapidated place. Once it was the home of some prosperous merchant. No more. Now it is 'dry lodgings'.

It changes again.

She looks through the window. Outside, in the courtyard where she stood, the river water has risen to ankle-deep. The water is rich in silted London mud, the primitive sludge of the river-bed, intermingled with the refuse of the residents of the surrounding buildings, and much worse besides.

How did this happen? she thinks to herself. Ah, yes. Grandmother refused to leave. Mother is shouting at her. 'Now we'll all be drowned and damned together.'

She watches the water. It comes in earnest, but not in raging torrents. It seeps in, steady and stealthy, drooling between cracks in the brick-work, up the old landings and steps. Gradually, it becomes so deep that the current flows steadily between buildings, and, piece by piece, washes the detritus of daily life out along the Thames. Chairs, tables, pots, pans. A skirt, a dress, a copy of the *Daily News*. Everything flows away.

But it is an awkward cleansing. She knows there is never cause for celebration when the tide subsides. How long does it take? She is not sure. None the less, in every house, and in all the warehouses and store-rooms that line the quays, the ousted inhabitants return to find that the river has left an indelible mark, signifying the limits of water's ambition. And everywhere Clara herself looks there is mud, a grimy syrup that adheres to the walls, inside and out, a filthy black sludge that must be thanklessly scraped and scrubbed away.

It stinks of dirt and decay, and Clara's mother cries. She does not often cry.

Outside, she can hear her little sister screaming.

———

'Lizzie?'

'What? Clara, wake up.'

'Lizzie?'

'Clara, wake up, you're dreaming.'

Clara White turns over, looking at the sloping ceiling of the attic, recalling the room and the voice of Alice the kitchen-maid, who lies beside her in the bed.

'You were dreaming about your sister, weren't you?'

'I'm sorry. Did I say something?'

'You were calling her name.'

Clara pauses, as if trying to recall her thoughts. 'She came yesterday, and saw my mother.'

'You said. What's wrong with that?'

'I thought she'd fallen out with her.'

'What for?'

'It don't matter. She ran off with someone, a man what we used to know, and we haven't heard anything of her, not for a twelvemonth.'

'Who was he then, this someone?'

'Tom Hunt.'

'That it?'

'What do you mean?'

'What was he? Butcher? Baker? Good-looking? Thin? Fat?'

'Tom? He's no good to anyone. Lord knows how she's fixed, or what she's doing.'

———

On the rise of Saffron Hill, Lizzie Hunt stands, glum-faced and bare-headed in the clammy night air, clapping her arms to her sides to keep warm, peering through the fog. A figure approaches her, indistinct at first, then becoming more visible, walking with a hesitant gait; he is a rough-looking man, with bushy unkempt whiskers and the familiar hint of gin on his breath.

'Can we go somewhere? Will two bob do it? I ain't got no more.'

She nods. 'I know a good little place, if you like. It's not far.'

She takes hold of his arm, and leads him away, turning towards Victoria Street.

PART TWO

CHAPTER SEVENTEEN

Morning.

The fog has lifted a little, but there is still a perceptible black-brown mist that dogs the streets, occluding roads and alley. Moreover, during the night, the outside atmosphere has crept into private homes, a stealthy intruder through letter-boxes and ill-fitting sash windows, and the smell of it clings to cloth and curtains. Indeed, as breakfast appears upon the dining-tables of the metropolis, so omnipresent is the residual stench of the night's 'London particular', that the pleasant aromas of the kitchen are generally mingled with an all-too-familiar scent of coal-dust and sulphur.

In the dining-room of the Harris household, however, Clara White is too preoccupied to give the ravages of the fog a second thought. Instead, she frowns in concentration as she strategically lays out the morning's copy of *The Times* upon the dining-table, aligning it precisely with the toast rack, a fine example of Sheffield plate, which takes pride of place amongst the Harrises' pre-prandial silverware. She only leaves the paper alone when she is quite sure that its positioning will not interfere with Dr. Harris's enjoyment of his breakfast, nor prevent him from casually perusing its pages. She then positions a tea service, also of burnished silver, to the left of the paper, in accordance with the household usage, with space remaining for an arrangement of plates and cutlery. If the teapot lid rattles somewhat as Clara deposits it upon the damask tablecloth, it is only because her worthy mistress, unlike the good doctor, has already come in and sat down at table. Mrs. Harris, in fact, observes her maid-servant's movements with the same critical attention that a lesser woman might reserve for discussing the talents of the Opera House's *corps de ballet*, and it comes as no surprise to Clara, therefore, when she learns that the position of the knives is 'altogether wrong', and her situation of the anchovy paste 'utterly remarkable'. Indeed, the pronouncement of such discerning judgements is an almost daily occurrence in the Harris household, and the prospect of such scrutiny fills Clara with dread every morning. It is only the sound of Dr. Harris upon the stairs, and his appearance in the doorway in his navy-blue dressing gown, that signals the end of her ordeal. A curt nod from her mistress, and Clara is dismissed, in order that she might hurry down to the kitchen, to retrieve the morning's boiled eggs, bacon and cold cuts.

Clara performs this task with admirable speed, such that, as she comes back into the parlour, the bacon still sizzles from its scorching, and the eggs still steam from the pan. And yet she does not get a word of thanks from her mistress, whose attention has turned to perfecting the drapery of her dress's pagoda sleeves, which are of sufficient breadth to be in danger of trailing over the toast rack. Clara's only encouragement is, rather, a smile from the cherubic doctor, who regards his prospective repast with satisfaction, and remarks with relish, 'Eggs!'

This simple and heartfelt comment is sufficient to send her back downstairs marginally more cheerful. The clock in the hall chimes nine o'clock as she descends the steps, and she smiles pleasantly at Cook as she enters the kitchen.

'Any bacon left?'

Cook looks at her with a certain degree of complacency and satisfaction, and dabs her salty lips with a dish-rag.

'Sorry, dear, no.'

———

As in any house, there are chores to be done after breakfast, and it is past ten o'clock before Clara White, wrapped in her winter shawl, can excuse herself, under pretence of pursuing Dr. Harris's missing book. Indeed, she climbs the area steps and sets off briskly along Doughty Street with a sigh of relief, thinking all the while of her mother.

Outside, the fog has nearly lifted. There are still a few office boys and copy-clerks on their way to Gray's Inn, but it is past time for them to be at their desks; the streets, in fact, are quite empty but for these occasional stragglers, and the odd delivery man on his rounds. There is still, of course, the constant rumble of traffic, the endless reverberation of iron-shod wheels in neighbouring streets, and it is not long before Clara hears the far-off shout of some itinerant street hawker, in the business of selling and mending old clothes. None the less, there is no-one to impede her as she goes along Jockey's Fields, the old mews that leads down by the high stone wall of Gray's Inn, and thence to Lincoln's Inn Fields. She walks quickly and, in her apron pocket, hidden beneath her woollen wrap, she keeps one hand carefully protecting the bottle she purchased for her mother.

Even as she climbs the steps to the refuge, however, she falters a little, since she can hear a pair of raised voices inside. In itself, this is not an unusual occurrence in Miss Sparrow's establishment, where some friction between the residents is an almost daily event. What is remarkable, however, is that one of the women speaking sounds akin to Miss Sparrow herself. Still, Clara goes up and rings the bell, conscious of the fact that she is well past visiting time. The door is slow to open, and reveals the nurse who spoke to her the previous day, her face a little flushed.

'Oh, Miss,' she says, startled, 'I wasn't expecting you.'

'No, I am sorry, I know it's past visiting, and I cannot stop. It's just that I have something for my mother,' Clara says, taking out the bottle. 'The medicine we talked about?'

The girl looks perplexed for a moment. 'Oh, I see. Yes, Miss, I think you had better come in. Have a word with Miss Sparrow.'

'No, really, there is no need for that. If you could just give it to her?'

'I think there is, Miss, if you will . . . it's a bit awkward.'

Clara White, confused, reluctantly follows her indoors, and waits in the hall as the nurse hurries into Miss Sparrow's office, exchanges a few hasty words, then comes out again, and bids her to go inside. Philomena Sparrow stands there waiting for her, with her hands behind her back, and her head held high. But her eyes do not quite meet those of her visitor, and she seems far from comfortable.

'We were not expecting you, Miss White.'

'I am sorry, ma'am. I did not ask to come in at all. I know the hours. I was asked in.'

'Well, in fact, I am glad Jenny did so. I am afraid I have to tell you that I have some bad news. Your mother, it appears, has once more seen fit to abscond.'

'Abscond?'

'She has gone, Miss White. Taken off without a by-your-leave.'

'But she is ill. When did this happen?'

'Last night.'

'She was allowed out?'

'We are not a Bastille, Miss White. As it happens, I was absent upon some other business, and I have remonstrated with Jenny. Nevertheless, we do not imprison our charges, as well you know.'

Clara frowns. Before she can gather her thoughts, however, there is a resounding knock at the front door of the house, where she herself was standing moments before. It echoes loudly through the hall. She watches as Miss Sparrow hurries to the window, and peers out at the step. When Philomena Sparrow turns back to face her, Clara cannot help but notice how firmly she grips the back of her chair as she speaks, with her arms held rigid as iron railings.

'I can say nothing more, Miss White. This is the last time. You may tell Dr. Harris that we can no longer keep a place for her here.'

'Really, ma'am, I promise you . . .'

Clara's pleas are interrupted by a knock at the study door, and Jenny cautiously enters the room. She is accompanied by the bulky figure of Decimus Webb, his features a little red from a swift progress, on two wheels, through the city streets.

Jenny blushes as she speaks. 'I'm sorry, ma'am, but the gentleman . . . well, being the police and all, I didn't think he should wait.'

Clara steals a look at the man and flinches. There is something in the word 'police', and in the sight of the blue uniform, that produces a subtle alteration in her posture, and a glance downwards at the floor, as if chastened by some unspoken word of reproach.

'Thank you, Jenny, that will be all. And I believe

we have concluded our talk, Miss White.'

Clara looks up, as if about to reply, then catches the eye of Webb once more, and changes her mind. She turns to leave. But before she can do so, the inspector politely interrupts her progress.

'One moment, if you please. Perhaps you might introduce us, Miss Sparrow?'

Miss Sparrow purses her lips.

'Very well, Inspector. This is Clara White, one of our former residents. Miss White – this is Inspector Webb.'

'Ma'am!' interjects Clara in an urgent whisper, far too late to prevent the revelation.

'Really, Miss White,' continues Miss Sparrow, ignoring her protest, 'there is no need to hide your old life from the inspector; indeed, we are all proud of your progress.'

Clara blushes, avoiding the inspector's quizzical glance.

Webb smiles. 'Ah, I see. Well, a success attributable solely to you, ma'am, I am sure. It is good to see your former charges doing so well, I suppose.'

'Indeed.'

'Well, ma'am,' says Webb, 'I do not suppose I need speak to former residents, so much as the current ones, eh?'

'No, indeed,' says Miss Sparrow hurriedly. 'You may go, Miss White.'

Clara nods and walks briskly out of the room, her face still burning red. As she enters the hallway, she finds Jenny, the nurse who spoke to her previously, standing remarkably close to the door, making a feint at adjusting the inspector's coat, which hangs from a nearby hook.

'I didn't know you used to be *here*, Miss,' she says in a whisper. 'You'd never know it, to look at you, I mean.'

Clara smiles weakly. She appears eager to change the subject.

'Why are the police here?'

'Well, you'll never believe it, but you know the girl what you were talking about yesterday . . .'

———

'A nervous creature, ma'am,' observes Inspector Webb, once Clara has left the room.

'Indeed,' replies Miss Sparrow, and smiles anxiously. 'I think we are all a little nervous. This is an awful business, Inspector.'

'Undoubtedly,' says Webb.

CHAPTER EIGHTEEN

Clara White leaves the Holborn Refuge for Penitent Women thoughtful and troubled, dwelling both upon the news of her mother's disappearance, and the nurse's revelations about Sally Bowker's death. It is, however, an instinctive eagerness to place some distance between herself and the figure of Inspector Webb, still dimly visible in Miss Sparrow's parlour window, that sends her walking briskly across Serle Street. She is too swift, however, since she does not heed the clattering approach of a hansom cab, which darts out from the gatehouse of nearby Lincoln's Inn. In fact, the vehicle flies into the road just as fast as if the horse had bolted. The actual cause is the promise of a half-sovereign made by its passenger, in the hope that the driver might proceed to London Bridge 'as quick as he likes'. It is a well-known fact that such an injunction is never wasted upon the Jehus of the cabbing profession, and inevitably leads to a liberal application of the whip. In this case, however, as in many others, it also nearly causes a collision. Indeed, in the end, it is impossible to say whether or not it is remotely due to the cabman's skill that he misses Clara, for he does so by no more than an inch or two. It is, perhaps, safe to assume that the driver himself would readily claim the glory. Certainly it is a tribute to his marvellous equanimity that, once he is satisfied that Clara is only sent tumbling on to the pavement, with nothing too much broken, he confines his observations upon the matter to a cry of 'Look it!', and turns the corner into Carey Street, wheels skidding on the slippery cobbles. And yet something is broken: the bottle of Balley's Quietener, intended for her absent mother, flies from Clara's pocket as she falls, and smashes into a dozen pieces beside her.

'Miss, here, let me help you up.'

Clara looks up, a little dazed but unhurt, and hesitantly takes the arm of a young man who seems to appear almost instantly at her side, a handsome man, although rather shabbily dressed. She is too preoccupied with the remains of the broken bottle to notice that there is something odd in his voice and manner that belies his poor appearance.

'Quite done for, I'm afraid,' he says, looking at the shards of glass, then carefully shunting them into the gutter with his foot. 'I hope it wasn't anything valuable. Still, you're lucky it isn't you in pieces. Are you hurt at all?'

Clara lets go of his arm, and dusts herself down. 'No,' she replies, a little breathless, 'not valuable. Not hurt either. I'm sorry, thank you, but I must go.'

At this, she says nothing more, and strides away, without even a smile for her saviour.

The man watches her hurry off into Lincoln's Inn Fields. He takes a long look at the Refuge for Penitent Women, as if pondering some question in his head, then turns and follows her at a distance, having made a note in his diary.

'Accident with a hansom'.

'So, tell me, ma'am, how many do you have?' asks Inspector Webb, as he takes a leisurely glance at the books in Miss Sparrow's study.

'You make it sound as if I keep prize cochins, Inspector. There are twenty or, no, I should say, nineteen women here at present.'

'Well, I will need to speak to all of them. Nineteen, not twenty? You were thinking of the dead girl, I suppose?'

'Well, no. Another woman left us yesterday.'

'Left you? Do you mean . . .'

'No, not died. She ran off last night, but I expect we shall see her again.'

'Ran off? You mean like Sally Bowker "ran off"?'

'Really, Inspector, nothing like that at all. What are you suggesting? Agnes White makes a habit of such petty recidivism; it is nothing out of the ordinary, I can assure you. She has never managed a full month with us without some infraction. Sally, on the other hand, was a good girl; she took well to instruction.'

'And you let this White woman offend with regularity?'

'We attempt to be charitable, Inspector. But this time is the last straw . . .'

'And did she know the dead girl?'

'They shared a room, but I do not believe they were close. Agnes has been ill for much of the time this past month or two. If anything, that alone has made her a little better behaved.'

'Shared a room? You astonish me, ma'am. Why was none of this mentioned before?'

'Agnes only went off last night. You think it significant?'

'It is something of a coincidence, is it not? One moment. Her name is "White"? The girl who I just saw . . .'

'Agnes's daughter. A much sounder proposition; one of our successes, as I said.'

The inspector smiles. 'The daughter? I see. Nice to keep a trade in the family, I suppose. I shall want to speak to the daughter again, I fear, when I am done here.'

'I am sure that can be arranged. But our work here is no laughing matter, Inspector.'

'No, ma'am. I don't honestly suppose it is.'

⸺

Clara White walks briskly around the square of Lincoln's Inn Fields. There is something agitated in her manner: her eyes are downcast, as if engaged in some awful contemplation, her hands busy in constant worrying of her dress. Moreover, she almost collides with several persons on the pavement, though she manages, upon each corner of the square, to keep clear of passing traffic. She only pauses, in fact, having almost completed a full circuit, when she comes near to the corner of Portugal Row, where the square abuts on to the narrow streets leading to Clare Market. At this junction, she halts, and looks up as if suddenly noticing something or someone. Then, for a moment she hesitates. But it is not for long; she leaves the square and walks briskly towards the alleys.

Clara makes swift progress, since the pavements of Clare Market, though littered with a confusion of market stalls and wagons, are empty of goods and persons, the market proper not being a daily occurrence. Admittedly, there are still some attractions for passing trade, principally the butchers' shops, which rarely close. Indeed, if a stranger were in any doubt as to whether, in these odd lanes, he or she had stumbled upon the famous market, he would only have to note the prevailing smell, distinctive to the district. It is an odour of old vegetables mingled with rotting meat, the pungent outpouring of local tripe-houses, the delicate scent of pig's blood and cabbage leaves. It is, say local wags, a meal in itself. In any case, the market is quite familiar to Clara White, and she readily ignores the stench, and the cries of the butchers. Likewise, where half a dozen or more purveyors of household stuff have cleared some ground to lay out their wares, she pays no heed and walks round them. Instead, her eyes are firmly fixed upon a person in the middle distance slowly weaving her way along in the direction of Drury Lane and the Strand. It is an old woman dressed in dark blue cotton and a rather dirty shawl, wearing a ribboned straw bonnet and carrying a small wicker basket hooked under her arm. The woman walks with a stoop and it is not long before Clara catches up to her. But she does not speak to her or detain her; rather, she ensures that she is a few yards behind the stooped figure, and idles a little, to guarantee that she does not get too near.

The old woman herself comes to a halt voluntarily some five minutes later in Wych Street. It is not a prepossessing place in which to stop, being a dog-leg continuation of Drury Lane that runs down to the Strand, famous only for the Olympic Theatre, a place grander in name than in reality. It does, however, possess a good number of print-sellers and bookshops displaying the latest prints and engravings in their windows, and the occasional cartoon from *Punch*; a few can even boast rather more immodest literature, pages and titles that would not be welcome in a decent household. In consequence, Wych Street, though narrow and gloomy, is never quite free of foot-traffic: in front of every establishment there are little crowds of window-gazers, both men and women, and even children, who come to press their noses against the plate glass and, in some cases, remark upon how shocking it is that such things are put on show. Indeed, a person might easily spend a whole day in Wych Street, moving from one window to another, pausing only occasionally to peruse the shops' books and antiquarian oddities, which are laid upon shambolic wooden counters upon the pavement. And it is, no doubt, with some such intention that the old woman stops in front of a particular print-seller where a huddle of half a dozen persons are already gathered. A sign in the window reads, 'Books and Prints: French curiosities.'

Clara White stops behind her.

—

'That is the entire list, ma'am?'

'Yes, Inspector, as I said. Every girl who has stayed with us in the last six months, and a list of family and visitors, with dates and times of visits.'

'Very thorough, ma'am. Commendable.'

'We do our best, Inspector.'

'I see Miss White has been a regular visitor these past few days.'

'She has been concerned for her mother's health. It is understandable, I suppose.'

'The same mother who pitched off into the night, yesterday, eh? Her health cannot be that bad.'

'My opinion also. If anything, I would say it is her mental state that is disturbed. I have never found much wrong with her.'

'She didn't see a doctor during her stay here?'

'Indeed, on two occasions, at considerable expense, I might add. They concurred with me.'

'I see. Well, may I have the daughter's address, ma'am?'

'As I said, Inspector, something can be arranged, I am sure . . .'

'The address will suffice, ma'am. Is there some difficulty?'

'No, it's merely that . . . well, Clara White is housemaid to one of our governors, Dr. Harris. He sponsored both Clara and her mother. I should not like him to think that there is anything amiss here.'

'You can't conceal a murder, ma'am. It is all over the papers already. I am surprised there is not a crowd of gawpers directly outside your window. There will be – you have my word.'

'Really? But surely this business with Agnes is something and nothing. It may rather sound to Dr. Harris as though we are in chaos here, Inspector, and that is far from the case.'

'I am confident no-one will think such a thing, ma'am. If it is any comfort to you, I will do my utmost to be discreet.'

'Very well. But I am sure Clara has nothing to hide, Inspector.'

'I never said she did, ma'am.'

—◆—

Outside the shop window, Clara White turns around, apparently intending to walk away. But, as a carriage passes by at the same moment, she happens to stumble on the kerb and falls back. As she trips she leans against a tall mustachioed gentleman in a dark green morning suit, also stationed by the window, knocking his walking cane to one side, and she herself lands clumsily upon the pavement. It is, however, a rather different kind of tumble from the incident upon Serle Street, though quite convincing to the uninitiated. Indeed, there is no-one more concerned for Clara's welfare, as she is helped up, than the old woman whom she followed. There are, in fact, expressions of heartfelt concern, pressing of hands, assurances sought, and received, as to her health and state of mind. And when Clara walks away with the old woman's purse, deftly retrieved from her shopping basket, the old party is none the wiser, and merely mutters 'poor soul' to herself as she watches the girl depart.

A few minutes later, Clara shelters in an alley just off Portugal Street, and counts the old woman's money; she finds it hard to stop her hands from shaking. It is, in truth, some months since she did anything so dangerous. The money, at least, is enough, she concludes, to pay for the broken bottle of medicine and to square the Harrises' account before a demand is made.

She takes a deep breath and heads back across Lincoln's Inn, somehow both ashamed and elated by her success.

For a moment, she has the peculiar sensation that someone is watching her.

CHAPTER NINETEEN

'LADIES AND GENTLEMEN, ladies and gentlemen! Three thimbles and one humble pea. I moves them around like so. A penny is the price to play, two pennies is what you win. Come now, don't be shy.'

It is well after midday, and Tom Hunt sits on a doorstep upon Saffron Hill, calling out to passers-by, a piece of card balanced upon his lap; on the card are the three thimbles, rusty little items made of some undistinguished metal, and under one he carefully places a dried pea, then shifts them around, slowly at first, then more quickly, shuffling them about. The only person watching, however, is a small ragged-looking boy who hovers nearby; he seems to regard this display as sufficient entertainment, without contemplating the investment of a penny into the proceedings, even if he had such an article.

'You, sir! How about you, sir? Would you venture a penny on a game of skill?' says Tom, addressing a man coming out of the alley opposite, the narrow passageway that leads to the Three Cups. 'Yes, sir. Skill. I won't say, "Try your luck", not me. It ain't luck what's needed. A good pair of eyes in your head, that's the thing for this game, sir. Not many as have 'em, mind you, but you look a sharp fellow.'

The man demurs, smiling but shaking his head. Tom

Hunt smiles back, albeit with less enthusiasm, and is about to continue his patter on the next person who chances to approach when he realises that the effort would be quite wasted.

'Bill!' he exclaims, seeing his cousin. 'You're up, are you? Ain't you on the night shift tonight?'

Bill Hunt shrugs. 'I couldn't sleep.'

'Is Lizzie back home?'

'Home?'

'A slip of the tongue, Bill. I mean to say your lodgings, of course I do.'

'You staying with us much longer?'

'Course not,' says Tom, emphatically, although his cousin does not appear reassured. 'So is Lizzie there?'

'She ain't there, least not when I woke up. What do you want with her?'

'A man can ask after his own wife, can't he?'

'If he likes.'

'Well, she should have some money for us, as it happens. Pay you back that half-crown what we borrowed.'

Bill Hunt pauses, frowning, as if framing his words carefully. 'Not sure I want it, given how she'll have earnt it.'

Tom Hunt laughs, an expression of amazement on his face. 'Not sure you want it?' he says, parroting his words in mockery. 'Well I never! You been going to church on Sundays, Bill?'

'It's a bad business for a young'un like her, that's all I'm saying.'

'Bad for me and all,' says Tom, reproachfully. 'Don't you think it weighs heavy on my head to have her doing that game?'

'Then you should do something.'

'I am, cousin, I am. Look at me, I'm sitting here now, ain't I? I ain't here for my health.'

'I could get you something regular, on the railway. They need men on the tunnel; they're taking it to Finsbury Circus in a month or two. There'll be lots of work for them as wants it.'

'I ain't that keen on picks and shovels, Bill. Don't have the bones for it. We ain't all cart-horses, are we? Wouldn't be natural if we were.'

Bill shrugs. 'I suppose.'

'Though you're right, this is slow going,' continues Tom, looking up and down the street, then staring disconsolately at his piece of card. 'What say you front us a drink, eh?'

Bill Hunt frowns, but acquiesces, and together they proceed down to the Three Cups. Although it is the middle of the afternoon, the smoke-filled room is busy enough: a pair of dustmen, still dressed in their greasy oilskins, sit at one table; at another a bare-armed costermonger downs a glass of pale ale; and several men and women, of indeterminate occupation, are dotted here and there, with blushing cheeks and bleary eyes, talking in gin-soaked accents. Bill makes his way to the bar and orders a mug of purl for himself and a measure of gin for his cousin; together they pull up a couple of stools around a small circular deal table.

'I've been thinking, old man,' says Tom, clapping his hand affectionately on his companion's shoulder, 'about the railway. A fellow might do a decent business on the railway.'

'What sort of business?'

'Well, take that girl what was killed, what you told us about. No-one saw nothing, did they? No-one stopped the devil who done it; even though he stuck right next to the bleedin' body.'

'So?'

'Well, don't get me wrong, it's a crying shame and all, but it tells you something that he got away with it, don't it? I bet, for instance, there's a lot of property what is lost, one way or another, on your blessed railway. And a fellow with light fingers, well, he might do all right out of it.'

'Nowhere to run neither, is there?'

'A fellow wouldn't need to. Not if he had someone looking out for the guard. And I bet you see a few things, working down them stations. I bet many an item goes walking from your works, don't it?'

'So that's your bright idea, is it? Well, I ain't helping you with that. Forget I said anything. I got enough troubles.'

'Just a thought, Bill. Perk up. I ain't never seen a fellow always look so bleedin' chopfallen as you, I swear.'

'Maybe I have reason.'

'Reason? You ain't got a care in the world, have you?'

'Just think of something else, that's all. I ain't helping you.'

Tom Hunt looks only a little downcast.

'I wonder where that blasted woman of mine's got to, eh?'

Lizzie Hunt stands by the imposing wall of Gray's Inn, near to the corner of Gray's Inn Lane, watching the traffic. There is something mesmeric in the shifting mass of bodies and vehicles, and she waits there for several minutes before moving on down Holborn Hill. Her face, however, looks tired and wan, and there is a certain listlessness in her movements that is noticeable to anyone who sees her. In her hand she clutches a small purse tied by a piece of cord to her wrist. She keeps a firm hold on it until she comes upon a solitary figure crouched upon the pavement. It is a man in his fifties, a grey-bearded, leather-cheeked old man in patched corduroys, with a little wooden tray set before him containing the sort of knick-knacks beloved by a certain class of pedlar.

'Anything you fancy, dear?' he says upon seeing her interest. 'Nice bit of stuff for a lady, this; set your pretty little head off a treat, it would.' The old man gestures at a row of ribbons laid out upon one portion of the tray.

Lizzie smiles involuntarily bringing her hand up to touch her touzled hair.

'How about this one?' he says, selecting a thin dark red strip of cloth. 'Genuine silk.'

She takes it and inspects it.

'That's your colour, that is, my dear.'

'I'll take it.'

—

'I've got to go,' says Bill Hunt to his cousin, an hour or more subsequent to their arrival in the Three Cups. Before them on the table lie half a dozen empty glasses.

'Already?'

'There's work to be done,' he replies morosely.

'Always work with you, ain't it, old man? Well, I reckon I'll stay here a short while.'

'I thought you was flat broke?'

'Oh, yes, I am,' replies Tom, 'well, near as damn it.'

Bill takes a deep breath, straightening his back and drawing himself up to his full height; to another man he might seem intimidating, but his cousin merely shakes his hand and wishes him well.

'Well, it's been a pleasure sharing a glass, ain't it? And if you see Lizzie, tell her to find us here.'

'Aye, I will.'

With that, Bill Hunt stands up, replaces his jacket,

and makes his way to the door. Once out into the street he does not turn his step towards Farringdon station, but returns instead to the tenement in which he has his meagre lodgings. His heavy boots echo on the creaking steps that lead to his door; it is never locked, as his few possessions can be readily accommodated upon his person: a razor, a pipe, a box of matches. He is not overly surprised, therefore, to find Lizzie Hunt inside, lying upon his bed. She sits up as he enters the room.

'You're back then,' he says.

'Halloa, Bill.'

'Tom's looking for you. Wants his money.'

'Well, he'll get it,' she says. 'I saw the deputy downstairs. Says you'll have to pay extra if we're staying here.'

'I'll set him straight,' he replies. 'Are you?'

'What?'

'Are you stopping here?'

'Up to Tom and you, ain't it?'

'I'm just asking,' he says, sitting next to her on the bed. 'I never know with him what he's up to.'

She shrugs. 'You and me both.'

'If it were just you, we'd do all right,' says Bill, looking down at the floorboards. 'He ain't no good for you, you know.'

'Good enough, I'd say.'

'Maybe,' he replies, placing a hand gently on hers.

She smiles, half-heartedly. 'No, Bill. Leave it. Not again. What about Tom?'

'He won't be back, not for a while. I left him drinking in the Cups.'

'He's my husband.'

'He don't want *you*, he just wants some mot earning for him.'

Lizzie scowls, upset by the slur on her husband's

character. 'That ain't true. Anyhow, I feel a bit queer,' she says, shifting away from him a little, 'I need a rest, Bill.'

He looks at her, his forehead creased in thought. 'I'll pay, if you like.'

'Bill! Don't be awkward. You're hurting me.'

Bill Hunt lets go of her hand. 'No, I'd never hurt you.'

She looks at him, smiling kindly. 'I know, Billy, I know. Not today, eh?'

CHAPTER TWENTY

'So, your ma's gone off again?' says Alice Meynell, slicing a piece of ham for herself then immediately returning to sweeping the floor. She does not glance at Clara White as she speaks; she is too busy for that. Indeed, although there is no clock in the Harrises' kitchen at Doughty Street, Alice knows the time full well: Cook has already returned home; her master and mistress have just retired to the upstairs drawing room with a full pot of tea. In other words, it is plain to Alice Meynell that it is nine o'clock or thereabouts, and, in twenty minutes, a fire will be required in each bedroom and the beds turned down. It is, moreover, the only time that Alice and Clara may take their evening meal.

'Yes, gone again,' says Clara, absent-mindedly echoing her companion's words, her face peculiarly pensive. Unlike Alice, she is seated at the kitchen table. She has a slice of bread and butter on a plate set neatly before her but has not touched a single crumb.

'And,' continues Alice, returning to spear the ham with her fork as she speaks, 'after you went and bought that tonic for her. Ungrateful, I call it.'

'That? Oh, I returned that to the shop,' she replies casually. 'That's all square.'

'Didn't make you pay for it? That's good of 'em.

But your ma don't know that, does she?'

'I'm not sure she knows much of anything. She ain't been herself.'

'She'll come back, she always does.'

'And then what do I do with her?'

Alice shrugs. 'Workhouse?'

'Alice!'

'Well, I'm just saying, Clarrie. You can't keep her here in the cupboard, can you? You can't afford to be keeping her anywhere.'

'I ain't sending her into the 'house. It'd kill her.'

'Fair enough,' replies the girl, putting down her broom and sitting beside Clara. 'But there's something else, ain't there?'

'Like what?'

'You tell me.'

'Nothing. Well . . . something she said. Or maybe she didn't even actually say it. I can't remember.'

'Lor!' exclaims Alice, reducing the ham by another slice. 'Will you ever just say what you mean, plain like?'

'Well, it was like she knew that girl was dead, even before anyone had heard about it. I even talked to the nurse about it, Ally. But how could she know? It don't make sense.'

'You're giving me goose bumps. Maybe she has the second sight.'

'Don't laugh at me.'

'I weren't,' replies Alice.

'Perhaps I should tell someone, the police. But then what will they think, with her running off like that?'

'Hmm,' replies Alice, her cheeks full of ham and bread. Clara is about to say something else when the front doorbell rings, the sound jingling in the hallway and in the kitchen.

'There ain't anyone expected, is there?' says Clara, surprised.

'I'll have a look,' says Alice, wearily, walking over to the kitchen window, and peering up the area steps.

'Well, now's your chance,' she says, squinting up at the road.

'My chance?'

'To tell the police. They're only here,' she says, grinning excitedly. 'Probably come to take you straight to the magistrate, I reckon.'

Clara says nothing, her mouth gaping in open-jawed surprise. After a few seconds' delay, she gathers her thoughts and hurries upstairs, brushing crumbs from her apron. The voice of Mrs. Harris can already be heard from the landing.

'Who on earth is that?'

'Don't know, ma'am.'

'Well, do find out.'

'Yes, ma'am.'

Clara reaches the hall and pulls back the thick velvet curtain that protects the front door, then unlocks it; there is also a bolt with a tendency to stick, which does not yield immediately to her nervous fingers. Finally the door is opened to reveal the presence of Inspector Webb and, behind him, sergeant Watkins.

'Ah, Miss White,' says Webb, laying a rather sarcastic stress on *Miss*, 'good evening. Allow me to introduce sergeant Watkins. I am afraid, following our little discussion this morning, we require a few moments of your employer's time, and likewise of yours.'

Clara hesitates for a moment, then recollects her duty and beckons the two men into the hallway; in her confusion, she almost forgets to take the inspector's helmet.

'Perhaps you had better announce us, eh, Miss White?' suggests Webb, observing her agitation.

Clara nods and hurries upstairs.

'Very nervy sort, ain't she?' remarks the sergeant. Webb nods.

—

'With respect, Inspector, this is a peculiar hour to be calling at my home,' says Dr. Harris, once Clara has ushered the men inside and left the room. Dr. Harris's normally beatific expression is marred by a slight wrinkling of his brow.

'Well, with respect, sir, it is a matter of some importance. Perhaps if we could speak in private; it is a little delicate . . .'

Mrs. Harris, seated opposite her husband, visibly colours.

'I am sure anything you might say to my husband might be said to me, Inspector,' she interjects.

'Really, my dear,' says Dr. Harris, 'I should think if the gentleman says the matter is delicate . . . well, I mean to say, I expect he knows his own business.'

Mrs. Harris appears shocked by this rare rebuke, however mild, and merely replies with one of the unique wordless exclamations she reserves for such occasions, something between a snort and a cough. None the less, she vacates the room, closing the door behind her with an eloquent thud.

Dr. Harris smiles at this small triumph, his features almost returning to their normal calm composition.

'Now, Inspector, do take a seat and tell me what can possibly bring you here.'

'Well, sir, I understand you are a governor of the Holborn Refuge for Penitent Women?'

'Ah, I see. Some difficulty with one of the girls, is it? Yes, I have the honour of supporting that institution.'

'Perhaps you know of a girl called Bowker, a Sally Bowker?'

'I cannot say I do, Inspector. Not all the girls are mine, as it were. Many are there upon recommendation of others.'

'Other governors?'

'Indeed. I confess, I believe I know the name of the girl, but I could not say much else. Certainly I could not personally vouch for her. Has she done something to, ah, bring herself to your attention, Inspector?'

'You could say that, sir,' interjects Watkins.

'How so?'

'She was the girl that was murdered on the railway two nights ago, sir,' replies Webb.

'Really? What was she doing there?'

'We cannot account for it as yet, sir,' says Webb. 'And so, to be quite clear, you are sure that there is no particular connection between yourself and the dead woman?'

'Indeed I am. I must say, Inspector, if that is all you came here for then you might have waited . . .'

'No, sir. There is a little more to it. You are also the sponsor of a certain Agnes White at the refuge, are you not?'

'Agnes White? Oh yes, that is the case; a difficult female. So unlike her daughter, which I suppose is something of a blessing.'

'Your, ah, maid?'

'Ah, I see that Miss Sparrow has acquainted you with our circumstances. I can tell you do not approve of me giving such a girl employment. What about you, sergeant? You look uncomfortable.'

'No, sir,' replies Watkins, 'though if you were to ask my opinion, I can only say I never knew any leopard what changed its spots, if you understand me, sir.'

'I do, sergeant. But, surely, we should allow for the possibility of repentance, should we not?'

'I couldn't say, sir.'

'I see,' replies Dr. Harris, a little curtly. 'But, forgive me, what has Agnes White, or Clara for that matter, to do with this awful railway business?'

'The mother shared a room with Bowker, sir. And she has now gone missing herself.'

'Agnes, gone missing? Well, I fear it is not for the first time. But I would not read much into that, Inspector. Miss Sparrow will tell you that Agnes White has the most refractory nature she has ever encountered.'

'And you would disagree?'

'Not at all. But I believe there is hope, even for her.'

'I understand she has been given several chances at the refuge? That is unusual, is it not?'

Dr. Harris frowns. 'In truth, Inspector, it is only for her daughter's sake that we have persisted with her. If you knew something of the history of the case . . .'

'Perhaps you could tell me, sir. And, if it is no trouble, perhaps Watkins here could go and interview the girl? I didn't know about her mother, you see, when I saw her this morning; we might have a few more questions for her.'

'This morning?'

'Yes, I met her at the refuge.'

'Ah, I see. Quite. Yes, well, I suppose your sergeant had best proceed with his business. What do you wish to know, Inspector?'

'Well, tell me about this Agnes White, sir. How did you come across her?'

———

Sergeant Watkins quits the drawing room of the house in Doughty Street, and almost collides with the figure of Mrs. Harris, whom he finds nearby upon the narrow landing, standing conspicuously close to the door.

'Sergeant.'

'Ma'am. Perhaps you can direct me to your maid-servant, ma'am.'

'White?'

'That's the one, ma'am.'

'I knew it!' exclaims Mrs. Harris, triumphantly.

'Ma'am?'

'That girl, sergeant, has been nothing but a trial.'

'Really, ma'am?'

'No grasp of the most basic household business,' she exclaims. 'A positive trial.'

'Really, ma'am?' repeats the sergeant, showing a polite but well-judged disinterest in Mrs. Harris's domestic afflictions. 'I'll perhaps find her in the kitchen, will I, ma'am?'

'I'll show you, sergeant.'

'No need, ma'am, no need. I'm sure I can locate it myself. You stay where you are.'

—❦—

'You ask me about Agnes White, Inspector? ' says Dr. Harris, sitting back in his chair. 'Well, let me begin by asking if you know of my own career?'

'Can't say I do, sir.'

'Well, that is understandable. I am hardly renowned for my work. Suffice to say, I was for many years a medical man and gave some of my time freely to the poor.'

'Commendable, sir.'

'I am glad you think so. Well, in that occupation, I became cognisant of the vast gulf between the various classes of our great metropolis, a gulf in both their material situation and health, and, worse still, in a gulf in understanding. We know so little of the poor, do we not, Inspector?'

'I suspect I know more than most, sir.'

'Well, that is surely so, but you are an exception. In any case, since my retirement from medical practice I have taken it upon myself to study the evils attendant upon the growth of our great city, with relation to the poorer classes, and to enquire into the, ah, darker recesses of the capital.'

'I'd say that sounds rather like my occupation,' replies the inspector.

Dr. Harris smiles. 'Please, Inspector, I fear you misunderstand me; I am no detective. I am, by nature, the most sedentary of men. My exploration is principally of the literary nature. I read, I write letters, the occasional pamphlet. If I am stirred to it, I rail against mankind's iniquities in the letters page of the *Chronicle*.'

'You are a reformer of sorts, then, sir?'

'Of course, my dear fellow. Nothing good prospers in darkness, does it? There are many stones in this city that ought to be lifted up, and a light shone upon what is found underneath.'

'My sergeant might say best to let them lie.'

'He might, but he would be thoroughly wrong-headed.'

Webb smiles.

'And Agnes White?'

'Ah yes, forgive my digression, Inspector. Well, upon rare occasions, I have also been obliged to confirm the reality of particular facts or observations, and made a few hesitant steps into the worse districts of our great city. It was on one such sally that I first came across Agnes White: a visit to Wapping, in fact, accompanied by one of your good constables. I believe his name was Broderick. Do you know him?'

'I do not believe so. I do not know the Thames Division so well.'

'Of course, foolish of me. Well, never mind. At all

events, I had a mind to enquire into low lodging houses, in particular around the docks, and I came across her in just such a place. She was quite a ruin, Inspector, though not the worst of her kind, not by a long way.'

'And you took pity upon the woman?'

'Not quite, Inspector, that is the curious thing. It was, and remains, my privilege, as a governor, to annually recommend a couple of women to the refuge; and, indeed, I do actively look out for suitable candidates if an opportunity arises. But there were several likely women that night, all seemingly earnest in a desire to improve their lot, all having a good character from Constable Broderick or, at least, as good as might be expected in their circumstances.'

'All whores?'

'That is rather blunt. None the less, as you say, Inspector. But White was quite singular.'

'How so?'

'She wanted nothing for herself. Rather, she impressed upon me her sole desire in life was to see her daughter "set right". She told me at length how the girl was likely to follow the same wretched course as she herself had taken, and how terribly the thought afflicted her. In short, Inspector, she seemed a peculiarly selfless creature, for one of her kind, and quite conscious of her own wrongdoing without any hopes for herself. I was so affected that I wondered whether it was not right that I should do something for the daughter, at the very least.'

'And so you . . . ?'

'I sought her daughter out; she was in lodgings near the Strand and, I believe, already semi-criminal in her ways. I offered her a place at refuge and the prospect of emigration at the end of her time there.'

'Emigration?'

'It is the principal hope of salvation for most of the girls. But what do you think, Inspector? Clara refused. She said that she could not contemplate leaving her mother behind. What perfect symmetry, eh? The estranged but devoted daughter, and the selfless *mater*?'

'If you say so, sir,' replies Webb, 'though I find it a little too romantic for my taste. In short, you gave the daughter employment?'

'Indeed I did, after she had benefitted from Miss Sparrow's training. I gave it much thought, but charity begins at home, does it not, Inspector? And I persuaded Miss Sparrow to take on the challenge of Clara's mother. Though I cannot help but wonder if that was a mistake.'

'A mistake, sir?'

'In truth, Inspector, Agnes White has been nothing but trouble to her keepers and, I suspect, a poor influence upon her daughter. But, come, surely none of this helps you with this awful railway business?'

Inspector Webb pauses and looks down at his shoes, a habit to which he is rather prone when contemplating a particular problem.

'I wouldn't assume anything, sir. I never do.'

—

Sergeant Watkins sits at the kitchen table, a cup of tea beside him, and Clara White on a stool nearby. Alice attends to some business in the larder, though keeping herself within earshot of the policeman's conversation.

'Now, Clara, is it?'

'Yes, sir.'

'Well, I'll wager you know our business. The poor girl that was strangled at Baker Street.'

'Yes, sir.'

'And do you know who she was, and where she lived?'

'The nurse at the refuge told me, sir.'

'Then we needn't beat about the bush. Did you know the Bowker girl?'

'Not to speak to, sir. I'd seen her about, that's all.'

'And what about your mother? Were they pals?'

'I don't think so, sir. My ma's been ill, anyhow.'

The sergeant pauses, nearing the end of his carefully planned questions. 'And why do you think your mother ran off, eh?'

'She just does it, sir. It's her way. It don't mean anything.'

'You'd reckon it was nothing to do with Sally Bowker, then?'

Clara pauses. Alice looks round, waiting for her to say something.

'No, sir. I don't think so.'

CHAPTER TWENTY-ONE

TEN O'CLOCK.

Webb and Watkins quit Doughty Street, having concluded their interviews, and continue northwards together along the gaslit street; the footfalls of the sergeant's heavy boots echo down the road.

'Where do you live, sergeant?' asks Webb.

'Me, sir? Paddington Green, a cottage, or that's what my Missus calls it anyhow, not far from the canal.'

'All bricks and mortar, now, is it not, Paddington Green?'

'You know the area, sir?'

'Not particularly.'

There is an awkward silence, as the two men walk together.

'Do we know,' resumes Webb, 'where Agnes White lived? Wapping, was it not?'

'The girl said as much, yes, sir; she was brought up by the river.'

'Send a message to Thames Division, see if anyone knows the mother or has seen her this past day or so, particularly in the lodging-houses and such.'

'You're certain this White creature knows something, sir?'

'I am rarely entirely certain about anything,

sergeant. But we must look at all possibilities. And have you found someone to translate that blessed scribble of our friend Phibbs?'

'I have, sir. Gentleman I know who reports on the Parliament for the papers reckoned he could help me out. Should have it tomorrow afternoon at latest. And the surgeon's report.'

'About time. And you learnt nothing more from talking to the daughter?'

'Not a thing your Miss Sparrow hasn't already told us, sir, no.'

'She is not "my" Miss Sparrow.'

'No, sir. Begging your pardon, sir.'

'If I did not know better, sergeant, I would think you enjoy provoking your seniors.'

'Me, sir?'

Webb falls silent, and a couple more minutes pass as they turn from Guilford Street into Russell Square.

'Not on your, ah, vehicle, tonight, sir?'

Webb narrows his eyes, and looks pointedly at the sergeant. 'It seems one of the wheels was damaged in the station house. Sergeant Tibbs cannot account for it.'

'Lord! You're not safe anywhere, are you, sir?'

Webb does not reply, and there is silence again.

'I think this is the parting of the ways, sergeant,' says Webb at length, as they come to the corner.

'See you tomorrow then, sir.'

Webb nods, and begins walking in the direction of King's Cross.

—

Wapping.

Agnes White can hear the men and women shouting, the raucous laughter of the High Street echoing in the courtyard outside the old house. She walks over and peers into the darkness; part of the window is broken, patched with shreds of brown paper that, if once considered a sufficient barricade against the elements, can now only flutter in the breeze. There is nothing to see in the courtyard itself. The voices pass by and now she can hear just the river, lapping silt water against the far side of the house, working upon the bricks.

She turns back, shivering, and goes again to sit near to the fire she has started in the hearth; it will soon go out unless it is offered another piece of wood. She considers using the floorboards, like has been done in other rooms, wondering if she can loosen them; they creak loudly enough.

No. They are all damp and half-rotten.

The river, she thinks to herself, is soaking up through her mother's house, waiting for its chance, waiting for the next flood.

And how long until someone finds her?

She looks at the clothes she has laid out upon the floor, and bundles them up together.

She best get going.

———

Midnight.

Decimus Webb sits down at his writing desk and unbuttons his waistcoat. Then, almost immediately, he gets up and pours himself a small measure of brandy from the decanter that sits upon his sideboard. He takes a sip. A few drops bring a welcome warmth to his body.

He turns up the gas-light to see more clearly and looks at the piece of paper he has brought home with him. On it he has written a series of names: 'Agnes White', then 'Phibbs, Sparrow, Bowker', and a simple question mark. He has also drawn a diagram of a railway carriage, and of the stations at Farringdon Street and Baker Street.

And there is also a list of station names along the line: Farringdon (11.30 p.m.), Kings Cross, (11.34 p.m.), Gower Street (11.41 p.m.), Portland Road (11.46 p.m), Baker Street (11.52 p.m).

He takes another sip of brandy.

———

A woman walks to the end of Tower Wharf, by St. Katherine's Docks. She scurries past the half a dozen lamps, strung up on poles along its length, until she is at the darkened end of the pier. It is nearly one o'clock. On the road behind her the occasional cab or carriage speeds past, pulled by horses that gallop as fast as they are able, revelling in the freedom afforded by empty streets. In six or seven hours it will be different; the roads round the Tower will be a bedlam of goods and persons; the only sound will be that of wheels grinding slowly from the docks into the City, and the tread of weary feet upon the paving stones.

But for now there is only the flowing Thames, and a solitary woman who looks down into the water. How easy, thinks Agnes White, to end it all here.

She throws her bundle of clothes into the river.

CHAPTER TWENTY-TWO

THE GRANDFATHER CLOCK, that watches magisterially over the hall of the Harrises' house in Doughty Street, chimes one o'clock.

The sound of its cold brass bell resonates throughout the darkened house, disturbing the nocturnal calm. For Clara White, climbing the stairs to her room, a solitary candle guiding her progress, the clock is an annoyance that regularly disturbs her sleep. None the less, she herself walks slowly, trying to keep silent as possible, measuring her steps so that she might not disturb her slumbering employers. But as she comes to the first floor, she realises that she is mistaken in assuming that Dr. Harris has retired to his bed. There is a light emanating from his study, visible through the half-open door. Moreover, as she tiptoes along the landing the door itself opens a little wider, and Dr. Harris himself stands there, watching her.

'Clara, my dear, I would like a word with you.'

'Sir?' she replies in a whisper.

He gestures for her to come inside the study, and so she mutely follows as he retreats back into the room and takes a seat in his best leather-upholstered armchair, the rich russet padding scratched and careworn through years of abrasion.

'You are working late?' he suggests.

'There was a good deal to clean up in the kitchen, sir, after dinner, and it was Cook's early night.'

'I see. Tell me, Clara, are you, how should I put it, content working here?'

'Content, sir?'

'There is no need, my dear girl, to parrot the question,' he replies, a tone of mild irritation in his voice, 'I merely ask if you are content in your situation.'

'Yes, sir. I am. Very much, sir,' she replies. She tries to sound calm but her voice flutters with nerves.

'I am glad to hear it, and yet, well, I must say it: what am I to make of this latest business with your mother? Miss Sparrow has said many a time that she is a lost cause and yet, foolishly, I have stood firm against expelling her from the refuge. Nay, I have even pressed for her to be permitted to return, despite all evidence against her. Have I been a fool, Clara, to indulge my sympathies. Have I?'

'No, sir.'

'Oh, but patently I have, my dear girl. For not only does she, your blessed mother, once more spurn our charity, but she is plainly enticing you to do likewise.'

'Me, sir?'

'There is no need to play the innocent. I spoke to the inspector. Where were you this morning?'

Clara blushes, but there is a hint of relief in her face as she fathoms the source of her employer's accusation.

'I went to the refuge, sir.'

'Precisely, Clara, precisely! Why? Do you suppose that we expect you to wander the streets, as the fancy takes you, when we have given you employment here? Indeed, when we have fed and clothed you?'

'No, sir.'

'No, sir. Surely not, sir! Indeed, you know full well that we do not. It is positively deceitful of you to do such things. I should be grateful, I suppose, that you even got my book at all!'

'It's just that my ma's been ill, sir. That's all.'

'Then you should ask permission of Mrs. Harris to visit her. You know that is the rule, do you not?'

'Yes, sir.'

Dr. Harris sighs, removing his glasses, and sitting back in his chair.

'It is a slippery slope you have embarked upon, my dear girl; and it is all too easy to stray from the path. Now, I have discussed the matter with Mrs. Harris just now, and I must confess that she was all for dismissing you with neither notice nor character.'

'Sir!'

'One moment, if you please. I pointed out to Mrs. Harris that this would serve little purpose but to return you to the condition in which we found you. And I am glad to say that, after much discussion, Mrs. Harris has shown her typical generosity of spirit.'

'Sir?'

'In plain terms, and my wife and I are quite agreed upon this matter, we must wash our hands of your mother. There, I have said it. Furthermore, we ask that you have nothing more to do with her. If,' he continues, laying much stress upon that word, 'you can abide by this, and give us no more cause for concern, then we are willing to give you another opportunity to prove yourself.'

'But what of my mother, sir?'

'Really, Clara! Have you not been listening? There is nothing to be done for her. Do you think I can subject Mrs. Harris to regular visits from the police, for your mother's sake?'

'But, sir . . .'

'No, Clara. You have heard the terms I have laid down. Now, will you abide by them, or do you too reject our goodwill?'

Clara frowns, a look reciprocated in the face of Dr. Harris as he realises that she is at least willing to consider the latter option. It is a moment or two before he can return to his usual calm expression.

'I will, sir,' she says at last.

'Nothing more to do with your mother? No more of these escapades? Do I have your solemn word?'

'Yes, sir.'

'Good,' he replies, allowing his face to relax into a smile. 'Then some benefit may have come of this evening, eh?'

'Yes, sir.'

'Good girl. Ah, now there is one more thing; a less weighty matter. Please tell Cook in the morning that we are to have a small dinner party tomorrow evening.'

'Tomorrow, sir?'

'Yes, I realise it is short notice, and Cook will not be happy, but none the less. I happened to meet a very interesting young fellow when I was out this afternoon. He has an interest in my writing, and so I have invited him to dinner tomorrow.'

'As you wish, sir.'

'Very well, off you go. And tell Cook that Mrs. Harris will speak to her of the menu, but I have a strong fancy for ox-tail soup.'

'Sir.'

Clara curtsies, and leaves the room.

~

'Well?' says Alice Meynell, as Clara finally creeps into their attic room.

'Well what?'

'Well, what was that all about, his nibs calling you in?'

'You're a little earwig, ain't you?'

'Never mind that, tell us.'

'He found out about me going to the refuge this morning.'

'Only the once, just this morning? You're doing all right then, ain't you?'

'He said I can't see my ma no more.'

'Well, he could have let you go, the way you've been carrying on. He'd be in his rights.'

'I know,' replies Clara morosely. 'He said the missus was all for that.'

Alice laughs. 'I'll bet,' she says. 'I'll just bet she would. Lucky he's so sweet on you.'

'Ally! There's nothing like that.'

Alice shrugs, as Clara takes off her dress and petticoats. 'If you say so. Lor. Get a move on, I'm freezing here.'

———

It is gone two o'clock when Clara wakes up. The room is in darkness, and she can hear the distant ticking of the clock some three floors below. There is something irritating in its monotonous repetition, and, in her half-waking mind, she wonders for a moment whether, as often happens, it has only just rung out the hour and disturbed her from sleep.

But there is another sound: footsteps descending the stairs; footsteps in the hallway.

She silently pulls back the covers, enough to creep from the bed. In the darkness she fumbles for her shawl, wrapping it hurriedly around her, then opens the door on to the landing. There is someone in the kitchen now, she is sure of it; the sound of someone unlocking the area door. In bare feet, she descends the stairs as quickly as she can and opens the door of the first-floor drawing-room. From the window she can see a man coming up the area steps, a well-fed, well-dressed man in a tweed great-coat, with a woollen scarf swathing his neck.

She follows him with her eyes, and, as the man passes a street-lamp, recognises the features of her employer.

For a moment she wonders if he sees her but, if he does so, Dr. Harris gives no indication of it. Rather, he lowers his head and walks in the direction of Gray's Inn.

CHAPTER TWENTY-THREE

MORNING.

Inspector Decimus Webb sits in his Marylebone office, scanning the *Daily Chronicle* newspaper with a glum expression.

> There are questions which must be asked regarding the conduct of the Metropolitan Police in the present 'Railway Murder'. It is remarkable enough that such a terrible offence has been committed within the confines of a railway carriage; it is more remarkable still that the offender appears to have escaped from the Baker Street station with complete impunity. It is not unreasonable to suggest there has been a want of vigour and decision in the prosecution of the police inquiry. In particular, it is understood that no member of the Detective Force has yet taken responsibility for this matter. It is to be hoped that the Coroner's Inquest, to be held today at Marylebone Town Hall, may throw some light on what seems to be a very dark corner indeed.

He looks up, alerted to the presence of sergeant Watkins by a polite cough.

'Watkins,' says Webb, acknowledging his presence.

'Morning, sir,' replies the sergeant.

'Have you seen this?' asks Webb.

'One of the lads showed it me,' replies the sergeant, 'but I thought you didn't set any store by the press, sir.'

'I don't, but you may be surprised to hear that the chief superintendent does. And he is most curious to know where we are, on the *third day* of our inquiry, as he put it.'

'So we're getting a gentleman in from the Yard, are we?'

'I believe it will be Inspector Burton, as soon as they can locate him; I gather he is not in London.'

'Well, two heads may be better than one, sir.'

'In some cases,' replies Webb, though he does not sound convinced of the benefits. 'We must do all we can, in the meantime, I think. And there is the inquest. An adjournment is needed. We do not have all the facts, I am sure of it.'

'I suppose we can have a quiet word with the coroner, sir.'

'Good. Now, come, we must forget about this newspaper nonsense and press on. Do you have the surgeon's report?'

'No, sir. Should be here this afternoon.'

'The transcript of the diary?'

'The same, sir,' replies Watkins, wearily, 'as I said last night.'

Webb breathes out, in a long contemplative sigh.

'You don't seem too happy, sir,' says Watkins, 'if I may say so.'

'No, I can't say that I am. Even if we discount the man upon the train, there is something we are missing here.'

'Something missing?'

'Or perhaps someone.'

Bill Hunt climbs the stairs of his Hatton Garden lodgings and opens the door into his room. It is midmorning, but only a modicum of daylight filters through the room's smeared window. His cousin Tom and his young wife both lie stretched upon the bed, sound asleep. Bill pauses on the threshold, watching the young woman breathe in and out, staring at the sallow milk-white skin of her neck, a contrast to the layer of brick-dust and dirt that encrusts his own hands and face. He squats down on the floor by the bed, looking at the curve of her body under the tatty woollen blanket pulled over her shoulders, and reaches over to touch her cheek gently with his finger.

Lizzie opens her eyes, frowning and half conscious of the figure watching her wake.

'Bill?' she says in a hushed whisper.

The man nods but says nothing. She turns over quietly to look at the slumbering body of her husband. Once she is assured that he is still asleep, she shuffles to the edge of the bed and sits up. She wears the same dress as the day before, since she possesses only one such article, but her feet are bare. Her boots are by the bed, and she slips into them, still careful not to disturb the sleeping form of Tom, who unconsciously pulls the blanket a little tighter around himself. She picks up her shawl from the floor, and wraps it around her shoulders, shivering a little.

'You're cold,' says Bill.

'You're dirty,' she replies, looking at the dirt on his cuffs and hands. 'Come outside, I don't want to wake him up. He won't thank me for it.'

Bill nods and they both step outside on to the landing.

'Here,' he says, seeing her still shivering, 'take my coat.'

'That thing? No thank you, Bill,' she replies, laughing, stopping him before he can take it off, 'I ain't no coal-miner, thank you. It's black as pitch, and you as well.'

'I'm on night shift all week; it's worse at night. I'm going to the baths anyhow.'

'I should think so. What are you doing here, then?'

'Nothing,' he replies. 'I came to see you.'

She frowns. 'Well, now you seen me.'

He pauses, as if willing himself to say something. 'My heart's bursting for you, Lizzie.'

She looks at him dumbfounded, half amazed and half amused. 'Don't be silly, Bill. Really, don't. I told you it was just the once. You go and get your bath.'

'Lizzie . . .'

His voice trails off; perhaps he hears the sound of the floorboards creaking back inside the room. In any case, Tom Hunt stands in the doorway.

'What's all this?' he asks jovially. 'You making love to my missus, old man?'

Bill Hunt blushes. 'No,' he stammers.

'Just my little joke, old man,' says his cousin, perplexed.

'Aye, well, I'll be off.' And with those words Bill Hunt turns his back and lumbers down the stairs.

Tom walks over to the banister, and waits until he has gone before addressing his wife.

'You watch him. He's a queer beggar. I sometimes think he ain't all there.'

'He's all right.'

'I didn't say he weren't. You just watch him, that's all.'

'I will, Tom.'

'Good girl. Now, go get us some grub. I'm starving.'

'Sir.'

Inspector Webb, for the second time, is woken from his reverie by the unasked-for presence of sergeant Watkins in his office.

'I take it you have news, sergeant?'

'Surgeon's report, sir.'

'Ah, now that is something, I suppose. Give it here. Strangulation, I take it?'

'Indeed, sir. Most likely by hand. Makes a change from the garrotte, don't it?'

'I knew this already. Anything else?'

'Surgeon reckons she didn't struggle much. Says you can tell from the bruising around the neck. And no scratches or marks on her hands, face, nor arms or anything.'

'But that is odd, is it not? Does he make anything of that?'

'Too drunk, sir. Stomach contents was mostly gin, a bellyful, and she'd taken a bit of something else and all.'

'Something else?'

'Laudanum, sir. A good dose of it.'

'Ah, yes, I see it down here,' he says, scanning the paper. 'Well, a lot of the street girls swear by it, do they not? I am told it keeps one warmer than gin.'

'I believe so, sir.'

'Ah! But have you read this, sergeant? "It is my opinion that such a dose as taken by the deceased would be more than sufficient to render the average female unconscious. The combination of such an agent with the active properties of alcohol would only tend to increase such a possibility." That tells us something at least.'

'Sir?'

'Consider this, Watkins. Do you think it likely she purchased her ticket sober, and then drank herself into

144

a stupor upon the train in the five or ten minutes before she was killed?'

'Well, I couldn't say, sir.'

'More likely there was someone with her from the beginning, if she was in such a state. Someone who got her upon the train.'

Watkins looks somewhat skeptical. 'Some of these girls have powerful constitutions, sir.'

Webb pauses, a thoughtful expression passing over his face before he speaks once more. 'No, I think someone was with her. Still, at least you will be kept busy, sergeant.'

'Me, sir?'

'Gin-shops, sergeant. I want someone to speak to the owner of every public, gin palace and wine-shop between Drury Lane and the Farringdon Road. Someone must have sold her a good deal of it, eh?'

'And what about the laudanum?'

'Now, I've a good idea where she got that. Send a note to Miss Sparrow, if you will, and ask her to check if her medicine cupboard matches her inventory.'

'She had it from the refuge?'

Webb nods. 'It is a distinct possibility. She has given me all her invoices and correspondence. It seems they keep a good deal of such stuff. '

'Well then,' says the sergeant cheerfully, 'that just proves what I've been saying, don't it? These girls don't change, however much you dose 'em with religion. That ain't what they're after.'

'You think not, sergeant? Miss Sparrow and Dr. Harris would disagree with you.'

'They don't change, sir. They just get more sly.'

CHAPTER TWENTY-FOUR

'WILL YOU HURRY up? They will be here any moment.'

'Yes, ma'am, sorry, ma'am.'

Clara White rubs the blacking diligently into the fancy iron-work of the fender; her fingers are quite as black as the metal of the fire-place, which has already been the recipient of two full coats during the day, and, if truth be told, her hands are numb with the exertion.

'Will that do, ma'am?'

'It will do, I suppose,' says Mrs. Harris, magnanimously. 'Just hurry and lay the fire, then do go and wash, for goodness' sake. I swear I do not know how you can get yourself into such a state.'

'Yes, ma'am.'

Clara returns her attention to the hearth, arranging coals and kindling neatly upon the grate, then lighting a match, which sparks a puny flame. It struggles to take a firm hold of its carboniferous tribute, and for a moment looks as if it might go out.

'Really,' says Mrs. Harris, anxiously, 'this is too much; and there will be an awful vapour, I know there will.'

'Should I remove some of the coals, ma'am?'

'There is no time,' replies Mrs. Harris, looking at

the clock upon the mantelpiece. 'Just go, go and make yourself decent, if such a thing is possible. If it is not too much to ask.'

Clara says nothing in reply, but gathers up her things: a box of brushes and blacking rags, a dustpan filled with ashes; as she leaves the room she hears a despairing exclamation.

'The poker! No blacking on the poker!'

Clara again does not reply to her mistress's words, and knows better than to return and face her. Instead, having checked her face for smudges in the landing mirror, she descends as swiftly as she can downstairs, through the hallway and down to the kitchen. There she stows her cleaning things in the pantry, dashes to the kitchen sink and wrings her hands under the tap, scouring them with a brush normally reserved for cleaning the saucepans. Cook is too preoccupied with the complexities of the range to notice this infraction of the domestic order; rather, she peers intently into the oven and returns to watching over the griddle, working with the same proprietorial interest that a captain takes in steering his ship as it comes into harbour. And if her face is even more ruddy than usual amidst the heat and steam of her work, her cheeks apple-red, then it is merely a flush of pride in her culinary achievements.

'What are you gawping at?' she says, finally noticing Clara.

'Nothing.'

The doorbell rings; it is a faint, high-pitched ring, a small sprung bell that vibrates above the kitchen door, but it is sufficient to make both servants jump, and is as effective as the loudest call to arms. Cook curses to herself, immediately removing a copper pan from the heat of the stove; Clara unties her apron, throwing it to one side, and hastens back up the stairs.

The hallway is in immaculate order with everything just so; even the tassels of the Persian rug have been arrayed in perfect alignment with each other. Clara takes a nervous breath and opens the door, ushering in the couple waiting on the doorstep, sheltering under a soaked umbrella. She recognises them both: acquaintances of her employer, namely a certain Mr. and Mrs. Carpenter.

'Devilish bad weather, is it not, White?' says Mr. Carpenter, cheerfully enough. He is an old man, of a similar age to Dr. Harris, but lean and wiry, with whiskery hollow cheeks that sink into his face; his wife is a little younger, a shy small woman, who smiles nervously as Clara relieves her of her mantle and bonnet.

'Awful, sir,' replies Clara, taking the umbrella from the man and carefully placing it in the coat-stand, along with his coat. 'Will you come up, sir?'

The guests follow her as she leads them upstairs and into the drawing-room. Following Mrs. Harris's instructions, she announces them as they enter. Clara cannot help but notice this provokes something of a wry smile in Mr. Carpenter; but if he is amused by the formality of being introduced to one of his closest acquaintances, he says nothing about it.

'Good to see you, old man!' says Harris, stepping forward and shaking his guest warmly by the hand.

'And you, my dear fellow.'

Clara slips unnoticed from the room, leaving the conversation and greetings behind her. It is not long after she steps out on the landing, however, that she hears the bell ring once more. She walks briskly down the stairs and once more assumes her post at the door, opening it to find a young man, not more than twenty-one years old, dressed in black evening wear. He is without the extravagant whiskers that are the fashion, but has a good head of dark brown hair, neatly combed through, and possesses what many would consider a handsome countenance. But there is something in the way he looks at Clara that disturbs her composure. It seems like a minute or more before either of them speaks.

'This is the Harris household?'

Clara blushes, realising how foolish she must look simply staring at the visitor.

'Y-yes, sir,' she stutters. 'May I take your hat and coat, sir?'

'I suppose that would be for the best,' he replies, following her into the hall. It is a thick winter great-coat, a little splashed by mud, and dripping with rain-water; she hangs it carefully on the coat-stand.

'If you'd like to follow me, sir.'

He nods and follows.

'What name shall I give, sir?'

'Name? Phibbs. Ernest Phibbs. I am expected, I hope.'

Clara leads the way into the drawing-room. Before she can speak a word, however, Dr. Harris steps forward with his outstretched arm.

'Ah, Mr. Phibbs,' he says, shaking his guest heartily by the hand.

'Dr. Harris. A pleasure to accept your hospitality.'

'Indeed, young man. Welcome! Carpenter, this is the young man I was telling you about. Met him quite by chance. He is a writer; he read my paper on the plight of the Streatham needlewomen.'

'I am glad somebody did,' replies Carpenter, addressing the new arrival.

'Really, Mr. Carpenter!' interposes Mrs. Carpenter, admonishing her husband with a stern glance.

Dr. Harris laughs. 'Really, ma'am, there is no need to protect me from your husband's cynicism; I have endured it for many a year. Now, Mr. Phibbs, you must come and tell us about the projects you alluded to yesterday. You wish to out-Mayhew Mr. Mayhew, eh?'

Henry Cotton smiles. 'You are not far wrong, sir.'

And, for a moment, his glance is directed toward Clara White, who stands inconspicuously in the doorway. Mrs. Harris is nearby but does not notice the focus of her guest's attention. She bids Clara, in an urgent whisper, to leave and assist Cook in her work, with an injunction that soup should be served at 'eight precisely'. Clara obeys and leaves the room, hearing her mistress's sonorous voice predominating in the chatter behind her.

'Tell me, Mr. Phibbs, have you been in London long? I would recommend the Crystal Palace. It *is* a sight, you know. Truly it is.'

⬥

Dinner begins in Doughty Street at eight precisely. Clara sits in the kitchen with Alice, watching Cook at work, waiting for the bell. There is something unsettling in waiting for the dinner party to finish its various stages. Each ring signals a course completed, another dash up the stairs with the tray to clear plates, remove crumbs, prepare for the next offering: mackerel after the soup; then fricasseed rabbit with oysters; boiled round of beef; roast quail and pigeon with bacon. And as each course is prepared, it is taken immediately upstairs, succulent and aromatic; and each time the plates return it has shrunk to slivers of abandoned gristle and carefully picked bones. Clara takes a taste here and there whilst descending the stairs, but never when anything is fresh, hot and plump.

And finally, plum pudding and cheesecakes; baked apples and ice creams.

Clara presents them upon the table with fresh napkins.

———

The bell is rung for the last time and Clara returns to the dining-room.

'I must compliment your cook, Harris, once again,' says Mr. Carpenter, a crumb of plum pudding upon his lips.

'Indeed, I second that,' says the young man. 'The food is excellent. You have excellent servants, all in all, I dare say, Doctor.'

Clara blushes at this remark, since the speaker's gaze is plainly directed at her as she moves round the table, collecting the plates and cutlery. Mrs. Harris looks at her guest with raised eyebrows, whereas her husbands smiles, raising his wine glass to his lips.

'There, my dear boy,' says Harris, his voice a little slurred with a surfeit of alcohol, 'is a tale to be told. But I dare say you are right, sir. Eh, Clara?'

Clara nods, not looking at her employer, a hot flush of embarrassment rising under her collar, hurrying to collect the last few plates. But then it happens; something catches her foot as she comes to the young man; her balance goes awry, and one plate, mercifully no more, slips from its position on the tray and spills its contents into the man's lap, melted ice-cream smearing his jacket and shirt. She cannot catch it for fear of losing the rest, and, in a moment, the room is utterly, dreadfully still.

'White!'

The unforgiving voice of Clara's mistress, as angry and strident as ever, breaks the awful silence. Clara puts the tray down, uncertain what to do.

'Sir, I am so sorry . . .'

She stammers the words, but the man waves his hand nonchalantly, as if to dismiss the matter.

'Really, do not trouble yourself. Do you have something to remove the stain?'

'Cook might have something, ma'am,' says Clara, eagerly, looking at her mistress for permission to retreat.

'Hurry and get it, then, you wretched girl,' says Mrs. Harris, her face fixed into a rigid look of profound displeasure with which Clara is quite familiar enough. She sets off to retrieve whatever chemicals Cook can conjure up, but the young man gets up from the table.

'Wait a moment,' he says, turning to his hostess. 'Ma'am, I'll go myself, if you do not mind. That will be less trouble, surely? And I can pay my compliments to your delightful cook.'

'Are you sure, sir?' asks the doctor.

'Yes, by all means.'

'Well, Clara,' Dr. Harris says, 'show the gentleman the way. Do what you can for him, eh?'

Clara nods, her face now bright red, and leads the young man from the room.

'Unorthodox young fellow, isn't he?' comments Dr. Harris.

Clara says nothing on the stairs, and it is only as they reach the hallway that the young man speaks.

'We've met before, you know.'

'Sir?'

'You don't remember me? I suppose you were a little flustered. Yesterday, on Serle Street, when you fell down.'

She turns and looks at him, perplexed, as the moment comes back to her. He nods, as if to indicate he understands her confusion.

'I was dressed a little differently, but it was me, I assure you.'

'Sir?'

'I am sorry, I am confusing you. Look, it is difficult, but you should understand that I came here to see you and you alone. But we can hardly talk now. We have ice-cream to dispose of, after all. I just wanted to tell you that I will come back tomorrow.'

'Tomorrow, sir? I cannot . . .'

'Tomorrow. Your master and mistress are at Sydenham, they told me. I will come back in the evening when they are out, and we may talk then.'

Clara looks at him. 'Sir, I don't know what you want from me, and I don't know what Dr. Harris might have said, but I ain't the sort of girl who . . .'

'Who follows old women and thieves their purses?'

'Sir?' she says, her voice trembling.

'I followed you from Serle Street. I know exactly the sort of girl you are. That is precisely why you intrigue me. And that is why we must talk tomorrow.'

Clara says nothing, feeling unsteady on her feet.

'Come,' he says, taking her arm, 'I mean you no harm. Know that much. Now, you best go and warn your worthy cook that I intend to meet her.'

She looks at him blankly.

'Come on. And I am sorry for tripping you, but,' he says, looking down at his shirt, 'but I believe I had the worst of it.'

—

It is ten o'clock when a carriage arrives for the Carpenters. Mr. Phibbs, meanwhile, announces that he will depart on foot, despite numerous protestations from his hosts that he must obtain the services of a hansom. At the door, Clara hands him his hat and

153

coat, and, just for a moment, she can almost swear that he winks at her.

Once all three guests have left, however, there is a lecture from Mrs. Harris; it revolves principally around the many reasons why it is unwise for a house-maid to spill food upon young gentlemen; why a particular housemaid is ungrateful and unreasoning; and why must that particular housemaid induce a migraine in all those who try to help her improve herself?

All in all, the talk does not last too long, since Mrs. Harris declares herself positively exhausted.

Then comes the washing of plates and saucepans, a task Clara shares with Alice Meynell, until the hands and wrists of both women are chapped and aching.

At twelve o'clock, Alice goes to bed. Clara lingers for a moment in the kitchen, thinking about the strange insistence of the young man as he spoke to her.

'I mean you no harm.'

Then there is a knock upon the kitchen door.

CHAPTER TWENTY-FIVE

CLARA LOOKS UP, startled. In the dim light of the gas, with rain still falling outside, the prospect of a nocturnal visitor instantly fills her mind with unwelcome visions of area-sneaks and burglars, and half-remembered ghost stories. Then it occurs to her that the strange young man has returned. It takes her a moment to realise, amidst the pitter-patter of the rain, that she can hear a female voice calling her name.

'Clara? Are you there? Don't jump. It's me. Let us in; I'm soaking.'

Clara looks in the direction of the door. Peering through the kitchen window, she can make out a figure standing in the rain. As she catches sight of the visitor's features, it somehow takes a few seconds for the face to register in her mind.

'Lizzie?'

'Come on. Who did you think?'

Clara unbolts the door. The girl that walks in is somewhat different from Clara's memory of her. Her girlish face is, undoubtedly, older and wearier, and she is, as far as Clara can recall, also a little taller. Clara stands back and stares at her.

'Lizzie?' she says, shaking her head in disbelief. 'Look at you!'

'Have I changed that much, then?'

'You have. You look so much like ma,' she replies, 'but when she was younger.'

Lizzie Hunt frowns. She unwraps her shawl from around her shoulders, shaking her head, dripping water on the stone floor.

'Well,' she says, 'if you say so. This is a fine halloa. Can't you start a fire up or something? I'll catch my death in here.'

'A fire? Not this time of night,' says Clara, taking the shawl and draping it over one of the kitchen chairs. 'Come here, stand by the range; that'll be hot enough.'

Lizzie does as suggested, standing with her back to the stove, looking round the room. As she does so, Clara notices a large black bruise around her wrist, and another on her neck, partially concealed by her trailing brown hair.

'Here,' she says, peering, 'who did that?'

'No-one. Just an accident, that's all.'

Clara looks at her skeptically, but lets the topic rest for the moment.

'It's good to see you.'

'You too.'

'You'll get us into trouble, you know,' says Clara, 'coming here like this.'

'Trouble? You've changed your tune, ain't you?' says Lizzie. 'Ma used to say you was the fearless one.'

'It's just that it's a good place here. I don't want to lose my character.'

'Your "character"?'

'Maybe I have changed. Maybe for the better, anyhow. What about you?'

'What about me?'

'Are you all right?'

'Yes, as it goes,' Lizze says, 'apart from being bleeding soaked.'

'That ain't what I mean. I mean, in yourself,' replies

Clara. 'Where have you been all these months? You could have sent word.'

'Here and there.'

'With Tom?'

'Yes, with Tom.'

Clara sighs, pointedly avoiding her sister's gaze. 'And where are you stopping now?'

'Tom's cousin's. He's got a room, off Saffron Hill.'

'Has he? Lizzie, tell us, why did you run off like that? Tom Hunt of all people.'

'He's been good to me.'

'I'll believe that when I see it. Does he thump you?'

'Not much. No more than most, I expect.'

'That ain't what it looks like.'

Lizzie scowls at her sister. 'What do you know anyway? You've never had anyone sweet on you, have you?'

'That ain't nothing to do with it. I just don't want you to get hurt. I know Tom well enough, don't I? He ain't good for you. Nor anyone else, for that matter.'

'I reckon I should never have come here,' replies Lizzie, tutting to herself. 'I thought you'd be pleased to see us.'

'I am.'

Clara sits down at the kitchen table and rubs her forehead with her palms.

'How are you managing?' she finally continues. 'Does he give you money? I ain't got anything I can spare. Not at the moment, anyhow.'

'Good, because I don't need it. I can take care of myself.'

She says it proudly and her sister looks at her from between her fingers, still pressed to her head.

'How?'

'How do you think?' she says, pushing back her hair from her face. 'I got my looks, ain't I?'

It takes a moment for Clara to grasp the meaning of her sister's words; she closes her eyes and mutters an oath to herself.

'Lizzie, you ain't serious? How could you?'

'Easy enough; you know as well as I do, you've seen ma do it often enough. Besides, it don't matter, I've got Tom, ain't I? It don't matter if you love someone.'

'You think Tom Hunt loves you?'

'I know he does. He went and married me. With a preacher, and all.'

Clara laughs; it is a sarcastic laugh that makes her sister glare at her angrily. There is a pause before either of them speaks.

'I should go,' says Lizzie. 'I don't want you to get into trouble, not on my account.'

'Don't be like that. Look, you know ma's gone off somewhere?'

'Has she?' says Lizzie, surprised. 'I only saw her a couple of days ago. She told us where to find you.'

'Did she say anything to you?'

'About what?'

'Anything.'

Lizzie shrugs. 'She didn't seem too good; she weren't saying much at all.'

'Do you know about the railway murder?'

Lizzie nods.

'The girl that shared the room with ma, she was the one that was killed. You probably even saw her. Anyhow, the police have been sniffing round. They even came here, asking after her.'

Now it is Lizzie's turn to laugh.

'The crushers think ma did it?'

'I didn't say that. But all the same, it ain't good, is it, if they think she's mixed up in it?'

'Perhaps she is,' replies Lizzie, with a hint of drollery in her voice.

'Lizzie, don't be stupid.'

'Well,' she says, picking up her wet shawl, hardly much drier than when she left it, 'I am sorry if I am too stupid for you, Clarrie dear. I hadn't meant to be such a bother, I'm sure. I was going to tell you, my sister, some good news, as it happens, but if I ain't good enough to be in your company . . .'

'Go on then, what was it?'

'Just something.'

'What?'

Lizzie falls silent, wringing out the water from her shawl, looking down at the floor. Suddenly she seems more serious and less confident. When she does speak, it is in a soft whisper. Unconsciously she puts her hand to her belly.

'I'm think I'm carrying.'

Clara looks at her in astonishment.

'You stupid girl. That's good news, is it?'

'Don't call me stupid! And I ain't a girl no more, neither. I knew you'd be like this. I knew it. I should never have come.'

Lizzie takes up her shawl, and throws it back over her shoulders as she talks.

'Spite, that's all it is. You think you're special, sitting there, do you, Clarrie? Better than me? Well, you ain't.'

'At least I ain't got myself bloody knocked up by . . . well, Lord knows who.'

'It's Tom's baby,' replies Lizzie emphatically. 'And if you think you're so much better than me, how did you swing this set-up anyhow? You in your pretty little Abigail's outfit, like you were born to it. That's a joke, ain't it?'

'I didn't go and sell myself, if that's what you mean.'

Lizzie is at the door now, her face flushed with frustration and anger.

'Well, ain't that bully for you. But you're no better

than us. And,' she says, her voice petulant and child-like, 'come the summer, I'll have Tom, and my babby, and what will you have to show for it, skivvying here?'

She does not wait for a response. She is gone, rushing up the area steps, the door slamming behind her.

If she was in her normal state of mind, Clara White might worry that the sound of raised voices would wake those sleeping upstairs and bring down the wrath of Mrs. Harris for the second time in as many hours.

As it is, she merely slouches forward on the kitchen table, her head in her hands.

Outside, the rain still descends, persistent and flecked with the evening's soot. It is a familiar companion for Lizzie Hunt as she walks through the city streets, and she barely notices it, her head swimming. As she approaches Saffron Hill, however, a man approaches her. Perhaps he mistakes the tears on her face for rain-drops, or perhaps he just has something else on his mind.

'How much, love?'

'Not tonight.'

'Go on, I'll see you right.'

'I said no! Not tonight.'

CHAPTER TWENTY-SIX

INSPECTOR WEBB SITS in his office at Marylebone police station, looking over the notes upon his desk, scraps of paper that he has been arranging and re-arranging for a good hour or more. There is also a book, *Uses of Opium, in Tincture and Solution*. His contemplation is once again disturbed by the appearance of sergeant Watkins at the door.

'Burning the midnight oil, sir?'

'I think you will find it is gas, Watkins.'

'That don't have the same ring to it, though, does it, sir? You been here all day? Seems like it.'

'You have news, I hope, sergeant? Or did you merely lack for conversation in the mess?'

'We're still waiting on the transcript of the diary, sir.'

'I know that all too well. I thought it was to be today?'

'My man had some business at the Commons suddenly, sir. Says he can't neglect his work.'

'Tomorrow?'

'Almost definitely, sir.'

'I hope there is more, Watkins. I can see from your face there is. Please tell me.'

'Wapping has just sent us word about Agnes White,' says Watkins.

'They've found her?' asks Webb, interrupting the sergeant.

'Well, in a manner of speaking. They found her dress washed up near the Tower. They reckon she's drowned. Quite fortuitous, as it happens; some mudlark or scavenger found it, took it to some clothesman, and the fellow there had heard we were looking for her.'

'One moment, sergeant; it is remarkable, but I confess you are racing ahead of me. How do they know this article is White's dress?'

'Ah, now that foxed me, sir, until I saw it. It's the refuge's uniform, a sort of gown, ain't it? Got her name sewn inside.'

'We have it here?'

'They sent it over, sir. No use to the Thames boys, really, is it?'

'Well, for God's sake, bring it in, Watkins, show me.'

Watkins leaves the room, and swiftly returns with a bundle of cloth wrapped in brown paper. He loosens the paper, and lays out the refuge's distinctive blue and white uniform upon a nearby desk. It is sullied by mud and dirt, and slightly torn in several places, but the pattern is quite clear, and the sergeant pulls up the hem, showing his superior the neat name tag that has been stitched on to it.

'What do you make of that, sir?'

'It has not been in the river long, I suppose.'

'I suppose not. Why do you think she did it, sir?'

'What?'

'Killed herself,' says Watkins.

Webb looks at him, raising his eyebrows skeptically.

' "Deeds to be hid which were not hid." '

'Sir?'

'It is a quotation, Watkins. Never mind. How do

we know she did kill herself? We only have the clothing, after all. Doesn't it strike you as curious that a
dress became detached from the body so easily? It is
pretty much of a piece, after all,' he says, fingering
the still-damp material.

'It could happen, sir.'

'It could. But what of the body itself?'

'Might have sunk down. Or drifted further on. We
don't find 'em all, do we, sir?'

'True.'

'You don't seem convinced yourself either way, if I
may say so, sir.'

'You may, Watkins, because I am not at all sure of
anything at present. Except that we are still quite in
the dark.'

'Come now, sir,' replies the sergeant. 'I wouldn't say
that. I'd say you should go home and get yourself
some sleep.'

'That is my intention. By the by, did you hear
anything from the refuge about the other matter,
sergeant?'

'The refuge? Sorry, sir, I forgot to mention it. You
were bang on there. At least one bottle is missing of
a patent mixture – containing laudanum, as it happens.'

Webb smiles. 'I thought as much,' he replies, looking
at the tattered clothing. 'I do not think we will find
Agnes White, sergeant.'

'If she's in the river, you mean?'

Webb shrugs. 'I do not think she is in the river.
Check with Miss Sparrow if she had a regular outfit
of her own clothes, as well as the uniform. I should
think she did, and I'll warrant she took them. She
wants to give us the slip, sergeant. I do not think she
wants to be found at all.'

⬤

Wapping.

The alley is a dark, foetid place, a narrow path with a watery channel running along the middle that serves as collective sewer for the surrounding buildings. It runs from Wapping High Street to the London Dock, but ends as a cul-de-sac, against the dock's high brick wall, which protects the warehouses and ships within. Agnes White knows it well enough; she follows the man halfway down, as the location is his choice, to an abandoned doorway with a nearby window-ledge on which she can balance herself against his body. She looks at his face, trying to remember what he looked like in the gas-light of the main road, as he raises her skirt with grubbing hands; he is dark and tanned, she remembers that much. She wonders idly if he is a Greek, or perhaps the son of some Ottoman pirate, the sort that kidnap decent girls and place them in some distant harem for the amusement of a brooding sultan; she has seen them in the three-act plays at the penny gaffs in Whitechapel.

It is over quickly enough. But he turns away too soon for her liking. She pulls at his sleeve.

'A shilling?'

She says it; he will know the word after all, even if he does not speak English. He turns away, and she grips his arm more firmly. He slaps her and pushes her away, so that she falls to the ground, amidst the rotting detritus and thick brown mud.

She does not get up immediately; she knows better than that. She waits until he has gone and then feels for the wall with dirt-soaked hands, clambering against it until she can support herself on two feet.

No-one will have her now, covered in muck. Not unless she is lucky.

She will have to stay in Gravehunger Court for at least one more night.

CHAPTER TWENTY-SEVEN

ACROSS THE CITY, in Doughty Street, a clock chimes two o'clock, echoing in the house's dark hallway.

Dr. Harris slowly opens his bedroom door and steps carefully on to the landing, bearing a solitary candle before him. It gives off a meagre light, but, even in the flickering shadows, it is clear that there is something peculiarly exuberant in his expression. Indeed, he creeps past the door of his wife's room with such a look of barely suppressed glee that, if said party were to wake and catch sight of him, she would most likely assume him to be drunk. His face, moreover, is particularly striking in that it can be compared with a countenance that, in normal circumstances, is generally perfectly composed and almost beatific. It may be that the whole effect is an exaggeration caused by the dim melting glow of the candlelight; but if his wife were to wake, she would, at the very least, observe that he smiles to himself as he passes by. She would, moreover, notice that he cups his hand around the flame to prevent it shedding its light too freely. She would also see that he is dressed to go out.

But, of course, Mrs. Harris does not stir.

Once he is upon the stairs, Dr. Harris allows himself a backwards glance, then walks softly down two flights, into the hallway. There he rests the candlestick upon the hall table. He sports an unremarkable black suit and completes his outfit by putting on his woollen coat and acquiring his hat from the iron-work stand beside the door. He does not attempt to open the front door, however; doubtless it presents too great a challenge to his silent progress, with its plush velvet draught-excluder and numerous bolts and Chubb lock. Rather, he takes up the candle and proceeds downstairs to the kitchen. Once there, carefully avoiding the mouse and beetle traps, and the scuttling progress of the 'black natives' for whom the latter nocturnal entanglements are intended, he proceeds to let himself out.

Outside, upon Doughty Street, there is a light mist, though it is not sufficiently soot-blown for any true resident of the capital to call it a fog. It is cold, however, cold enough for his breath to be visible in the air. He pulls his coat collar tight about his neck, and proceeds down the road, in the direction of Gray's Inn.

Upon the corner there stands a cab, manned by a cabman dressed in a thick overcoat, and wide-brimmed hat pulled down over his ears, such that only his puffing tobacco pipe projects beyond it, and his face is quite hidden from view. Without removing the clay from his mouth, he nods at Dr. Harris and addresses him.

'Usual place, sir?'

Harris says nothing, merely nodding in return, and climbing into the hansom.

Even with the doors closed, the vehicle affords little protection from the chill night air. Dr. Harris shivers a little, and watches through the window as the cab passes familiar streets and heads eastwards, turning north by Clerkenwell Green and past St. James's Church. Still, it is a short journey upon the empty road, and in little more than five minutes he has arrived at his destination, a rather decrepit Georgian terrace hidden amongst the squares of Islington. Indeed, it is not a particularly respectable-looking street; there are signs of disrepair abounding, from cracked paintwork upon window and door-frames, to iron railings that lean ever so slightly in arthritic contradiction to their intended alignment, buckling inwards or outwards. None the less, it suits Dr. Harris to stop outside a particular house, and he alights from the hansom with only two words to the driver.

'One hour.'

'Aye,' replies the man, and gently provokes his horse onwards.

There are thick curtains at the front windows of the house in question, upon all of its three floors, and it is impossible to guess whether anyone within might be awake to receive guests. It is remarkable, therefore, as the visitor approaches the front door, that it opens silently almost before Dr. Harris has a chance to set foot upon the threshold; moreover, he seems quite unperturbed by such prescience and walks confidently inside.

A maid-servant greets him politely in the hallway, closes the door, and takes his hat and coat. He is shown through into a downstairs parlour, but, apart from a pair of matching sofas and a mahogany table and chairs it is barely furnished; indeed, there are only two fading watercolours badly hung above the mantel-piece, a wilting fern under dusty glass, and numerous dents and cracks in the undistinguished wainscoting. It has the appearance of a station waiting-room on a barely used branch line.

A woman enters, a matronly figure, a similar age to Harris's wife; she smiles and nods acknowledgement of his presence, then settles herself on the sofa.

'Good evening, sir.'

'Ma'am.'

'Twice in two nights, sir? We are honoured.'

'As I said last night, ma'am, there are now two places begging at the refuge, and I wish to interview as many candidates as possible, before I make a recommendation. You said there was another girl?'

'Oh, several, I should think.'

'A young girl, though.'

'Don't worry, sir. No more than thirteen years, I assure you.'

'And virtuous?'

'I can produce a doctor's certificate, if you like.'

'I do not think that necessary. I have medical experience enough.'

'Thank you, sir. I'm sure that's a relief for all parties.'

'Indeed. Shall we say the same fee for the interview?'

'Interview? Two pounds, for a full discussion with the young lady.'

'She is not a "lady", I trust.'

'I believe she is a stay-maker's daughter, sir, lately arrived in Islington from the country – Tottenham, she tells me. Hoping to make her fortune, or some such nonsense. Full of odd fancies, as young girls are at that age. You know the sort.'

'How many nights have you had her?'

'Five nights and days. She's accustomed to the house now, I'd say. I don't think she'll give you any trouble, sir.'

'I may have difficult questions.'

'You question her as long as you like, sir. Won't be anyone eavesdropping, rest assured. You ask anything you like of her.'

'I am glad we understand each other, ma'am.'

The woman smiles politely.

———

'Tell me, what is your name?'

'Eliza.'

'That is a pretty name. Come, there is no need to be scared of me.'

'I ain't.'

'Good. This is a nice room, is it not? Fancy sheets, a nice bed. All for you. Mrs. F. is a good woman, is she not, treating you to this?'

'I want to go home, I swear it.'

'Come now, it is a little late for that. And at this time of night?'

'I'd go. I would.'

'Sit a little closer to me. That's better, isn't it?'

'I suppose.'

'Do you wish to improve yourself, my dear?'

'I suppose.'

'Naturally you do. My dear, I know a place where they help women like you, women who have gone wrong. A home for young women, with the promise of a fresh start for those who would care for it, all paid for. I could recommend you to the governors.'

'Fresh start?'

'Emigration. Perhaps to Van Diemen's Land. A beautiful country, I assure you.'

'But I ain't gone wrong.'

'But why do you think you are here?'

'I don't know.'

'Then I shall show you.'

'Let me go, won't you?'

'Come, just here.'

'No!'

'Yes. Place your hand just here. Don't struggle. There! That's my girl.'

CHAPTER TWENTY-EIGHT

Noon.

Lizzie Hunt wanders through the back streets of Saffron Hill. The sky is covered by a coal-black sheet of cloud, but the rain of the previous evening has lifted and the air is cool and crisp. She turns from the main road into the little alley that leads to her husband's preferred meeting-place. Indeed, Tom Hunt has become quite a fixture in the Three Cups in the past few days; he has a talent for making himself at home in such establishments, and possesses a particular expertise at ingratiating himself with any landlord or barmaid, whether it is by flattering words or his winning smile. Moreover, the fact that he can make a small measure of gin last for an hour or two is rarely held against him. In fact, once he is settled, his very presence is generally deemed to be something of a testimony to the excellent character of any public house he frequents. The Three Cups is no exception and Lizzie is not surprised to find him there; it is a little more remarkable that he has accrued to himself not only a table, but some writing paper, pen, ink, and inkwell.

'There she is,' he exclaims, seeing Lizzie approach.

'Here I am,' she says, pulling up a stool and sitting down beside him.

'How much was it then?' he says eagerly. 'Good night, was it?'

'A few bob,' she says, handing him a handful of coins.

'Is that it?' he asks, counting them.

She shrugs; her face looks drawn and tired, and there are dark shadows under her eyes.

'What you doing?' she says, after a moment.

'Writing a letter,' he says irritably, dropping the coins in his trouser pocket.

'Let's have a look,' says Lizzie, leaning over him, trying to read the words aloud, slowly forming them with her lips.

'Here,' he replies, perhaps with a little pride, 'I'll read it myself. See if it don't sound a smasher. This, my darling, will revive our flagging fortunes, or I'm a Dutchman:

'Dear sir,
'I address this letter to you, being assured by your renowned compassion towards suffering human-ity that you will forgive my presumption in doing so. I am compelled to write by circumstances which would reduce any man to a state of perfect misery and wretchedness, and it is only the thought that a fellow Christian may look kindly upon my appeal that keeps me from absolute despair. It is painful to relate the nature and causes of my embarrass-ment, and I hope it is sufficient for me to say that though I am a working man, I have suffered the loss of both my mother, father, and wife, all in a matter of weeks. I have three children remaining to me, who are a great burden, and my infant daughter is sick with fever. I now have not even a sixpence with which to buy her either medicine or food. I freely confess I am reduced to abject

beggary, and forced to make others my creditor, if I am to keep my little ones from death's door. I know you will consider me bold when you hear these entreaties, and can only plead the lives of my children as excuse for such an importunate missive. If you have some small compassion towards my unfortunate condition, I beg you to send some token of your feelings addressed, Smith, T. M., Post Office, High Holborn.'

Lizzie smiles. 'You ain't half good, Tom,' she says admiringly.

'You better hope this fellow replies,' says Tom, pleased with her praise. 'I paid Honest Charlie two bob for the name and address. For some of the words and all.'

'He will,' says Lizzie, and leans forward to kiss him. As she does so, her arm inadvertently makes contact with the bottle of ink; it rattles from side to side for one moment, and then tips over. Both Tom and Lizzie watch it, unable to move, as the blue-black fluid spills over the table and stains its contents. It seems a slow progress, but there is enough of it to seep across the letter itself, obscuring the words on one side of the page in a dark viscous pond. Tom instinctively tries to pick the paper up, but ink just trickles down the sheet, ruining it in its entirety.

'You clumsy little bitch,' he exclaims, turning on her, raising his hand.

'Tom! Don't!' she shouts. 'It was an accident.'

A voice from the bar, the landlord, joins in: 'Here! None of that!'

Tom Hunt draws back his hand, and breathes a deep breath. Even the three or four blank sheets that he had nearby are all blotted with spots of ink, spattered from his attempt to recover the letter itself.

'Wasted!' he exclaims. 'All bloody wasted, you little bitch!'

There is a long pause. Lizzie steals herself to speak, though she cowers a little beside her husband, her back and shoulders curled up and tense.

'I am sorry, Tom,' she says, her voice low and timid. 'Really I am. It was an accident.'

Tom Hunt looks at the mess on the table.

'You best go get a cloth to clear this up.'

Lizzie nods, and stands up.

'What'll we do now, eh?' he says, angrily.

'I saw my sister last night,' she says, eager to change the subject.

'Clara?' he replies, saying the name almost fondly, looking up at her. 'How is she doing? Where did you catch her? Prigging some gent's wallet, was she?'

'She ain't in that line any more.'

'After all I taught her? That's a crying shame. She had good hands for it, not like some clumsy little madams I could mention. What's she doing then?'

'Housemaid.'

Tom looks astonished and abruptly all signs of petulance and anger disappear from his unshaven face. Instead he laughs, thumping the table with his fist, griming his hand with ink even further.

'Maid? Clara White? You are having me on, my love, ain't you?'

Lizzie shakes her head. 'She's changed, different from when you knew her.'

'I never heard so much gammon,' he says, laughing in between words. 'Here, come here, will you?'

He leans forward and beckons Lizzie to come closer. She leans towards him, warily, and he whispers to her, 'What sort of place has she got? Big house?'

'A place on Doughty Street, by Gray's Inn. Three or four storeys.'

'A gentleman's house, then?'

Lizzie nods. Tom suddenly leans a little more and grabs his wife by the back of her neck, pulling her face an inch from his, his mouth by her ear.

'Get this mess cleared up, then come back and tell me everything about it.'

Lizzie nods; as she goes to the bar for a cloth, Tom Hunt sits back in his chair.

'No-one,' he mutters to himself, 'no-one changes that much.'

He smiles.

'Clara bloody White. Ha!'

CHAPTER TWENTY-NINE

CLARA WHITE STANDS nervously outside Doughty Street, watching the brougham containing her master and mistress depart to the manifold delights of Sydenham. Once it is out of sight, she returns to the kitchen, where Alice Meynell is sweeping the floor.

'Wish I was going with them,' says Alice.

'With them?'

'Well, not with *them*,' she replies. 'They're going to the opera, ain't they? I've never been to the Palace, though.'

Clara smiles. 'Well, maybe if you work that broom hard enough, I'll get some Prince Charming to whisk you off.'

'I can't even get the baker's boy to look at me.'

As Clara is about to reply, the front doorbell rings.

'Ain't that typical, when they've only just gone,' exclaims Alice. 'They ain't expecting anyone, are they?'

Clara says nothing, but runs upstairs, with a mixture of trepidation and excitement agitating her stomach. She opens the door to find Henry Cotton. He is dressed in a decent suit, though not the formal evening wear of the previous night, and smiles as he sees her.

'Miss White.'

Again Clara stands there, uncertain what to say or

do. In consequence, the visitor lets himself into the hall.

'May we talk?' he says, offering her his hat and coat. She does not take them.

'No,' she replies hesitantly. 'Alice is downstairs.'

'No Cook? She was a charming woman, I must say.'

'She don't live in.'

'Perhaps in here, then?' he says, opening the dining-room door for himself, and walking briskly in, before Clara can object. She follows him, looking nervously back towards the stairs, in case Alice might appear.

'What do you want with me?' she says in exasperation, once inside the room, closing the door behind her. 'Alice will know something's up. She's no fool. And neither am I.'

'Clara . . .' he says, sitting down on a chair beside the fireplace, but pausing in his speech. 'May I call you Clara?'

She nods mutely; it is not the sort of question to which she is accustomed.

'Clara, I know you must think me a lunatic or worse, but as I said yesterday I mean you no harm. Please rest assured, you have nothing to fear from me. I am, well, for want of a better term, a journalist of sorts. And I believe you can be of immense assistance to me.'

'Journalist?'

'Well, a writer, at least.'

'And how can I help you?' she says, frowning, disbelief in her voice.

'Dr. Harris has told me something of your history, and I have seen your handiwork myself . . .'

At this, Clara blushes. She starts to speak, but Cotton raises his hand.

'Wait. I was going to say, please understand that I

have no great wish to see you before the Bench. Rather, it was fortunate that I saw you because you could be so invaluable to my work.'

'I ain't prigging nothing for you.'

'Lord! Do you take me for some Fagin? Rather, I want your help.'

'I still don't understand you,' says Clara, anxiously, glancing out of the front window lest her employers should unexpectedly return. 'I don't understand anything you're saying.'

'Forgive me, I am not making myself clear. Clara, I know your background, your past. I know also that you are a clever girl, who has found a place here with Dr. Harris. And I know you are not averse to lifting a woman's purse, even now, so please do not tell me you are quite reformed, for I do not believe that. The reason I am speaking to you like this is that I am hoping to write at length about the various evils of our society. Indeed, I believe I can make my name by doing so. But I have found that I can only do so much unaided. I have even disguised myself to penetrate the worst sort of places, and converse with the folk who inhabit them, but my words always give me away the very instant I speak. I confess, it is hard for me to gain their trust, and I can never rely upon what I am told. You, on the other hand, are a unique find. You can help me uncover places and people . . .' He pauses for breath, as if coming to the conclusion of a complex piece of logic. 'You, Clara, can show me the *underworld*.'

There is a pause, and Clara looks at the young man astonished. He seems breathless and excited, but she cannot help her reaction. It starts as a half-smile, then a wide grin, then an out-and-out laugh, her hands clutching her waist as she steps back, supporting herself against the nearest chair.

'The "*underworld*"? You sound like some penny dreadful!' she exclaims.

'Do I?' he replies, mildly annoyed but almost laughing with her. 'Don't you see? That is why I need someone who knows what it is to live . . . well, as you have lived. Someone whose guidance I could rely upon. Just think of it. I might even pay you a little something.'

'Pay?'

'I cannot afford much. But I know you wish to better yourself, otherwise you would not be working here.'

'What about the purse? Will you tell?'

'I saw your agitation before you did it. It was not quite the work of a hardened criminal, I know that. But you know that life, do you not? That is why I need you.'

'How can I do anything like what you want? Mrs. Harris would never hear of it.'

'Mrs. Harris need never know.'

'And I can't go behind her back. Nor the doctor's, either. They've been good to me.'

'Come, you've done it before. Besides, they are out tonight, are they not? I saw them leave, that is why I came now. We have a good three or four hours; come with me.'

'Now?' she replies, amazed. 'And do what?'

'Well, let me see. For a start, you might show me the area where you were raised. I believe you had an exciting youth, so Harris told me. Wapping, was it not?'

'To Wapping?'

'To begin with. I will take some notes, and then, for tonight, we are done.'

'What about Alice?'

'You can get round her, surely. I will bring you back

in good time, I promise. We can take a hansom, if
needs must.'

'What if I don't want to? Will you tell them, about
what you saw?'

'But don't you want to?' he says eagerly. 'It will be
a marvellous adventure.'

She looks at him, undecided.

'Come,' he says, offering her his hand.

CHAPTER THIRTY

CLARA SITS BESIDE Henry Cotton as their cab rattles along the muddy cobbles of Wapping High Street, nervously tapping the straw-covered floor of the carriage with her foot. Though it is almost dark, she peers between the warehouses at the river. She can make out the tall masts of ships; in the blackness they resemble the tree-tops of some barren forest, swaying gently in the breeze. Cotton watches his companion, a notebook in his hand, and makes the occasional annotation. Finally, about halfway along the road, Clara bids the cabman to stop; this information is then passed to the horse by means of a shout and a sharp tug upon the reins, such that the vehicle pulls up with a jolt. Cotton smiles at Clara's discomfort as she is thrown forward by the sudden movement.

'You don't travel by cab too often, I expect,' he says, opening the door and descending on to the road.

'No,' replies Clara, tartly, accepting his hand as she follows him. 'And I can't believe I was fool enough to come here.'

'Clara, I swear you can trust me.'

The cab leaves them standing upon the High Street in front of a tavern named the Black Boy. It is a small riverside place, less ostentatious than many of its rivals, with only its sign to herald its function as a place of entertainment: a clumsy representation of a naked black child; he seems content enough, though in constant danger from an unprotected jet of gas that flares directly above his head. Inside, however, the warm glow of a fire can be seen through the steamed-up windows and the sound of numerous voices raised in animated conversation can be plainly heard from the street.

'Well, like I told you, I was born here,' says Clara, gesturing towards the door. 'By the hearth, so my ma told me. Do you want to go in?'

'Born in a public house?'

'Do you want to go in?'

'No, not for now. We shall come back here. First take me to the house you used to live in, the one by the river. Harris told me of it. He said it was a very curious place.'

'Gravehunger Court.'

'That was the name?' says Cotton, clearly amused by the sound of it.

'It was. But it's deserted now.'

'Why?'

'There was hardly anything left of it. It got flooded almost every year we were there.'

'None the less, take me there, if you will.'

'We can't stay too long, you promised.'

'Clara, we have only just arrived. If I am to make a study . . .'

'You promised,' she says again, emphasising the latter word, looking nervously around. 'What if someone sees us?'

Cotton touches her arm. 'Please, just take me there. We won't stay long, and I will get you back, I assure you, in good time. Surely it is not far?'

She concedes, and the pair of them walk east along the High Street, past the outfitting warehouses, ships' chandlers, sail-makers, and a dozen more types of maritime establishments that appear upon every corner. Though the road is not particularly busy so early in the evening, they pass men of several nationalities, from Swedes and blue-jacketed Germans, to swarthy Lascars. It is possible that some of these sailors pass ironic comment on seeing such a respectable-looking gentleman and servant-girl together in such a location, but their words and accents are incomprehensible, even to Henry Cotton.

After five minutes or so, they finally come to a particular alley; at its entrance, a small row-boat is upturned upon the pavement, smelling of fresh tar upon its meagre hull. For a moment, it appears that this obstruction, the pride of some local river scavenger, is the point of interest for a gang of young boys who loiter nearby. As they draw nearer, however, it becomes apparent that the alley itself is a hive of activity, with a good few locals pushing past them, pressing to gain access.

'I thought you said it was deserted?' asks Cotton.

'It was,' replies Clara. 'Something's going on.'

There is something strangely fearful in her voice and, without waiting for Cotton to catch up, she joins the push and shove of bodies that crowd down the narrow passage. Moreover, she moves her way through to the front of the crowd with forceful and colourful language that quite belies any impression given by the neat servant's uniform beneath her shawl. Cotton follows reluctantly behind, jostled and jeered by several larger men, whom he guesses to be dockers. At some point his hat goes flying; at another, he is sure he feels a hand tugging at waistcoat buttons in the hope of finding a watch-chain. His struggle is rewarded, however, as the alley opens into a courtyard. He recognises the large dilapidated house of

Clara's childhood as soon as he sees it. Moreover, in front of it there is a well in the centre of the yard, a small cylinder of brick work around which stand two men, pulling at ropes that dangle into the narrow shaft. And, nearby, a trio of blue-coated policemen, each with a bull's-eye lantern. One peers anxiously into the well, the others vainly attempt to keep back the heaving crowd that has gathered. Cotton finds a place by Clara's side at the front of the mob.

'What on earth's going on?' he asks, but she merely stares at the scene in front of them.

There is a shout, and the policeman stands back. One of the men on the ropes leans over and grabs hold; a wet and twisted bundle of rags is dragged from the mouth of the bricks and laid carefully upon the ground. All three of the policemen shine their lights upon it.

Clara White recognises the face of her mother.

CHAPTER THIRTY-ONE

'CLARA! WAIT!'

Henry Cotton calls out anxiously as Clara turns and pushes her way back through the crowd. She does not hear him, or chooses to ignore him. Whichever is the case, she does not wait. Instead, she fights against the surging tide of men and women, all keen to witness what the police have found, until she finds herself once more back on the High Street. There, with nothing to struggle against, she halts.

''Ere, what's all this?'

A woman stands before her, dressed in ragged clothing, nodding in the direction of the alley.

'I don't know,' replies Clara, brushing her aside and walking blindly down the street. 'Leave me be.'

She stumbles along until she comes to another alley. In this case, however, it leads down to a set of steps, and then to one of the old wharfs by the river. Picking her way down the mossy stones, she continues on to the platform, where a half-dozen small boats are tethered. There is no-one else to be seen; and the only sound is that of the river lapping at the wooden supports. She sits down and looks into the black water. All along the bank, the lights of the warehouses and pubs are visible, but the water does not so much reflect them as absorb them, dissolving their brilliancy in its silt depths.

'Clara!'

There are footsteps behind her and she turns her head to see Henry Cotton, hesitantly picking his way along the slippery timbers of the wharf. It takes him a little while to come up next to her.

'Why did you run off like that? Did you know that wretched woman?'

'My mother.'

'Lord,' says Cotton, stammering. 'I am so sorry. I did not mean to . . .'

He stops short, looking down at her, quite lost for words. Clara takes pity on him, and breaks the silence.

'I used to come here,' she says, looking out along the curve of the river. 'Or, at least, not far from here, when I was a child. I used to think the river was beautiful at night.'

'It is beautiful, after a fashion,' says Cotton, unsure of himself. Gingerly, he sits down next to her.

'No, it's just mud and dirt.'

'Clara, look, I am awfully sorry. I can't begin to . . . Perhaps I should get you home?'

'I'm all right. I thought I'd done with Wapping, you see? I thought ma would be fine in the refuge, and that was that. But she had to come back to it, didn't she? I should have known she'd be here.'

'But why did she come here? How . . . ?'

Clara shrugs.

'Here,' he says, getting up. 'Take my hand. I will take you home. Unless you want to . . .' His voice trails off; again he's uncertain of the words, merely inclining his head in the direction of Gravehunger Court, further down the river.

'No, I don't want to go back there,' she says vehemently. 'I don't want to go back there ever again.'

He nods, and offers her his hand. She takes it and he helps her upright.

'My own mother died when I was a boy,' he says, feeling that he should say something appropriate to the situation. Immediately, however, he feels it is quite inadequate. Clara, for her part, looks up at him. Then the blank mask of her face cracks and she begins to cry, tears welling in her eyes, streaming down her cheeks.

'Ah,' he says, releasing her hand. He pulls out a handkerchief from his pocket. 'Here, take this.'

But she does not take it; rather, she just stands still, sobbing. For a moment, he fears she might faint, and takes hold of her arm. Nervously he reaches out and dabs her cheeks with the cloth.

'Here, I am sorry. Please.'

She takes the handkerchief from his hand, and collects herself enough to wipe her eyes. Without thinking, she mutely offers it back.

'No, please, keep it,' he says, looking at her face in the darkness. 'You may need it.'

She shakes her head, but she is still crying. He puts his hand to her cheek, wiping away a tear.

Then, without a word of warning, he leans down and kisses her.

PART THREE

CHAPTER THIRTY-TWO

'WE THEREFORE COMMIT her body to the ground; earth to earth, ashes to ashes, dust to dust; in sure and certain hope of the Resurrection . . .'

A wet wintry day in February.

Heavy rain bounces off the black umbrella held aloft by Henry Cotton. He looks down at the lowered head of Clara White, who stands by his side, under its protection; together, they listen to the clergyman complete the last few words of the simple funeral service. When he is finished, the man nods, pulls up the collar of his coat, and dashes away along the muddy path that leads out of the churchyard.

The churchyard itself is an old, run-down place, situated east of the Limehouse Basin, by the side of the Bromley Canal. Although it is not a quarter-mile from the grand church of St. Anne's upon the nearby Commercial Road, it bears no relation to that well-known edifice. Instead, the plot maintains a peculiar freedom from any such ecclesiastical attachment. The small country church, to which it once belonged, was, in fact, levelled long ago, although whether this was achieved by the ravages of time or the work of a speculative builder, no-one can recall. Now the plot merely abuts the backyards of a hastily constructed row of cottages, and, to all appearances, is quite neglected. The land itself is, however, property of the parish of Wapping, though the circumstances under which the parish made such an acquisition have, likewise, slipped from popular memory. None the less, a wooden sign testifying to ownership, and addressing various cautions to trespassers, is posted upon the stone gateposts. Likewise, the churchyard is girded around by iron railings, to ensure its tombstones and solitary weeping willow are free from the unwanted attentions of local children, or any passers-by who might wish to loiter amongst the graves. But no provision has been made to protect the place against greedy Nature, and the spread of weeds and briars that accompanies the passing of each year. In consequence, what must once have been a neatly kept patch of consecrated earth resembles the unworthiest piece of wasteland. It is, regardless, the best resting place that the Parish of Wapping can provide for Agnes White, and, if truth be told, her grave is better than many a pauper's lot. True, all the coffins that reside within it, half a dozen or more, are made of unplaned wood and stacked with only an inch of earth between them; but such are the pitfalls of relying upon the Parish.

In any case, once the clergyman has departed, a grave-digger, who has been lingering by the gate, comes forward wordlessly, spade in hand. Although the rain still falls in dense black sheets, he begins to fill in the ground, shovelling in the clay-rich clods on to the wooden lid, which itself rests only a couple of feet below the surface.

Clara, meanwhile, raises her head, covered by a tatty black bonnet, and looks up at Henry Cotton. He stands there silently, observing the man at his work.

'I must thank you for paying for the service, sir,'

she says, her voice quiet and subdued. 'I cannot think why you should, but I thank you.'

'It was the least I could do,' he replies. 'If I had not taken you to Wapping . . . well, besides, the man hardly said a couple of dozen words.'

'Still, it was more than I could do for her.'

'Surely Dr. Harris might have made some arrangement?'

Clara frowns. 'No, not even a kind word. I had to beg him to let me come here.'

Cotton raises his eyebrows, but says nothing in reply. A minute or two passes.

'Shall we go then?' he says at last. 'It sounds as if you will be missed before long, even today. Were you expecting any others to come?'

Clara hesitates, looking at the grave and the simple wooden cross that marks it.

'I had thought my sister might be here. Perhaps Miss Sparrow.'

'Miss Sparrow?'

'The superintendent of the refuge. She was at the inquest yesterday.'

'Ah yes, of course. I would have gone myself, but I had business to attend to.'

Clara stares at the grave.

'Still, I do not think anyone is coming,' says Cotton, observing that his companion still seems rooted to the spot.

'No, it seems not,' she replies. 'We ought to go.'

Cotton takes Clara's arm, and leads her gently away, through the gateway to the churchyard. From there, they take a track that joins the footpath by the canal, and leads back towards Limehouse. The canal path is empty of traffic, as no-one else is promenading in such weather. None the less, Henry Cotton looks anxiously about before he speaks.

'Clara,' he says, 'I hope you do not think too badly of me?'

She says nothing, but it is plain from her face that she does not fully understand his meaning.

'Why should I?' she asks.

'I mean to say, two days ago, when your mother was . . . when I found you by the river, and I took advantage of your distress.'

She stares at him blankly.

'Damn it!' he exclaims to himself nervously. 'I mean to say, I am sorry that I kissed you. It was not the act of a gentleman.'

Clara looks at him in surprise. Her face is still wet with tears, but a slight smile comes to her lips.

'You're a queer sort of gentleman, Mr. Phibbs. I know that much.'

'I have made you laugh,' he says, half annoyed with her gentle tone of mockery, half pleased with the result.

'No,' she says, though her lips still suggest a smile.

'Very well, then. I know this is not the best of moments, but I merely wanted to say that, if I have not offended you too much, I would still like your help.'

'I cannot go back to Wapping,' she replies, her voice suddenly losing its warmth.

'No, not that. Not at all. But I would still like to talk to you, about your history and so forth. We never had a proper chance, and I confess, you interest me greatly. As a study, I mean to say.'

She looks at him doubtfully.

'Please,' he continues, 'let me at least take you for some food. I am sure we can find a chop-house or some such when we get back upon the road.'

'It ain't proper, you being seen with me.'

'Then we will find somewhere suitably disreputable. We are in Limehouse, after all. And you look half starved in any case.'

'I'll be missed.'

He smiles, seeing the steps that lead up to the Commercial Road.

'Not, my dear girl, if we take a cab. Will you come?'

She hesitates for a moment.

'If you like.'

—

The chop-house is almost empty. None the less, its booths, separated by rickety oak partitions, smell of roasting, burnt toast, and spilt porter, and everywhere there is the all-pervasive scent of tobacco smoke.

'So, Clara, where shall we begin?'

'Where would you like?'

'Well, you were born in the public house which you showed me. When is your birthday?'

'The twelfth of March, I think.'

'You are not sure?'

'There was only my ma to remember it. And she was never that good at marking days.'

'I see. And where did you live at first?'

'In different places, then with my grandma.'

'In the house by the river?'

'Yes.' She looks down, frowning.

'I am sorry,' says Cotton. 'If it is, well, awkward to talk of it now . . . I did not mean to . . .'

'I do not mind.'

'What about the other places? Were they lodging houses?'

'If ma could afford the doss.'

'If not?'

She shrugs. 'Doorways, alleys, any place. There was a boat for a while.'

'You slept in a boat?'

'When it moored up, at night. My sister was good as born in it.'

'Really?'

'I ain't making it up.'

'I am sorry. It merely sounds rather, well, colourful.'

'It weren't.'

—

Step back.

A small boat floats upon the river, tethered to the pier at Hermitage Stairs; in it are a woman and child, curled together under a heavy canvas, a makeshift bed of folded sails and twisted rope beneath them. The woman has a round belly, and turns uneasily, this way and that. The little girl is awake and watches her shifting about.

Now the little girl is dragged to her feet, and they are up once more on the pier. She looks up at the woman. Her back is bent double and she holds her stomach, repeating an inaudible prayer, again and again.

The woman squats on the muddy shore. She groans like an injured animal, and the girl watches her closely, remembering a horse she once saw fall on the Ratcliffe Highway, with its hind leg quite broken. She does not know how long it takes to come: an awkward, squeezed bundle of skin and bones, wriggling and bloody-blue, that appears between her mother's thighs.

Some stranger hears the noise: a coal-heaver, his hands black as soot; the woman begs him for a knife and cuts the baby's cord.

'Clara?'

'Clara, say halloa to your sister. Ain't she a beautiful little thing?'

—

'Clara?'

'Your toast is getting cold.'

'I'm sorry.'

'That is quite all right. What became of you after your sister was born?'

'That was when we went to my grandma's.'

'But you had not lived there before? Why was that?'

'They never got on, her and my ma. They used to argue.'

'I see. Your grandmother did not, how shall we say, approve of your mother? Was she a very moral woman?'

Clara laughs. 'No. She kept the worst cadging-house north of the river.'

'Then what was the source of the trouble?'

'I don't know,' she says, buttering another slice of bread. 'I think they were too alike. It's often the way in families, ain't it?'

'Perhaps. How were they similar?'

'Both hard and stubborn, the pair of them. Ma would storm out after some row, and we'd be back on the street until the next time.'

Cotton smiles. 'Are you, then, hard and stubborn too?'

'Don't tease me.'

'I'm sorry. But you did not think much of your poor mother, I would say?'

She shrugs. 'I looked after her. She would have gone to the workhouse if it weren't for me talking round Dr. Harris. That's enough, ain't it?'

'I suppose so. And she is at peace now.'

'I hope so, for her sake.'

'Tell me about the rest of your family. Your grandmother?'

'She's dead. Three years last Christmas.'

'I'm sorry.'

'No-one else was.'

'Not even you?'

'Not much.'

'And what about your sister? She is still alive, is she not?'

'She is.'

'What does she do now?'

A pause; Clara looks away.

'She's gone the same way as ma, except she went and got herself married first.'

'She is married, but on the streets?'

Clara nods, not meeting Cotton's glance, looking down at her plate.

'The man she married, does he not object to it?'

'Him? I very much doubt it.'

'Ah, I see. It is like that?'

———

Tom Hunt. Clara can picture his face.

How old was she when they first met?

Seven years. Her mother brought him to meet her.

'Clarrie, this is Tom. You're to go with him today and be a good girl, do as he says.'

She looks up from her dinner and sees a boy, fifteen years old. A handsome boy, dressed in a neat waist-coat and jacket, though of cheap cloth, with a narrow-brimmed tall hat, cocked casually to one side of his head. He scrutinises the little girl standing in front of him.

'Ain't you pretty? Show us your hands.'

She stretches out her arms.

'Good hands. But you'll need nimble fingers for this game, my little darlin'.'

'Go on, Clarrie, go with the nice man.'

She looks at her mother.

'Don't you worry, Aggie,' says the young man,

winking. 'I'll teach her how to prig a man's pocket at twenty paces. She'll be a little goldmine, this one.'

He looks down at her.

'A little treasure with a face like that, eh? Butter wouldn't melt.'

———

'Tom Hunt? So it was this man Hunt who taught you how to thieve, at your mother's request?'

Cotton looks at Clara intently, assessing her response. She merely nods.

'I declare,' he continues, looking down to scribble in his notebook, 'it is like some penny serial! I never thought such things to be arranged quite so romantically.'

'Please, keep your voice down.'

'Bless you, Clara, no-one here imagines either of us to be particularly respectable. Besides, it is so intriguing a story.'

A pause.

'It is not a "story". I should like to go now, if you please.'

'You have not finished your meal.'

'Mrs. Harris will be waiting. You promised me a cab.'

'And you shall have one, you have my word. But there is one thing I would ask.'

She sighs. 'What now?'

'I would very much like to meet your sister, and this fellow, this Tom Hunt.'

CHAPTER THIRTY-THREE

'Useless.'

'Useless, sergeant?'

'A waste of time, sir, this diary business, even now we have the blasted transcript. It's all the same, ain't it? Here's one, "November the fifteenth 1863":

'Went for walk along the Haymarket; it was a cold night, quite bitter, but I confess that the area quite lives up to its reputation, and not merely around the night houses and such. I was immediately accosted by two girls; asked me directions, then enquired if I wished to go with them; one had a broad West Country brogue, and said she was new to the city. The other, I believe, was a native, though she affected ignorance of the streets (claimed they were both quite lost!). For all that, I am quite sure both would know of a house-of-call within walking distance, but I did not pursue the matter. For some reason I took a dislike to both of these females.

'It took a shilling to rid myself of them.

'Dozens of them. Night after night. And he writes it all down. Never says nothing about himself. I can't make no sense of it. It's an obsession, if you ask me. He's a deviant, like what I said.'

'Does he bed these girls?'

The sergeant snorts, as if to indicate the naïvety of the question. 'Never says so. But it ain't normal, is it?'

'Maybe. He is a writer of sorts, I think. He writes well enough.'

'If you say so.'

'A journalist, or some such. There is a line here, in January: "Took mss. to B. says he would be interested in monthly series on the 'social evils'."'

'B.?'

'Yes. It is little help, I know. Perhaps if we made a few enquiries around the newspapers.'

'It is something, I suppose,' says Watkins, glumly, envisioning a wasted afternoon in the dingy offices of a dozen sub-editors.

'It is, Watkins, the only blessed clue we have to our Mr. Phibbs' identity. Besides, the book is not "all the same", as you put it. It falls into a pattern: he makes brief jottings, always in shorthand, then writes a fuller diary entry upon the subject, presumably when he is at home and free to do so.'

'Oh, well then,' says Watkins, affecting a sarcastic tone, 'I can see that's very different. Anyhow, I thought you reckoned he didn't do it? With respect, sir, if that is the case, why are we wasting all our time on this fellow?'

'I have never said we should not find him.'

'Well, be that as it may, I'm done with this,' says Watkins, putting the papers down. 'I'll be off, if it's all right by you.'

Webb nods distractedly, still reading from his section of the transcription, while Watkins puts down the sheaf of paper and gets up. Then he calls the sergeant back.

'Wait one moment.'

'Sir?' says Watkins, wearily.

Webb smiles; a smile of quiet satisfaction.

'I have found it, sergeant. I have found it. Although I wonder why it was not right at the end, in sequence. Perhaps he was running out of paper. It explains everything.'

'Found what, sir?'

Webb looks at him eagerly. 'You ask if I thought that he did not kill her. Listen to this, in the fellow's own notes:

'Few people upon the streets; no suitable girls, or they have avoided me; once accosted, near Saffron Hill; did I want to "give her a good ride"? I said not; asked if I may put usual questions, if she did not object; I paid; she cursed me foully and hurried off! pretty though – wretched creature!'

'Just like the rest of it,' says the sergeant. 'Though I'd say that one had the right idea.'

'Please, Watkins, do not interrupt; I am coming to it.

'Followed the girl; lost her by Farringdon Stn.; took fancy to go down, catch last train, bought ticket; found solitary red-haired girl lying asleep on train; smell of gin; street girl?; odd sort to find in 2nd class; grand-dame comes on at King's Cross, gives her a <u>strong</u> look; sniffing air, full of crinoline and dignity;

'Mem. article on the Underground Railway?

'He stops there. It is dated the night of the murder.' Webb's face is bright with excitement. 'The night of the murder. Do you not see what this means?'

202

The sergeant raises his eyebrows. 'I can see what you're getting at, sir. That's all well and good, but a man can't write himself his own alibi, can he? I wouldn't want to rely on it, not if I was him, anyhow.'

'Really, Watkins, you can be obtuse. In this case, he did just that, though he did not know it. I swear he did not kill her, I am sure of it. Why would he be so elaborate? Besides, you are missing my point entirely.'

'Perhaps you could spell it out for me, then, sir.'

'Don't you see, sergeant? What if the girl was already on the train when he got on?'

'What of it? She got on before him. He strangles her.'

'At the station, in full view of the platform?'

'He waits till the train's moving, like we thought.'

'No, the diary explains why no-one at Farringdon remembers her. Don't you see? What if she was left there? She came down on the train from Paddington, and was missed when the train came to the terminus. They were short of guards, were they not? She was missed when the train emptied, and just left lying there, dead. She could have been killed at any time before the train reached the station. We have been thinking it must have happened between Farringdon and King's Cross, whereas, if I am right, it was just the opposite, if not earlier.'

Sergeant Watkins frowns. 'But even if that's true,' he says, 'and it's still an odd business if it is, where does that leave us?'

Webb looks thoughtful for a moment, but his face visibly sags, losing the brilliance in his eyes and the smile upon his lips.

'Not much further on, really, are we, sir?' says Watkins.

Decimus Webb sits in his office. Sergeant Watkins has long since disappeared home. Before him, Webb has sketched in pencil a rough map of the Metropolitan Railway, and the relation of the various stations to the Holborn Refuge, with approximate distances clearly marked. He idly traces his finger over the route, then turns to one side and picks up a nearby folder, marked 'Agnes Mary White; Coroner's Verdict'.

He opens the folder and reads through the contents once more, staring at the words 'broken neck' and 'Verdict of Accidental Death'. He returns to the piece of paper with his map, and writes out very deliberately, in his neatest handwriting: 'Agnes White is the link.'

He ponders this for a moment, then underneath 'Agnes White' writes: 'Phibbs?'

Decimus Webb sighs, and gets up in search of coffee.

CHAPTER THIRTY-FOUR

'Is THIS THE place, do you think?' asks Henry Cotton.

'I don't know. She said Saffron Hill, I told you. It was your idea to come here, weren't it?'

'Clara, it did not have to be today. Besides, we have been in half a dozen places already, and no-one has seen them. I thought you wanted to get home.'

'No, I want to get it over with. And I want to see Lizzie anyhow.'

'Very well,' replies Cotton, following her down the muddy alley. 'Let us try this one, although if I had known, I believe I would have worn something less formal.'

Clara looks back at him as she opens the door to the Three Cups public house.

'You'll do,' she says, stepping inside.

Cotton follows her. The interior is as ill-ventilated and poorly lit as any place they have already visited. It is, however, rather smaller, and thus it is impossible to remain anonymous. Only a couple of loafers stand by the bar, and a dozen more are seated at the various tables, illuminated by the flickering light of the fireplace. None the less, all of them spare the newcomers a quick glance, and most exchange some waggish comment upon the incongruity of seeing such a prim servant-girl and gentleman together in such an establishment. Indeed, it is almost certain that several prepare themselves to go further, and say something 'telling', and at a volume such that everyone may enjoy their wit. They are all spared the opportunity by a voice that booms from the back of the room.

'Well, blow me tight!'

Clara looks, and sees the figure of Tom Hunt rising from his seat to greet her.

'There he is,' she whispers to her companion, almost ruefully, 'you have your wish now.'

'I had forgotten you said he was so young,' he replies. 'Something of a swell about him.'

'You expected an old Jew, did you?'

Cotton does not have time to reply, as Tom Hunt comes up and extends his arm, snatching Clara's hand and kissing it.

'Clarrie! How long has it been now?'

'A good twelvemonth,' she replies coldly, removing her hand from his. Hunt, however, ignores the severity of her tone.

'Too long, now we're related and all, eh? And ain't you going to introduce us to this gentleman? Halloa there, sir!' he says, extending his hand to Cotton.

'This is Mr. Phibbs,' she replies, uncertain what more she can say on the subject.

'I say, Clarrie,' says Hunt, smiling, 'he ain't your . . . I mean, you and him ain't . . .'

'I am just an acquaintance, Mr. Hunt, I assure you,' interjects Henry Cotton.

Hunt falters for a moment, surprised to hear his own name. He glances at Clara, though retaining his cheerful demeanour.

'I see our Clarrie must have spoken of me,' he says. 'Nothing too bad, I hope.'

Cotton coughs. 'In point of fact, I had hoped to meet you.'

'Now,' says Hunt, a little mystified, 'you have the advantage of me, sir. Why is that?'

'I have a proposition for you,' says Cotton, choosing his words carefully. 'A matter of business.'

'Ah, now that is interesting,' replies Hunt, his curiosity piqued. 'Well, what say we take a seat, like old friends, share a drop of something suitable?'

Cotton nods, and the three of them make their way to the table where Tom Hunt was sitting.

Clara looks around the room. 'Is Lizzie not here?'

'She'll be along later, I should think. You wanting a word with her? And I thought it was me you'd come for.'

Clara does not reply.

———

Tom Hunt downs his second pint of porter, purchased by Henry Cotton, who sits opposite him, still drinking from his first. Clara sits by his side, with no drink before her, looking at the door in case her sister should arrive.

'I'm not sure I get your meaning, sir,' says Hunt, wiping his lips.

'Well, I am an author, you see. Or rather, a journalist.'

'That writes for the papers?'

'Well, I would like to, yes. You must have seen the sort of thing that I am talking about – studies of London characters and such like.'

'And you consider me a character, do you, sir?'

'Clara tells me you know a few dodges. Is that not true?'

'What you been telling this fellow, Clarrie, eh?' says Hunt, a little nervously. 'I fear the girl misled you, sir. She's always been a bit fanciful. Just because a man is alive to a few fakes, that don't make him no cadger, nor a thief.'

'Wait, you misunderstand me,' says Cotton. 'I wish to make a study of such things, but I assure you I will not give your rightful name when I write my piece.'

'How do I know that?'

'You have my word. And I would pay, of course.'

'How much?'

'That would depend on what I find.'

Hunt fails to reply, as he sees the diminutive figure of his wife enter the room.

'Over here, Liz! Just look who's here to see you!'

Lizzie Hunt frowns and walks cautiously towards the table. Henry Cotton stands up, a display of manners that causes her husband to grin in amusement.

'Here, please,' says Cotton, offering her his seat.

'Who's this?' she says, ignoring him and finding another stool, pulling it up next to her husband.

'Now, Liz,' replies her husband, 'no need to be rude. This gentleman is Mr. Phibbs, who is an acquaintance of Clarrie, and who has just made me an interesting little offer.'

She does not reply, looking sideways at her sister. Clara herself, however, speaks up.

'You missed the funeral.'

'Did I? I didn't want to go anyhow.'

'You knew it was today then?'

'No. Tom saw something in the papers about . . . well, what happened.'

'You should have come to her funeral. You owed her that.'

Lizzie shrugs. 'I didn't know it was today.'

'You could have asked me.'

'It's a crying shame,' interjects Hunt. 'Nasty way to go, that.'

'Who's asking you?' says Clara, a hint of anger in her voice.

Hunt smiles thinly and glances away. Clara turns and looks at Cotton. 'I'd better go,' she says, standing up.

'Clara, wait a moment,' he replies, 'I will see you home. Mr. Hunt, so do we have an agreement?'

'If we can settle terms.'

'I will come back tomorrow, then, as we discussed?'

'If you like.'

'Good. I will make it worth your trouble, you have my word.'

Hunt nods and watches Henry Cotton depart, together with Clara White, who studiously avoids his gaze.

'What was that all about?' asks Lizzie, when the door of the Three Cups has closed behind the pair of them.

'Apparently, my dear, I am a "character", and it seems "characters" are at a premium with that young gentleman.'

'I don't much like the look of him,' says Lizzie Hunt.

⎯

Ten minutes later, and Henry Cotton and Clara stand upon the corner of Doughty Street.

'Don't come any further,' she says, looking warily along the road. 'They might see you.'

'And then I would have to say we met by chance here. Would that be so terrible?'

'Not for you, maybe.'

'Well, thank you for introducing me to Mr. Hunt.'

Clara looks at him. 'I owe you that much, sir. I hope you don't live to regret it.'

'I do not think I will. It is a shame your sister is, well, shy of me. I would like to talk to her too.'

'I'm sure Tom will fix you a price.'

'I only wish to talk to her, you realise that, I hope?'

'If you say so, Mr. Phibbs. Talking won't help her, in any case.'

'How do you mean?'

'You didn't see the bruises on her arm, I suppose?'

'No, I can't say I did.'

'Well, I best be going.'

'I hope we shall meet again at least?'

Clara merely turns away.

CHAPTER THIRTY-FIVE

THE THREE CUPS.

The clock upon the wall strikes four in the afternoon and, though it is an inoffensive little timepiece, the landlord of the establishment looks at it with a peculiarly grim expression, as if the passing of the hour only brings him sixty minutes nearer the final judgment of his maker. He is a heavily jowled, snub-nosed man, and his features bear a passing resemblance to those of the average British bull-dog. In consequence, his expression rarely wavers from a look of perpetual melancholy, regardless of the object of his contemplation. In this case, however, the diminution of the evening light is under consideration, and, after a good deal of thought, he finally puts a match to a taper and goes out to light the gas-lamp. As he leaves, the words 'I won't be but a minute' are muttered indistinctly, but with a slight undertone of menace, to no-one in particular. He feels no need to make any more particular statement; he does not say, for instance, that he emphatically does not expect the contents of the whiskey bottle to diminish in his brief absence. None the less, this much, at least, is understood by the few drinkers who loiter in the smoky comfort of the Three Cups. At a corner table, Tom Hunt and his wife are still part of the Cup's clientele, their conversation having turned back to their encounter with Mr. Phibbs earlier in the afternoon.

'He was a queer one, though, Tom. What if he's police?' says Lizzie.

'That young scrub? Hardly, darlin'. You saw him.'

'Plain clothes,' she replies. 'What if he's plain clothes? He could be, you know.'

'Then he would be not plain, but very fine clothes, I must say,' says Tom, amused; he has a drink in his hand and a merry look on his face. 'The police have worse suits, and worse manners.'

'I'm not sure,' says Lizzie.

'Your Mr. Plain-Clothes will do us fine. He talks smart, but he's green as the grass. I'll tap him easy. Your Clarrie's done us a favour, Liz. It's good of her.'

'If you say so.'

'Here now,' he says, taking her hand and squeezing it hard, 'who else is there to say different?'

She bites her lip and looks away. He tuts to himself, and releases his grip.

'You said for me to tell you when you got ratted,' she says, stealing a glance in his direction.

'Well, I ain't.'

'If you says so.'

'Lizzie, dear, I ain't drunk,' he says, though the words are a little slurred. 'You know what I am?'

'What?'

'Happy. And you know why? Because I smell money.'

'You think he's got money?'

Tom taps his nose. 'I can smell it, darlin'. Plenty of it.'

'That's the beer, I reckon.'

Tom smiles, and swills the dregs of brown liquid around his glass.

'I don't think he's a peeler,' he says, more contemplatively, 'but maybe you should go and have a word with your blessed sister anyhow, see what's what. Find out proper how she knows this fellow. Maybe have a good look at that grand mansion what you say she's living in, while you're there. Likely she could put something our way.'

'Tom,' she says, pleadingly, 'do I have to? It ain't no mansion, and she was so off with me last time, I told you she was. And she weren't much better today, was she? She hardly said a word. She thinks she's better than the likes of you and me.'

Tom shakes his head. 'That's just the business with your blasted mother, ain't it? Can't blame her being upset, can you? Just do as you're told,' he says emphatically. 'You'd do well to keep in with her. And with me and all.'

Lizzie says nothing in reply. Instead, she reluctantly stands up, leaning against the pub's dark green wallpaper, which itself seems to trap something of the gin-sodden atmosphere of the place, and is slightly damp to the touch. She looks a little unsteady.

'Here, how much have you had?' asks Tom, eyeing her suspiciously, wondering, perhaps, if she somehow has acquired a personal supply of liquor.

'Hardly anything,' she replies, steadying herself. 'I ain't eaten much, that's all.'

Tom raises his eyebrows, adopting a mocking weary expression, as if to indicate that he cannot understand why any woman of his should declare a want for food. He reaches into his pocket and gives his wife two pennies.

'Get yourself something.'

Another woman might dash such meagre house-keeping to the ground, and demand more. Lizzie Hunt, however, is not such a female; she merely takes it meekly from her husband's palm.

'Tom,' she says, as she takes the money, 'there's something I've been wanting to tell you . . .'

'I don't want to hear your troubles. Will you just get gone?' he says, ignoring her words, impatiently downing the last of his drink.

She looks at him for a moment, but thinks better of speaking, and turns away. With a nod to the sullen landlord, returned from his lamp-lighting, she walks out into the evening air.

Outside, though the rain has ceased, the alley is still wet with mud, the viscous mixture of dirt and dung that clings to London's side streets, places where no crossing-sweeper would ever ply for trade. Lizzie sighs to herself, hoists her dress above her boots and makes her way expertly along the slippery surface and down onto Saffron Hill. It is an old thoroughfare, and the area surrounding is often invoked as exemplary of the worst sort of slum. Indeed, the street itself is lined on both sides by second-hand sellers of this and that, from clothes to old iron, knives to neckerchiefs. If there is a saving grace to Saffron Hill, it is the gas-lights, which can be found upon every corner. They range from the ornate projection of a distant gin palace, bigger even than that which heralds the Three Cups, to simple jets of naked flame that sprout unexpectedly, like fiery buds, from rain-soaked shop-fronts. And it occurs to Lizzie Hunt, as she makes her way along the road, that there is something of beauty in the sight, the fluttering of yellow flame against a soot-black evening sky. But it is because of such fanciful thoughts that she does not hear footsteps splashing upon the pavement behind her, nor pay any attention to the man to whom they belong, until he puts his arm around her shoulders. She gasps in surprise, and looks up.

'Bill!'

Bill Hunt smiles, touching his cap.

'What you doing out in such weather?' he says, pulling her closer.

'You scared me half to death, creeping up on us like that.'

'Creeping up? You was day-dreaming, I reckon.'

'Maybe,' she says, shifting a little from his grasp. 'Have you been following me?'

He winks. 'What if I have? You need someone to keep an eye on you, I reckon.'

There is the smell of beer on his breath; it is not an unfamiliar smell to Lizzie Hunt, but in this instance it is sufficient excuse for her to step away.

'You've been drinking, ain't you, Bill? Steering clear of the Cups now?'

He shrugs, and looks a little shame-faced. 'He's there all the time, and I ain't got enough money to be giving it away.'

She smiles a wry smile. 'You shouldn't let Tom bully you, a big man like you.'

'Neither should you,' he says. As he speaks, he abruptly reaches out and touches her face, stroking her cheek with a gentleness that belies his bulky frame.

'Bill!' she exclaims, pushing his hand away. 'Pack it in, will you? Besides, he don't bully me. I love him.'

Bill Hunt visibly winces at the words, and he frowns, a look of frustration etched on his face.

'No you don't,' he says emphatically.

Lizzie sighs.

'You can go now, Bill. I'll be all right from here.'

'I'll come with you.'

'I can't go and see my sister with you in tow, can I? Tom will be so angry if I don't.'

'Let him try being angry with me, if you likes,' says Bill Hunt, with drunken belligerence.

'Bill, don't be silly. Just leave me be, will you?'

Bill groans, but reluctantly turns away, muttering something indistinct to himself. He is inebriated enough to stumble as he walks along the pavement, but soon disappears into the distance. Lizzie, on the other hand, once she is certain her unwanted companion has gone, turns the corner and walks in the direction of Doughty Street.

In less than five minutes she is outside the house where her sister is employed. She stands upon the opposite side of the road, surveying the windows. For a moment, she considers whether to try the kitchen door, or if it might be sensible to return at a later hour. Then she can make out a girl busying herself, closing curtains on the first floor. Is it her sister? There is another figure behind her.

Lizzie Hunt stares fixedly at the window as the curtains are drawn. There is an odd change in her posture, a peculiar tension, a look of utter disbelief. Suddenly she turns and flies back along the road, running as fast as she can. With quick, anxious breaths she reaches Gray's Inn in seconds, tears welling in her eyes.

Chapter Thirty-Six

It is gone midnight when Bill Hunt stumbles out of the Old Friar public house upon Saffron Hill, pausing in a doorway to light his pipe. He has not stopped drinking since he saw Lizzie Hunt, and he struggles to find the box of Vesuvians in his coat pocket. In fact, his fingers fumble with the match, with the result that he almost drops the pipe in the process. Cursing himself, he finally lights the dry Virginian tobacco, putting the clay to his lips, taking a deep breath, drawing in the smoke, and puffing it back into the cold night air.

He is not alone, since the pubs have all begun to disgorge their clients on to the streets. He watches the steady stream of passers-by; most are working men at the end of the night's spree, steeped in drink. His reverie is interrupted by a melody playing in the distance, steadily becoming louder. It is a boy with a fiddle, working through the late night crowds, his brother beside him with an upturned cap, both of them olive-skinned Italians, no more than eight years old. A pair of costers chip in a couple of pennies, and the boy grins like a lunatic. Then a trio of young women, laughing amongst themselves, do likewise. Bill looks at the women. They are all older than Lizzie Hunt, though not by much, and dressed in gaudy colours. One, the tallest of the group, wears a hat tipped with a white feather, the others are bare-headed, but all wear thick woollen shawls around their shoulders, and huddle close to one another as they walk.

Bill Hunt shuffles out into the gaslit street, and follows a few yards behind them. He has a tendency to stoop as he walks, and it is hard to say whether this is due to a natural shyness, or a habit formed whilst working underground with pickaxe and shovel. In any case, he dogs the three girls, unnoticed, for a good minute or more before the tallest of the group chances to look round and see him. It is a quick, appraising glance, a business-like look with which Bill Hunt is quite familiar. In turn, he catches her eye, and jerks his head, as if to indicate a nearby alley.

The woman leans towards her companions, and whispers a few words; both turn briefly to look at him, then move away, hastening down the street. She, on the other hand, splits away from them, and waits for Bill to come closer.

'I ain't going down there, dear,' she says, looking at the alley. 'It stinks something awful.'

Bill looks at her. 'I know another good place, just round the corner.'

——

Midnight. Doughty Street.

A conversation in the front parlour.

'I trust your mother is quite dead, Clara?'

'I believe so, ma'am.'

'Well, I am glad of it. I cannot abide sloppiness in these matters.'

Wait. No.

Clara White wakes up, perspiring.

——

'Where we goin'?' asks the girl with the feathered hat.

'It's not far.'

'I don't give a fig, darlin'. Long as you see me right.'

'Here, careful,' says Bill Hunt. 'Now keep your eyes shut, and I'll surprise you.'

'Why?'

'It's a surprise, I told you. Watch out for the steps.'

'What steps? Oh, bloody hell, you'll kill me, you will.'

'Here, I've got hold of you, ain't I? It's not far, I told you. Mind while I undo the latch.'

'Can I open my eyes yet?'

'Go on then.'

'Well, ain't this a little nest? Blankets and all. Very grand.'

'We won't get any trouble here.'

'If you say so, love. It's your shillin'. Easy now, no need to paw us like that, is there?'

'It's my shilling.'

'You could be a bit . . .'

'Shut your hole, will you?'

'Charming. Here, what's that noise?'

'Nothing to be afraid of.'

—

Wapping by night.

The man clasps her hand in his and gently brings her palm to his breast; she can feel his heart beating.

'Mr. Phibbs, I can't . . .'

'Hush,' he says, and kisses her, touching her cheek with his fingers.

'I've never really . . .'

'Clara, hush,' he says. 'Tell me about your sister.'

'Lizzie?'

—

'Lizzie.'

Bill Hunt says it in a whisper but the woman hears him. Her mouth curls, sardonically, teasing him, even as he keeps going at her as hard as he can.

'Who's Lizzie, darlin'?' she asks, between breaths; she is laughing at him, he is sure. He puts his hand over the woman's mouth; she talks too much. She still looks at him, mocking him with her eyes; for a moment, he thinks he should hit her.

But the moment passes; then it is but one brief second of pleasure.

He collapses on top of her, blood pounding through his veins. He smells of sweat, and steam, and coal-dust; the girl quickly wriggles free of his bulk. For a moment, she fears he might be asleep, but then he turns over and stares at her.

'Who's Lizzie?' she asks, tugging down her petti-coat.

'Never mind.'

'I don't. I just want my money, dear.'

'Wait there, I'll see if it's safe to go out.'

Doughty Street.

'Clara?'

'Yes, sir?'

'I am sorry about your mother.' Dr. Harris takes her palm, and places it between his own hands. 'Perhaps it is for the best? She is at peace now, after all.'

'I hope so, sir.'

'And, I think, there is no need to speak of the matter again.'

'Sir.'

CHAPTER THIRTY-SEVEN

MORNING.

Henry Cotton walks the length of Saffron Hill, past the peculiar arrangements of stands and props that project from the old-clothes establishments. As he walks, a shaft of sunlight briefly penetrates the clouds, and, for a few seconds, the washed-out cottons and tattered silks almost seem bright and gay. Indeed, it strikes him what a remarkable difference the light makes when it disappears once more, as abruptly as it came, and the road reverts to its gloomier aspect.

In truth, his own garments contribute to the drabness, since he has abandoned his decent suit for an old and care-worn example of the mixed-cloth variety, giving himself an altogether shabbier appearance, more in keeping with such humble streets. In fact, no-one spares him a second glance as he comes to the alley that leads to the Three Cups. He does not enter it, however, but looks down at the figure of a man squatting on a doorstep, a board and three thimbles on his lap.

'Hardly recognised you, sir,' says Tom Hunt, plainly amused by Cotton's appearance. 'Here, look out,' he whispers, as he notices a group of factory men approaching, 'now, what we was talking about, see how it's done . . .'

Hunt takes a deep breath, and shouts out along the

street, 'Come on, ladies and gentlemen. Try your luck, won't you? I've already lost a shilling today. I know my luck's got to turn.'

The men laugh, but seem to be bent on passing by. Hunt, however, addresses himself loudly to Henry Cotton.

'You, sir. I'll give you one more go, if you like, though you've robbed me blind already.'

Hunt raises his eyebrows conspiratorially. Cotton, realising he has a part to play, mumbles his agreement.

'Ah, now, how much will you wager, sir? I can't speak for more than a shilling, not when you can double your money.'

'A shilling then.'

'A shilling it is!' he exclaims at the top of his voice. A couple of the men going past turn their heads, slowing their pace. Hunt takes a shilling from Cotton and displays a hardened pea between thumb and fore-finger, placing it under the middle thimble. In time-honoured fashion he begins to swap one with the other, sliding them in ever-quicker movements around the piece of card. By the time he is finished, three of the factory men stand by Henry Cotton's side, expectantly waiting for the result.

'Your call, sir,' says Hunt, addressing Cotton.

Cotton deliberates, and picks the middle one. The thimble is slowly raised, to reveal the shrivelled pea beneath.

'Damn me,' exclaims Hunt, vehemently, taking a pair of coins from his pocket with great show of reluctance, 'I never knew a fellow with such keen peepers. That's it! I'm finished at this game.'

Cotton takes the money that is offered him. No sooner than it changes hands does one of the factory men step forward.

'Here, I'll have a go,' he says cautiously.

Hunt smiles, but shakes his head.

'Sorry, my friend, this young swell here has cleaned me out.'

———

It is a few minutes before Henry Cotton, having once more traversed the length of Saffron Hill, returns to the Three Cups, following Tom Hunt's instructions. He finds Tom Hunt seated inside.

'Made sure they were gone, did you?' asks Hunt.

'Quite gone.'

'Good. Better safe than sorry, eh? Even if I don't catch them today, there's always tomorrow. Now, you see how easy a rig it is? He would have put down a shilling, that fellow, mark my words.'

'And he could not win?'

Hunt answers by retrieving the thimbles from his pocket, placing the pea down under the middle one once more, and rotating their positions at half the speed of his previous display.

'Now pick one.'

Cotton chooses the thimble to his left. Hunt raises it up to reveal nothing, then likewise with its compatriot in the middle, and upon the right.

'Now, where do you think it went, that pea?'

Cotton smiles, admiring the man's skill. 'I don't know.'

Hunt raises his left hand, and proudly shows Cotton his thumb. The pea can just be seen under his thumb nail, trapped against calloused skin.

'What do you reckon to that then?'

Cotton smiles. 'I have read about the trick, of course,' he says. 'But it is remarkable to see how it is done. Does it always need an accomplice?'

'Accomplice? Ain't that a bit grand? It's just a fellow

223

what jollies things along, that's all. And he ain't always needed, if your luck holds good.'

'You would lose some money to start with?'

Hunt smirks. 'Have a look at them coins what I gave you.'

'They seem all right,' says Cotton, taking them out into the light.

'You rub them hard against each other.'

'Ah.'

'Paint. They're queer as you'll ever find. But there ain't many who will know the difference, not if they think as they've gained something for nothing.'

'Tell me,' says Cotton, eagerly, examining one of the thimbles, 'would you do it all again, but slower? I would like to make some notes.'

'I think I'm in need of a reviver before that,' says Hunt, nodding towards the bar.

'And there is more you can show me?'

'I should think so,' says Tom Hunt. 'Now where's that drink? And then there's the small matter of payment, ain't there?'

CHAPTER THIRTY-EIGHT

EVENING, IN SAFFRON Hill.

'Tom, is that you?'

Lizzie Hunt sits, curled up on the bed, alone in Bill Hunt's room.

'Aye.'

'What you doing in the dark, anyhow?'

'I didn't want to waste the matches.'

'Here,' he says, striking a light, and illuminating the candle beside the bed. His voice is unusually cheerful. 'Look at this.'

Tom stands in front of her, turning a little to the left, then the right. In the dim light it takes his wife a moment to realise he is wearing a jacket and greatcoat that look smart enough to be new. She sits up, staring at him.

'Where did you get those?'

'I bought them off a man in Monmouth Street, not an hour ago. And,' he says, pulling a little bundle from inside his coat, 'who do you think this is for?'

The bundle falls open to reveal itself as a thick woollen shawl, dyed dark red, wrapped around a silk bonnet of similar hue, slightly crushed by its confinement.

'Tom!' she exclaims, snatching them from his hands and wrapping the shawl around her shoulders. 'Where did you get the money?'

'Let's just say I had a very satisfactory afternoon with your Mr. Plain-Clothes. It was so satisfactory I even forgot that I ain't seen hide nor hair of you since yesterday. Where've you been? I thought you was going to see your sister?'

'Tom, don't be angry, please.'

'I ain't,' he replies, looking at her quizzically, 'not now, anyhow. There's nothing like ready money to lift a man's spirits. What say I treat you to supper?'

She nods, a response containing less enthusiasm than might have been anticipated.

'Here, have you been crying?'

'A little,' she replies, 'and thinking.'

'Too much of that ain't good for you.'

'Tom, there's something I should tell you. You'll be good about it, I know you will, but . . .'

'What?' he says, unease in his voice.

'I think I'm expecting.'

He does not reply. In the half-light of the candle she merely watches him as he brings his hand to his mouth and tugs fretfully at his lip.

'Tom, say something. It's your babby, I know it is.'

He leans forward, picking up the candle and bringing it closer to her face.

'Tom?'

'How far gone are you?'

'I don't know.'

'How far gone?'

'A couple of months?'

'Good,' he says, breathing a sigh of relief, putting the candle back down.

'What do you mean, Tom?'

'You ain't got the brains you were born with, have you?' he says softly. 'It ain't mine, you stupid sow. How could it be? When you've been giving it up to half of bleeding Clerkenwell?'

'It is Tom,' she says, standing up, clutching his arm. 'If you want it, it is.'

He is silent for a moment, then looks at her, his expression almost kindly.

'What I want, Liz, is for you to put things right. Will you do that for me?'

'I don't understand,' she says, looking at him blankly.

'I know a woman, St. Giles's way, who'll do it for two bob.'

'Do what?'

'Get rid of it.'

There is silence again, as her mouth drops open. Her eyes fill with tears before she can say a word. Finally, she speaks.

'I won't.'

Tom Hunt pushes his wife back on to the bed.

'By God, you little madam, you bleeding will,' he says, loosening the strap of his belt.

~

'Clara? What you doing skulking down here?'

'Leave us, Ally. I'll be all right.'

'Is there something wrong with you?'

'Just a twinge, that's all. It'll pass.'

~

The noises that echo round the yard off Saffron Hill are not unfamiliar to those who live nearby. The raised voices and sound of Tom Hunt's belt strap being brought down upon his wife's unprotected body – such things can be heard many an evening from any number of rooms and lodgings. It is perhaps a little odd that it is not a Saturday, since that is the night most favoured for such domestic disturbances, but not so odd as to make anyone do anything other than raise their eyebrows and quietly get on with their own business. In any case, it is done with in a matter of minutes, and, if the ragged tribesmen of Saffron Hill follow any etiquette in these matters, it is the tried and trusted prescription not to 'interfere'.

In consequence, there is no-one banging at the door when Tom Hunt returns his belt to his waist, and leaves his cousin's room. Nor is there anyone but his wife to hear his parting words, to the effect that if the cause of his displeasure is not removed, he will 'get rid of it' himself. Moreover, since Bill Hunt is still working upon his evening shift, there is no-one who will come and comfort the fragile, bruised likeness of a woman that lies cowering upon the bed, as the solitary candle burns down and finally splutters into nothingness.

How long Lizzie Hunt remains there in the darkness is impossible to say. She sobs for a while and then eventually falls into a disturbed sleep, with dreams of her mother, and her husband, and the spectre of a man whose name she cannot quite place.

~

'Clara?'

'What?'

'How are you?'

'I'm sorry, Ally, I was somewhere else.'

'You look awful pale. Shall I get his nibs, get him to have a look at you? What is it?'

Clara White shakes her head. 'I felt like this when ma died.'

'You didn't say anything.'

'I didn't know what it meant.'

'Come on, let's go to bed. You'll feel better after some sleep.'

~

Lizzie Hunt is awake. She clambers off the bed; her arm is swollen and she has to twist her body, counter to her natural inclination, in order to move herself without too much pain. She pulls the new shawl around herself, concealing some of her bruises, and opens the door into the hallway, walking slowly down the stairs.

CHAPTER THIRTY-NINE

Dr. Arthur Harris waits for the sound of the clock, sitting in his bedroom, fully dressed. It has, he realises, become a ritual with him that he should listen for the bell tolling two o'clock, before he leaves the house. Midnight, he muses, would be more poetic, if remaining unobserved were not a consideration.

There. The sound of the church bell, and the clock in the hall, barely a second apart. He allows himself a smile and creeps on to the landing, treading on the rug as softly as he can, conscious of the slightest creak of the floorboards. Indeed, although two o'clock is an inconsequential hour, there is something rather melodramatic in the way he sneaks downstairs upon tiptoe, bearing his solitary candle. It is done in a manner that would be quite suited to a pantomime clown, or the music-hall antics of 'Burglarious Bill'.

But there is no audience, and that, of course, is precisely his intention.

―――

'Did you hear something?'

'Clarrie, go back to sleep, will you?'

―――

Dr. Harris frowns as he approaches the end of Doughty Street. He feels cold despite the thick cloth of his great-coat, and the hansom, which normally waits for him by arrangement, is quite absent. He walks a little further in case the man is late, contemplating his options; the thought of proceeding the whole distance on foot is not appealing to a man of his years, and yet there is something equally unsatisfactory in the prospect of returning to his own cold bed. As he turns the corner, considering whether it would be wise to wait for a passing cab, he notices a figure loitering nearby, a tall, heavily built man, a labourer of some sort by the appearance of his clothes, a scarf wrapped around his face, and cloth cap on his head. The man is watching him.

Dr. Harris clutches his walking stick more tightly and hurries on, but the man walks over to him.

'Sir?'

Harris stops moving, seeing that the man is bent on speaking to him, and turns nervously to look at him.

'I have no money, I am sorry.'

The man shakes his head. 'I ain't asking for any. I've a message.'

'A message? My good man, I think you've mistaken me for someone else.'

'About a little girl, what needs your attention.'

Harris looks at him, intrigued, the skepticism vanishing from his face.

'Did Mrs. F. send you?'

The man nods.

'Well,' replies Harris, visibly relieved by this communication, though still a little nervous, 'I have lost my cab. Tell her I shall come tomorrow night. It is getting late.'

'She said tonight. She ain't far, just down the road. Said I was to take you there.'

'She is not at the . . . regular place?'

The man shakes his head. Harris thinks for a moment.

'Very well, lead the way. I suppose it would be churlish to refuse her my assistance.'

The man says nothing, but begins walking eastwards along the road, indicating for Harris to follow. Harris does so readily enough, his walking stick tapping out a steady rhythm on the pavement.

In truth, there is a slight smile upon his face.

———

'He's gone out again. I had a look in his room.'

'Who?'

'Who do you think, Ally? Himself.'

Alice Meynell sits up in bed; Clara White is pacing the attic room that they share.

'What's it to you, anyhow?' says Alice.

'Nothing, I just heard him go out, that's all.'

Alice sighs. 'I wish you could just sleep. You're wearing me out.'

She says it in a kindly, humouring way, but Clara does not notice.

'I'm sorry, I was just . . .'

'Thinking about your mother?'

'Maybe.'

'I'm sorry.'

'No need for you to be sorry.'

Alice Meynell pauses, sucking her thumb as she ponders changing the subject. 'You do know,' she says at last, 'what he gets up to at nights?'

'What?'

Alice frowns. 'You mean you don't? I always thought you and him had been . . .'

'Ally, I don't understand you.'

'You know he likes his girls? Young ones and all.

That's why he disappears of an evening.'

Clara shakes her head. 'That's just for his writing. That's how he finds girls for the refuge, talking to them and that.'

'And "that" all right. You mean he's never done you?'

'Ally!'

'If you say so.'

'Well, he ain't. Listen, it's all just gossip, that's all. I know what the girls at the refuge were like. All talk. You shouldn't pay any heed to it.'

'Maybe you was just too ugly for him, eh?'

'Ally, it's not funny. I won't hear it.'

Alice Meynell falls silent again, and when she speaks her voice seems more serious.

'Look, Clarrie, I don't want you thinking I'm a liar.'

'Ally, don't be like that. I just don't think . . .'

Alice interrupts her. 'How do you think I got this job? It weren't a good character, I can tell you that much.'

———

Dr. Harris comes to a halt, standing in a narrow cobbled passage not far from Gray's Inn Lane. If there were sufficient light his besuited figure would look incongruous in such a place, a grimy back street, set at the rear of smoke-black tenements, littered with refuse. As it is, however, he can barely see the tall man a few yards in front of him.

'Is it far?'

'Just round the corner here.'

'You said that five minutes ago. I swear we have gone round in a circle. I am not a young man, you know.'

The man turns round and walks back to him, so that he can just make out his face in the darkness.

'I know.'

'And I am not a fool.'

'I know what you are.'

There is something cold in the man's voice, in his grim, monotonous delivery, that turns Harris's stomach. Instantly, some primitive instinct takes hold of the doctor; a sudden wave of fear floods his body, sweat pouring from his brow.

'I was lying before,' says Harris hastily. 'Here, I have five pounds in my pocket. It is yours, if you leave me be.'

The man smiles. 'That's an odd reckoning. What's that to me?'

'What do you want from me? I shall call out, I swear.'

The man shakes his head, reaching suddenly forward and grabbing Harris's mouth.

'No, you shan't, you dirty old bastard.'

CHAPTER FORTY

DOUGHTY STREET.

Daylight streams into Mrs. Harris's room as her maid gently pulls back the curtains and opens the shutters. Mrs. Harris herself, bathed and dressed, is seated at her dressing table, selecting earrings from her jewellery box; she chooses a pair made of jade.

'Is the master awake, White?'

'No, ma'am, he ain't in his bed.'

'Not in bed? What do you mean? Surely he is, therefore, awake.'

'I couldn't say, ma'am,' replies Clara, emptying the liquid remainder of her mistress's bath into her pail, and applying a fresh rag to clean the metal.

Mrs. Harris nearly pricks her ear in annoyance, turning to stare at Clara. 'Really,' she says, the tone of her voice conveying ineffable exasperation, 'I beg you, for once speak plainly and sensibly.'

'He ain't in the house, ma'am.'

'Well, then, what time did he say he would be back?'

'He didn't say, ma'am.'

Mrs. Harris puts down her earring, which she has still not fixed in her ears, and gives her maid-servant what she considers a stern and demanding look. 'Now, I can hardly believe that. Surely he left us a note on his desk, or some such? You know that is his custom.'

'There's no note, ma'am, and . . .'

'What? Speak up, will you, girl?'

'His bed ain't been slept in, if you'll forgive me saying so, ma'am.'

For once, Mrs. Harris is quite lost for words. She gets up and walks briskly to the door that joins her bedroom to her husband's. Opening it, she looks at the unruffled sheets and coverlet neatly square on the bed, the pillows unmarked by any impression. She turns back, and, not looking at Clara, sits down at her dressing table once more.

'You may go,' she says.

'How long's she been up there?' asks Alice Meynell, looking pointedly up the stairs towards her mistress's bedroom.

'A couple of hours, I suppose.'

'That ain't like her. Hang on a minute . . .'

As they speak, the door to Mrs. Harris's bedroom opens and the lady herself steps hesitantly on to the landing; she is dressed in an expensive mauve day dress, but her hair looks less than neat, and her face a little paler than usual. She peers down into the hallway.

'Who's that?'

'Just me and Ally, ma'am.'

'Of course it is. White, will you come here?'

Clara hastens up the stairs. There is something strangely distracted in her mistress's expression as she speaks to her.

'White, I am afraid there must have been some accident for your master not to have returned home. I would be greatly indebted if you could go and speak to the policeman who came here last week – Inspector Webb at Marylebone police station, I believe – and ask him to come and see me.'

'Ma'am?'

'Did you not hear me?'

'Not Bow Street, ma'am? It's a lot nearer.'

'I know very well where Bow Street is. Do not contradict me. I wish to speak to Mr. Webb in particular, do you understand me? Him in particular.'

Clara turns to hurry down the stairs, but then stops and looks back at her mistress, who stands there like a statue.

'Ma'am . . .'

'What?'

'It ain't nothing to do with my ma, is it?'

'Heavens! Does the world revolve around your troubles? Will you just do as you are told!'

'Yes, ma'am.'

Clara runs down the stairs, trying to remember whether her shawl is in the kitchen or her bedroom. In the end, it proves to be the former; a few words are exchanged with Alice, and then with Cook, and with the latter issuing the age-old wisdom that 'no good will come of it', Clara leaves the house by the kitchen door. She has barely stepped upon the pavement, however, when a man's voice whispers her name.

'Clara.'

She turns, and finds Henry Cotton walking beside her.

———

'You know what we need, sir?'

'Enlighten me, sergeant.'

'Another murder. Give us some more clues, wouldn't it?'

'Very amusing. I'll tell that to the superintendent, shall I?'

'Maybe not, sir. But you've looked through those

papers a dozen times today, and I don't think you'll be finding fresh answers there.'

Webb puts down the folder he has been reading.

'You may jest, but I think there's already been another.'

'Agnes White?'

'Indeed. Why do you think her clothes were found in the river?'

'Say she was going to pawn them, dropped them in by accident?'

'She was trying to make someone think she was dead. She knew they would most likely be found, and thought it might help matters.'

'Maybe she just didn't like those clothes. Miss Sparrow said she was a little, well, disturbed.'

'All the same, why throw them in the river?'

'Good as anywhere.'

'No, I think she knew someone wanted her dead.'

Sergeant Watkins shrugs his shoulders, as if to say 'if you say so'.

'You're too skeptical, sergeant.'

'I find it helps in this line of work. Leave the thinking to Inspector Burton.'

'If we are finally graced with his presence.'

'Due tomorrow. Something will turn up, sir, don't you worry.'

'Watkins, that is precisely what worries me.'

—◆—

'I was just coming to see you,' says Henry Cotton, as he strolls beside Clara.

'You know you can't, Mr. Phibbs, not when I'm working.'

'But you're working all the time, are you not?'

'Yes.'

'I would have made some excuse to see Harris.'

238

'You'd be lucky.'

'How so?'

'He ain't been home since last night. The missus has sent us to get the police.'

'The police? She thinks it so serious?'

'I suppose.'

'You are going the wrong way, surely.'

'She wants this fellow at Marylebone. Webb.'

'Ah, that is the man you told me about? Lord, does she think it is something to do with the business on the train?'

Clara looks at Cotton, surprised by his particular interest. 'I don't know, do I?'

'May I walk with you some of the way, at least?'

'Ain't you got nothing better to do?'

Cotton smiles. 'No, I fear I have not. Although I was going to ask you a question.'

Clara sighs.

'I saw your Tom Hunt yesterday . . .'

'He ain't nothing to do with me.'

'He speaks fondly of you. He says you were an apt pupil.'

Clara shakes her head but says nothing.

'Well, at all events, he showed me a couple of his tricks, and, I swear, I feel I could almost write a book about him. He is a fine rogue, is he not?'

'Did you give him money?'

'Yes, I did.'

'Then he'll be all right with you. He don't want nothing else. That's all there is to know about him.'

'You think? What about your sister? Surely he is fond of her, at least?'

'He'll drop her when he's done with her.'

'That's awfully harsh, Clara. I confess, I am not overly impressed by his morals, but for a man of that class . . .'

'I thought you wanted to ask me something.'

'Well, I did. Tell me, does Tom . . . well, has he ever done anything in the way of houses?'

'Houses?'

'I mean to say, house-breaking. Burglary.'

She pauses for a moment, as if wondering whether it is safe to vouchsafe the information. 'He might have, once or twice, when he was desperate.'

'He knows something of how to go about it, then?'

'I should say so. What do you want to know that for?'

'It is an idea, nothing more. Do not worry.'

———

Mrs. Harris sits by her bedroom window, looking outside at the dead winter garden behind the house. At length, she gets up and walks downstairs to the study on the first floor. Her husband's writing desk is locked, and she wonders for a moment whether there is something she can do.

She sighs, and begins to pace the room.

CHAPTER FORTY-ONE

'Ahem. Message for you, Inspector.'

Inspector Webb sits back in his office chair, his eyes half closed, in a position that makes it impossible to say whether he is sleeping or engaged in deep contemplation. He slowly opens his eyes, and looks at the station's office boy, standing by his door.

'What?'

'A Mrs. Harris, Doughty Street, asking you to call on her.'

'Mrs. Harris?' replies Webb, taking a moment to recall the significance of the name. 'Really. Well, does she give a time? Show me the letter.'

'No letter, sir. Her maid came in, well, somebody's maid anyhow. She didn't say much, and then she went off, all rushed, wouldn't wait.'

'When was this?'

'A minute or two ago, sir,' replies the boy, defensively, fearing his punctuality to be in question. 'I waited a moment before I knocked, like. I didn't want to disturb you.'

Webb, however, springs out of his chair and grabs his hat and coat.

'Tell Watkins where I am going, will you?'

'Where, sir?' replies the boy, quite confused.

'To see Mrs. Harris, of course.'

'Miss White!'

Clara White turns, finding herself accosted for the second time in as many hours. On this occasion, however, it is the bulky figure of Decimus Webb, astride his repaired velocipede, cycling along Marylebone Lane beside her. The effort of maintaining his balance and shouting out makes him quite breathless, and, as he dismounts, Clara stares at him in amazement.

'Ah, I see I startled you,' he continues. 'You did just visit the station, did you not? You might have waited for a reply.'

'I'll be wanted back home.'

'I suppose you will. You don't much like the police, do you, Miss White? Old habits die hard, eh?'

Clara frowns, but says nothing. Webb ignores her silence, motioning her to walk on, and he continues by her side, pushing his bicycle.

'I take it Mrs. Harris is at home, then?'

Clara nods.

'Do you have any idea why she has asked me to call on her?'

'I don't like to say.'

'Well, I think you had better, all the same.'

'Dr. Harris ain't come home since yesterday.'

Webb frowns. 'Ah, I see. Well, I confess, that hardly seems too peculiar. Perhaps he stayed at his club, or with a friend?'

Clara shrugs. 'None of my business, is it?' she replies.

'Has he ever done so before – stopped overnight somewhere?'

'I don't think so.'

'I see. Well, that is something, I suppose. Did your mistress ask for me by name?'

242

'Yes.'

'Now, that is odd, is it not, Miss White?'

Clara says nothing, and the inspector does not press the point. After a minute or more of silence, they progress awkwardly together from the quiet confines of Marylebone Lane on to the pavement of Oxford Street. The road itself is busy with carriages. Many, no doubt, contain ladies of rank and distinction, contemplating the particular shop or store upon which they should bestow their generous patronage. The remainder of the great thoroughfare, however, is the exclusive property of the omnibus. There are dozens to be seen along the length of the street; they are all of different liveries and lines, and, near to Marylebone Lane, several have somehow contrived to come together, forming a snake-like train that obstructs any traffic attempting to cross. In consequence, Decimus Webb gives up on any idea of utilising the roadway, and pushes his bicycle along the pavement beside Clara White. They attract a few curious glances, and doubt-less there are some who assume that the girl with downcast eyes is in the custody of the uniformed gentleman who accompanies her. As they approach Regent's Circus, Webb speaks once more.

'About your mother, Miss White . . .'

'Yes?' she says. It is the first time she has looked him straight in the eye.

'I didn't get a chance at the inquest to offer you my condolences.'

'Thank you.'

'Tell me, were you happy with the verdict?'

'What do you mean?'

'Would it shock you if I told you I believe she was killed?'

Clara stops walking. 'It's occurred to me. Of course it has.'

'Of course it has? Why?'

Clara sighs. 'You know what sort of life she had.'

'Ah, you think it was . . . a gentleman she was entertaining, shall we say?'

'Who else?'

'It was merely a coincidence that she shared a room with Sally Bowker?'

'I never knew the girl, I told your sergeant whatever-his-name.'

'Indeed, I read his notes.'

'Then why are you asking me?'

Webb smiles. 'Idle curiosity.'

Clara says nothing in reply, but walks a little more briskly.

Mrs. Harris sits nervously in the front parlour of Doughty Street, fiddling with her sleeves. She rises to greet Decimus Webb, as her maid-servant shows him into the room.

'Thank you, White, that will be all,' she says, though her voice lacks a little of its usual imperious rigour.

'Well, ma'am,' begins Webb, taking a seat as Clara leaves the room, 'perhaps you can tell me why you wished to see me?'

'Did White not tell you?' she replies anxiously. 'I felt sure she would. I swear, she is not to be relied on in anything.'

'I merely would prefer to hear direct from your own lips, ma'am.'

'My husband has vanished, Inspector.'

'Vanished, ma'am?'

'He went out last night, and has not returned home, nor sent word to me.'

'You had some argument?'

'Not at all!'

'Please, do not distress yourself, ma'am. I merely ask for information. I would ask the same of anyone. Is there not some relative or acquaintance with whom he might have stopped?'

'And not told me?'

'Regrettable as it is, ma'am, I understand, from those colleagues of mine blessed by matrimony, that they aren't all in the habit of confiding absolutely in their wives.'

'I cannot speak for them, Inspector,' replies Mrs. Harris coldly, 'but my husband would not abandon me so. I fear for his safety.'

'His safety?'

'You know he visits the most awful places, to inform his writing. Slums, Inspector. Rookeries. Anything might have happened to him.'

Mrs. Harris looks tearful, and Webb, even as he speaks, wishes he had a pocket handkerchief to give to her.

'Well, I am sure there is no need to worry,' he replies. 'But I will take a few details and circulate the information to our men, just in case we can be of service. Can I ask, however,' continues Webb, 'why you asked for me by name? Surely, you have a local constable who might have sufficed to bring this to our attention?'

'You met my husband, Inspector. You know him to be a good, kind man who would stoop to raise any poor wretch from the gutter. If something has happened, if he is found in some awful place that would not be . . . oh, I cannot say it. I mean, a place that would not reflect well on his position in society.'

'Ah, I see. Well, you can rely on our discretion, ma'am, but I am sure he is safe and well.'

'But where, Inspector? Where?'

❦

In the tap-room of the Old Friar, Bill Hunt looks at his hands. They are large, workman's hands, hard with calloused skin, without any delicacy of shape, like clay modelled by a child. A couple of others in the pub give him a quizzical glance, wondering why he looks so distracted and leaves his pint pot sitting idle in front of him.

Bill Hunt looks at his hands, and remembers strangling Arthur Harris; it strikes him as strange and wonderful that it is possible to do such a thing, to extinguish human life, with such simple tools.

CHAPTER FORTY-TWO

HENRY COTTON GINGERLY opens the door that leads
into the Three Cups tavern. It is his third visit and
the landlord, first to see him, gives him a broad smile,
which does not make him entirely at ease; if anything,
it has the opposite effect. Cotton peers through the
smoky gloom of the pub and sees Tom Hunt sitting
at his usual table, though he is dressed in a new jacket
and coat, rather less careworn than the apparel he
wore previously. His young wife sits next to him,
passive and unanimated, and two glasses of spirits sit
half empty upon the table in front of them. Hunt, in
fact, is engaged in debate with a man nearby, but he
breaks off his conversation as he sees Cotton
approaching. He greets him like an old friend.

'Sir! Make room for the gentleman, Liz! This is a
surprise, sir. I thought we agreed it was tomorrow
we'd meet again?'

Cotton attempts a similarly joyous greeting, though
his eyes are distracted by the patches of dark bruising on Lizzie Hunt's face. Hunt follows his gaze, anticipating what he might say.

'Don't be alarmed, sir. Lizzie here is tougher than
she looks, ain't you, love?'

Lizzie mumbles something indistinct.

'And shy too,' continues Hunt. 'I tell you, when I

find the fellow what did that, I'll give him what for, won't I just?'

Hunt laughs, as if pleased with some personal joke, and Lizzie steals a nervous glance at her husband.

'I hope this is not a bad time, then?' ventures Cotton.

'Not at all, not for an old pal like yourself, eh?'

'No, well, that is good of you.'

'We had a fine time of it yesterday, did we not?'

'It was very instructive. In fact, that is why I came today.'

'No money returned,' replies Hunt, laughing, but looking at him a little warily.

'No, nothing like that. It's just that I had an idea, something where your particular knowledge and, ah, expertise, might assist my understanding. A different arena, as it were.'

'I ain't following you.'

'No, I should speak more plainly. As you know, I intend to throw light, in my writing, on the workings of the, shall we say, criminal classes.'

Hunt looks ready to make his usual objection to such a slur on his character, but Cotton holds up his hand, and continues.

'And I know that you yourself, by chance, have been exposed to all kinds of criminality and have a good knowledge of such persons and their manners.'

'That's no lie, I confess,' replies Hunt, affably.

'Well, the "dodges" you showed me yesterday . . .'

'Merely for instruction,' interjects Hunt.

'Indeed,' continues Cotton, 'they were remarkable, but such things have been written of before now.'

'I should not be surprised,' replies Hunt.

'But if I am to take firm hold of the public's attention, then there must be something novel.'

Hunt raises his eyebrows, but says nothing in reply. Cotton lowers his voice to a confidential whisper.

'It came to me last night. I am thinking, Mr. Hunt, of a burglary.'

Hunt looks perplexed, uncertain whether to laugh or take the suggestion seriously.

'I am sure,' he replies, 'though I ain't no scholar, that such things have been written of.'

'Oh, they have. But not first-hand.'

'First-hand?'

'I know of a house, near the Edgware Road, whose owner is absent from the property. He is, in fact, a friend of mine. I would like you to show me how you would go about it.'

'About what?'

'Breaking in, of course.'

'Come, Mr. Phibbs, you are joking. You want me to crack this place of your pal's?'

'Do not get me wrong, Mr. Hunt. Nothing must be taken. It is merely so that I might attempt an article on the subject.'

'You're a queer fellow, you know that.'

'Will you do it?'

'But I take nothing?'

'I'll pay, of course.'

'How much?'

'A pound.'

'For breaking a drum? Two guineas.'

'Done,' replies Cotton, eagerly, his face as bright and enthusiastic as a schoolboy planning a visit to a sweet-shop.

'And what if we're caught?'

'Well, I will explain the circumstances; my friend would not press charges. Besides, he is not even in London. I will fix everything, before and after.'

Hunt still looks a little doubtful. 'And when do you propose we have this little adventure?'

'Tonight.'

'Tonight!'

'Two guineas, Mr. Hunt, if we do it tonight. Think on it.'

Hunt breathes out, thinking the matter through.

'Done.'

'Now,' says Cotton, taking out his notebook, 'tell me how you intend to go about it.'

'I think, Mr. Phibbs,' says Hunt, downing the remainder of his drink, 'my head needs a little lubrication before I can do any serious thinking.'

———

Phillip P. Butterby, sub-editor of the *City and Westminster Press* ('The Oracle of the Metropolis') looks up in surprise.

'Phibbs?'

'That's the name, yes, sir. We wondered if you knew anyone of that name?'

'Is he in trouble, then, sergeant?'

'Then you do know a gentleman by that name, sir?'

'In a professional capacity. I was expecting a set of articles from him for the paper last week, as it happens, but they never arrived. A most unreliable young man.'

'What were these articles?'

Butterby looks in his desk drawer, and pulls out a sheet of paper.

'We had a title. Wrote it myself. Ah, here you go. "London's Hidden Deeps: An Exploration of Persons and Places Unknown and Unmourned: by One Who Has Seen Them".'

'Very colourful, sir.'

'Well, such things tickle the public's fancy, sergeant.'

'I am sure, sir. Now, do you have an address for the gentleman?'

'Ah. I believe I do not. He was rather a secretive young fellow. I know very little about him. Met him a few weeks back, gave us a smart little submission on "Our Social Ills". Told him I wanted more before we might publish, and haven't seen the blessed chap since.'

'Well, do you expect to see him, sir?'

The sub-editor sniffs. 'Doubtless he has some masterpiece to finish before then. If I have learnt one thing in my years here, sergeant, it is that you can never trust a literary gentleman to deliver on time.'

'I see. Perhaps you could give me a full description of the man.'

'Of course, sergeant. Do tell me, what has he done?'

CHAPTER FORTY-THREE

FARRINGDON CUT.

'Here, Billy boy, slow down, will you?'

The railway foreman, a stout man, his face covered in dirt, shouts out to Bill Hunt, as Hunt pushes past him, red-faced and sweating, with a wheelbarrow full of earth and rubble, almost clipping his leg. Bill scowls at him, making no apology.

'What?'

'Mind where you're going. What are you day-dreaming about?'

'Nothing.'

'Well then, take it slow. You'll do someone a bleedin' injury.'

Bill Hunt nods, and continues. He stops a few yards away by a mound of refuse, the accumulation of a day or two's excavation, and empties the barrow. He does it rather hastily, and the anxious look upon his face suggests he would like to be somewhere else. The foreman watches him from a distance, and shouts out once more.

'You ain't ill, are you?'

Hunt shakes his head.

Doughty Street.

Clara White hears the noise in the Harrises' study as she ascends the stairs. It is past the dinner hour, and, for a moment, she fancies it is her master who has quietly returned home. But the sound itself is of something metallic clattering off several surfaces, combined with her mistress groaning in frustration. Clara peers round the half-open door, and sees Mrs. Harris sitting upon her husband's chair by his writing desk. She is in the process of picking up a paper-knife from the rug. Once she has retrieved it, Clara watches as she attempts, for a second time, to wedge it into the locked desk drawer in a vain attempt to prise it open. It is a remarkable and almost frantic exertion, but the result is merely that the knife itself is visibly bent out of shape, and the drawer scratched but still sealed tight. Mrs. Harris looks round and notices her maid-servant watching her. The ringlets of dark hair that normally adorn her cheeks appear somewhat disordered.

'Can you get me something else, White?'

'Ma'am?'

'A stronger knife. I imagine Cook has something more durable.'

'Actually, ma'am, that was why I came up. Cook says dinner won't keep no longer.'

'I am not hungry.'

'No word from the master, then, ma'am?'

Mrs. Harris does not answer the question. 'Will you,' she says emphatically, 'get me a knife, or must I go downstairs myself?'

'Sorry, ma'am. I'll go and ask,' replies Clara, backing out of the room.

Mrs. Harris returns to her task.

'What you playing at, Billy Hunt?'

The foreman's voice booms from outside the workman's hut; Bill opens the door and finds the man in question waiting for him.

'What d'you mean?'

'How long you been in there? Having a little nap?'

'I was looking for a new pick,' he replies, rather sullenly. 'The shaft on this one's gone, see?'

He holds up a pick-axe with a broken handle, but the spectacle makes little impression on his interrogator.

'That don't take a half-hour.'

'I weren't gone a half-hour.'

'Listen, Bill,' says the foreman, lowering his voice, and clasping Bill Hunt round the shoulder, 'I know these larks ain't like you. But if you keep this up, I'll soon be having to let you go. And I don't want to lose a good man, see?'

Bill looks at the ground, but nods acknowledgement.

'Good,' replies the foreman. 'Now you just get back to work.'

Bill closes the shed door, broken pick-axe still in hand. He can hear a strange pounding in his head; he realises it is his heart beating.

—

Mrs. Harris cuts an incongruous figure, cutting away at the ornate mahogany with a kitchen knife. It is, in all probability, the most manual labour she has ever carried out in her life. For this reason, though the task is not that difficult, it takes her some minutes. Eventually, however, the little brass lock that fastens the desk drawer is free of the splintering wood. She sits back, looking at the ruined desk, nervously biting her lip. She realises that she has lived with her husband for thirty years, but only once questioned him on what he keeps locked away in his desk.

'Confidential papers.'

She pulls out the drawer gingerly in stages, as if it contains some cornered animal, and lays it on the desk, picking out the various notebooks and papers contained within.

CHAPTER FORTY-FOUR

'Is this the place?'

Tom Hunt surveys the corner of Meulton Street; it is a quiet side street, not far from the Edgware Road, near enough that the clatter of horse-drawn traffic can still be heard, even though it has gone midnight. Meulton Street, in darkness, has none of the nocturnal bustle and disorder of Saffron Hill, but rather contains a row of unexceptional town-houses, sound but small places, where, Hunt imagines, little of note ever happens, and, doubtless, the daily delivery of groceries is considered a cause for excitement. There is, admittedly, a light in one house, but every other building appears to be in darkness, shuttered and bolted for the night. The property upon which Tom Hunt focuses his attention certainly falls into this category. However, the house in question seems not half so grand as Henry Cotton's description had suggested. In consequence, Tom Hunt gives the appearance, at least, of being almost uninterested in the business at hand. His wife, however, seems anxious, frequently looking left and right, though there is, as yet, no requirement for her to do so. Henry Cotton, if truth be told, seems no less apprehensive, and nervously toys with the buttons on his coat.

'Is there some difficulty?'

'I thought it would be bigger,' replies Tom Hunt.

'Does it matter? Remember, we must take nothing, in any case.'

'The bigger the place, the less likely you are to be noticed, that's all. We can't go round the back for starters; there ain't even a way round it.'

'There are stables at the back, I believe, if you go round to the next road.'

'Well, where there are stables, there are horses. And they don't take kindly to being woke up, in my experience.'

'True.'

Hunt rubs his chin.

'Then what,' continues Cotton, 'shall we do?'

'It's plain enough, ain't it? Down to the kitchen, unless you fancy the front door's open, that is.'

'Yes, well, I suppose you are right.'

Hunt looks at him. 'What you waiting for, then?' asks Hunt. 'You first. Walk past, all casual, like, but open the gate and get down there, and do it sharpish.'

Henry Cotton nods. He takes a deep breath, stepping out from the doorway in which the trio are standing, and crosses the road, his figure briefly illuminated by the light of the nearby gas-lamp. He briskly crosses the street, where it is somewhat darker, and strides purposefully along, albeit rather stiffly, until he reaches the house on the corner. There he struggles clumsily with the catch on the iron gate that protects the area steps, and then disappears from view. Tom Hunt, a cautious man for all his bluster, waits a moment or two before following him. It is not long, however, before the two men are both standing in the dark well that fronts the basement kitchen.

'What if someone comes?' asks Cotton.

'Then Liz'll shout.'

'What will she shout?'

'Whatever she damn well likes. Be quiet, will you, or someone'll hear us.'

Hunt strikes a match, then takes off his hat, holding it a little above the lit flame so that any light it gives out is not so visible from above. He bends down and peers closely at the lock on the kitchen door, then at the glass panels above it.

'Can you pick the lock?' whispers Cotton.

'Well, it ain't one of Mr. Chubb's, so maybe I could. But I ain't going to try it in this case.'

'What then?'

Hunt motions him to be silent, and blows out the match. He takes from his pocket a small sheath knife and chisel, and begins applying the implements to one of the glass panels in the door. Rather than hacking noisily at the wood surrounding it, he adopts a chiselling motion that gradually strips away the splintering frame, until, after no more than a couple of minutes, the glass itself is so loose that he can easily lever it free into his hands. He handles the panel carefully, slowly laying it on the ground, then looks at Henry Cotton triumphantly.

'The door is still locked,' replies Cotton, confused. 'And even an infant could not get in through that space.'

'No,' replies Hunt, a little annoyed that his genius is not apparent, 'but that window there is just on a latch, ain't it?'

Hunt leans into the door, reaching through the gap; there is some distance between the door itself and the window, but he skilfully flips up the latch with the end of his knife, his arm fully extended. In one swift movement, he opens it, and then clambers through into the kitchen.

'You coming then?'

Cotton follows behind him, glancing back up at the street as he climbs inside.

'Confidentially,' says Hunt, cheerfully, 'busting the glaze is always easier than locks. Though I don't suppose your pal will be too happy.'

'My pal? Ah, yes, well, I will have it repaired first thing tomorrow.'

'Well, then,' says Hunt, looking around the kitchen disinterestedly, 'what do you want us to do now?'

'Perhaps if you show me what you would look for if you were here to take something.'

Hunt shrugs. 'It's plain enough. Anything what you can carry. Silver, plate, money, jewellery. Let's have a look-see.'

Before Cotton can reply, Hunt is up the stairs, lighting another match to see the way. Cotton follows him.

'Bachelor gentleman, is he, this friend of yours?' asks Hunt, surveying the hall.

'How did you know that?'

'Ain't nothing fancy in it, is there? You can tell a woman's hand on a place, can't you?'

'You look for such things?'

'Won't be no jewels about for a start, will there? Although, I'd know a bit about the place before I came in, in the regular way of things – scout it out.'

'Would you go through every room?'

'Depends on the house . . . here, what's that?'

Tom Hunt asks the question, but it is somewhat rhetorical, since he recognises his wife's voice crying out his name.

'Keep quiet,' says Hunt. 'For God's sake.'

The two men stand stock-still in the hall. The distinct sound of boots descending the area steps can be heard. Then of someone trying the handle of the kitchen door.

'I thought you said no-one was home,' says Hunt in a whisper.

'There isn't,' replies Cotton.

'Then it's the bleeding peelers, ain't it?'

'But no-one ever comes by here.'

'Don't they?'

Again, the question is left unanswered, as the sound of the kitchen window opening and closing can be heard downstairs.

'There is no need to be alarmed,' says Cotton, 'I swear. Remember what I told you.'

'I don't care what you say, I'm hooking it.'

Before Cotton can reply, Tom Hunt dashes into the front parlour, heading directly for the sash window that overlooks the area steps below, half-tripping on the rug as he does so. Despite his panic, there is something remarkably assured in the way he immediately locates and breaks the lock upon the shutter, smashing it forcefully with the end of the chisel. He pulls up the window, looking out on to the street. Without even glancing over his shoulder, he springs out into the road; easily clears the iron railings that guard the house, but falls awkwardly on the stones.

Henry Cotton, uncertain if he might be able to duplicate such athletics, merely stands at the window, staring out at the street. He loses sight of Tom Hunt, stumbling along the road, but can hear the sound of a policeman's whistle. In the strange excitement of Hunt's abrupt flight, he almost forgets the reason for Hunt's departure until he hears a man's voice behind him.

'Don't you bleedin' move. You're under arrest.'

Even in the darkness, Cotton turns his head and can make out the helmeted figure of a constable standing by the door to the parlour, his gutta-percha truncheon raised above his head.

'Really, Constable,' says Cotton, taking a deep breath, 'there is no need for that.'

'Ain't there? I think I'll be the judge of that. Hold out your hands.'

'What is the charge?'

'Don't come that with me.'

'No, you don't understand. You see, Constable, this is my house. I live here.'

CHAPTER FORTY-FIVE

DECIMUS WEBB IS alone in his office when he hears the sound of raised voices. Such raucous interruptions are not uncommon in the confines of the Marylebone Lane station, and he pays little heed to it. Instead, he turns to look at the clock, which, in the dim light of the brass oil-lamp that sits upon his desk, is barely visible; it is, he realises, two o'clock in the morning, and he has been asleep for an hour or more. Wearily, he prises himself from his chair, and goes to pick up his coat from the stand.

Outside, a man can still be heard complaining loudly from one of the cells situated at the rear of the building. Webb makes his way to the entrance hall of the station, in which the sergeant on duty, Tibbs by name, sits in a rather slovenly manner at his desk, his head propped up on his hands, lolling forward over a copy of the *Daily News*. On seeing the inspector, he sits up straight as a ruler and ineffectually attempts to conceal the paper beneath a pile of more official-looking material.

'Lor, you gave me a scare,' exclaims the sergeant.

'Am I that terrifying, sergeant?'

'I thought you had gone home, sir, that's all,' replies Tibbs. 'I would have called you out; you've missed some fun and games.'

'I am glad you didn't,' says Webb, making to leave.

'Constable Evans,' continues Tibbs, warming to his subject, 'took this cracksman in Meulton Street; regular Spring-Heel Jack he was! Jumped out the window of the place, then fought like blazes when he caught up with him. Took three men to get him here.'

'Ah, well, my congratulations to Evans.'

'You ain't heard the funniest part, sir, if you'll forgive me.'

'Haven't I?' asks Webb.

'His chum, who weren't so hot on his feet, says he owns the place what was done over; well, that he rents it, anyhow, or something. But the first fellow, he denies it. Frankly, sir, between the two of them, we can't make head nor tail of it.'

'Had he merely lost his key? Perhaps this man was helping him?'

'Oh, no, sir. Evans recognised the first fellow; used to see him about Saffron Hill when he was posted there a year or two back. Name of Thomas Hunt. Notorious rogue, sir, so Evans tells me. It was only a chance he saw him, as it happens. Dogged him from Regent Street, all the way till when he cracked the place. A regular ghost is Evans, when he wants to be.'

'And do we know the second man?'

'Well, we'll leave him to the magistrate, I reckon, sir. Says his name is Cotton, but the other fellow swears he told him it was Phibbs. Now, what do you make of that?'

Webb looks at sergeant Tibbs. His large heavily lidded eyes, suddenly quite alert, fix on Tibbs' face and narrow in an unmistakable expression of anger.

'Sir?' says Tibbs, nervously.

'Sergeant,' says Webb at last, 'do you ever read my memoranda? Perhaps it has escaped your notice that I am engaged in the investigation of a murder? Or do you imagine I am merely indulging a peculiar fancy for late nights in your company?'

A look of comprehension passes across the sergeant's face, as the name of Phibbs, mentioned in several papers circulated by Webb to his fellow officers, stirs something in his memory. He coughs, nervously.

'You'll want to see the man directly, I suppose,' says the sergeant, retrieving the keys to the cells. 'I'll get one of the lads to . . .'

'Give that here,' replies Webb, taking the keys. 'And for pity's sake, find out who does have that house in Meulton Street.'

'It's two a.m., sir,' says Tibbs, pleadingly.

'I don't care if you personally have to wake all his blasted neighbours one by one.'

Before sergeant Tibbs even contemplates an answer, Webb has turned and is walking back into the rear of the police station.

<hr />

Decimus Webb finds Henry Cotton, also known as Phibbs, sitting mournfully in his cell, on the palliasse mattress provided by the Metropolitan Police for the comfort of their guests. The curses of Tom Hunt, similarly accommodated, can be vaguely heard in the distance. Cotton looks up at Webb, and smiles nervously.

'Ah, good, Inspector. I asked to see someone more senior. There has been an awful misunderstanding.'

'I should say so, Mr. *Phibbs*.'

'Phibbs?'

'No need for that gammon, sir,' says Webb, pulling a leather-bound article from his pocket. 'I know who you are. I assume this is yours?'

Henry Cotton looks at his notebook, last seen at

Baker Street. He toys with the idea of remaining silent, but decides, in the end, to speak.

'Ah. Yes, it is,' he admits reluctantly. 'You say you know me? Then, really, Inspector, you must let me explain . . .'

Decimus Webb sighs. 'That is exactly what I would like you to do.'

'Well, I don't know quite where to begin. What can I tell you?'

'The truth, if you will, Mr. Phibbs. Or should I say Cotton? Is that your real name?'

Henry Cotton blushes. 'Yes, it is. Phibbs is something of a *nom de plume*, if you will.'

'You consider yourself a writer, then?'

'I aspire to be, sir, yes.'

'And your subject matter is vice.'

'I see you have deciphered my notes.'

Webb nods, as if realising the solution to a particular problem.

'But it is not just a *nom de plume*, is it, Mr. Cotton? You have gone to some pains to keep yourself hidden away from the world. It is your house in Meulton Street, is it not?'

Cotton smiles with relief. 'Thank the Lord you believe me. Yes, of course it is. I rent it by the quarter.'

'We can check that, Mr. Cotton, and, rest assured, we will. But you are accustomed to take lodgings elsewhere, in Clare Market, to pick one instance, for your, ah, research?'

'For convenience, Inspector. I believe there is a great advantage in being something of a chameleon when one is acquainting oneself with the evils of our society. I have taken lodgings in two or three places.'

'I see. Even so, I think there is more to it than that. You might begin by telling me, if you please, why you ran from Baker Street station that night?'

'Well, you don't suppose I killed that poor girl?'

'I don't suppose anything, though there's plenty who do. Tell me why you ran.'

Cotton looks awkwardly down at the ground, speaking hesitantly. 'There are reasons, quite delicate and personal to me . . .'

'Do you wish to hang, Mr. Cotton?'

Henry Cotton blanches. 'Hang? I am sure it could not come to that, could it?'

'Are you really, Mr. Cotton?'

Cotton pauses, then hesitantly speaks. 'My family, Inspector, have no knowledge of my particular studies of the metropolis. They believe me in Italy.'

'Italy?'

'On a tour, viewing Roman antiquities.'

'Good Lord!' exclaims Webb. 'That is your reason? You ran because you are commonly supposed to be in Italy?'

'If my father knew where I was, worse, the subject matter on which I am writing, how I have been spending my annuity . . . I mean to say, if any of it got out, well, he would cut me off without a penny.'

'But the blasted girl was dead!'

'Well,' says Cotton, trying to instil some degree of self-justification into his speech, 'what of it? I did not kill the wretched creature. She must have been dead before I even laid eyes on her. I thought she was asleep.'

Webb looks at him intently. 'Do we have that right, Mr. Cotton? Before you set eyes on her?'

'Well, yes, she was already on the train.'

'She had got on before you?'

'I assume so.'

'Tell me, Mr. Cotton, for this is important, exactly what happened that night. Why did you catch the train?'

'I decided to return home, to a decent bed.'

'A decent bed? To Meulton Street, you mean?'

'Yes.'

'Do you keep servants, Mr. Cotton?'

'No, I generally shift for myself, Inspector. It would be, well, difficult to do otherwise; and my, ah, financial situation is not the best.'

'And so, thinking of your bed, in your empty house, you purchased a ticket, and went down to the station platform, yes?'

'Indeed.'

'And then?'

'I waited for the train.'

'It was not there already? Were you alone?'

'No, there was myself and a few others, though I do not recall much about them.'

'No young women? Not Sally Bowker?'

'Well, I do not know. I did not see her, come to think of it. Then the train arrived, a handful of persons disembarked . . .'

'And you alighted?'

'No, not immediately at least.'

'Why not?'

'There was some business with the carriages. A man told us to wait while they "coupled" one more to the end of the train, or whatever they call it. I think he said it was something to do with the works at Paddington; they needed it for the morning or some such nonsense. He was quite apologetic about it.'

'How long were you waiting?'

'Five minutes or so.'

'And then you got on the train, and saw the girl?'

'Yes. Well, not quite. The first carriage I tried had little gas, and I could hardly see to read my notes, or write for that matter. So I got out and wandered down to another. Then I saw the girl. She was obviously drunk, or so I thought. I thought it would be instructive to watch her, if only to see her reaction on waking. I tell you, Inspector, I thought she was merely in a stupor. I swear it, on my life.'

Webb looks at him, amazed. 'The carriage was at the far end of the train, was it not?'

'Yes, what of it?'

Webb whispers through clenched teeth, 'You, Mr. Cotton, are a selfish idiot. And I am a complete fool. Though Lord knows why no-one told me.'

'I do not understand. What could I have possibly done? She was dead.'

'You could have told me all this two weeks ago. Do you not see? The girl was in the last carriage, which they added at Farringdon. It was probably sitting in the blasted sidings all day. She never even caught a train. She was killed in the bloody station.'

'Well, I hardly see . . .'

'Stand up, man. You're coming with me.'

'Where?'

'Farringdon.'

CHAPTER FORTY-SIX

HENRY COTTON FINDS himself in a cab, seated next to Inspector Decimus Webb. Acquired from a rank on Marylebone High Street, the vehicle speeds through the empty city streets at an alarming pace. To Cotton it seems that the whole of London is a blur of smoke-filled streets and half-glimpsed gas-light.

'Surely this could wait, Inspector?'

'I don't think so, sir. You should be grateful I haven't charged you. Not yet, anyhow.'

'I have done nothing wrong.'

'You have been hindering my enquiries, for a start. Not to mention the matter of breaking and entering.'

'It is *my* house, Inspector.'

'I believe you rent it, do you not? And what about your chum Hunt? Broke one of our fellow's ribs, they tell me.'

'Well, I had nothing to do with that.'

'I am sure your dear father would agree, sir.'

Cotton looks aghast at the suggestion. 'What,' he says, catching his breath, 'do you need me for? Surely the place is closed at night.'

'I need to know exactly where everything was. And there is a night-watchman, so I understand. I have waited long enough on your account, Mr. Cotton.'

'I see.'

'It is all very well saying, "I see", but it is too late,' says Webb, taking Cotton's notebook out of his pocket and throwing it into Cotton's lap. 'Look! You made all these blasted notes, and nothing in them of any use to anybody!'

In less than half an hour, Decimus Webb, Henry Cotton and the night-watchman of Farringdon station, an elderly man, less than happy to be woken from his customary state of slumber, find themselves standing on the platform where Cotton stood two weeks earlier. Both the watchman and the policeman carry oil-lanterns that send out faint orange beams over the darkened rails before them. Cotton shivers slightly. A vague rustle of movement prompts Webb to turn round, shining the light back along the length of the platform.

'Rats,' says the old man, cheerfully.

Webb takes a moment to compose himself, looking at the discomforted figure of Henry Cotton and, despite his opinion of the young man, he feels a trifle sorry for him.

'Tell me, Mr. Cotton, where was the train?'

'Where on earth do you think? Here beside the platform.'

'Yes, but from where to where? Show me where it began and ended.'

'It is some time ago.'

'Nevertheless, as best you can.'

Cotton walks tentatively, guided by the watchman's lamp, to the end of the platform facing the tunnel entrance.

'The engine was here, I should think.'

'And the rear carriage?'

Cotton walks back along the platform.

'Here.'

'Before the carriage was added?'

'I should say, in fact, after. I remember getting out and walking back to about here.'

'Too exposed,' mutters Webb.

'Forgive me?'

'No-one put her in the carriage there. Anyone might have seen it. You,' he says, addressing the watchman, who observes the proceedings with a look of bemusement, 'where would a carriage be kept if it was spare?'

'Spare?'

'Surplus to requirements. Damaged. Awaiting a train to connect to it. For whatever reason.'

The old man shrugs. 'The line goes back there, see, to the side? There's points, so you can switch it to the left there. By them works for the new station.'

Webb shines his light in the direction indicated by the watchman. The tracks recede back into the darkness, giving the impression that they might carry on for ever.

'What is that? By the scaffolding?'

'That? Just the men's hut, that's all. They keep tools in it.'

'It is beside where the carriage would have been, is it not?'

The old man shrugs once more.

'I believe it is,' says Webb. 'Come on.'

'I ain't going down there,' replies the watchman. 'It ain't safe, not in the dark.'

'If you brought your light it would not be dark. Oh, very well, give it to him,' he says, indicating that the man should hand it over to Cotton.

'Me?'

'You owe me that much, Mr. Cotton. Come.'

Cotton gingerly takes the lamp and the two men walk to the end of the wooden platform, and then clamber off the raised edge down on to the gravel below. Even with the two lamps it is difficult to cross the tracks, and they make slow progress, though it is but twenty yards to the wooden shed. To Webb's surprise, the door is not locked.

'Come out,' he says, his voice echoing in the empty station.

Nothing happens.

Webb grabs the door, throwing it open and shining his light inside. It is quite empty, but for the various tools of the workmen, neatly arranged on shelves. In one corner, however, there are two or three blankets lain against the wall, and an empty bottle beside them. Webb bends down, examining the cloth.

'You expected someone to be waiting here?' asks Cotton, incredulously.

'Can you smell it?'

'What?'

'Gin. And it is quite warm in here, is it not?'

'I do not know.'

'Someone has been in here, not that long ago.'

'It will be one of the workmen. I am sure they are not averse to a drink.'

'At this hour?'

'Perhaps it is the night-shift . . .'

Cotton stops midway in his sentence as Webb puts his hand to his mouth, beckoning him to keep silent. The sound is quite clear: footsteps on the gravel, not many yards distant.

'It is the watchman,' whispers Hunt.

'He said he would not come down here.'

Webb takes up his light and walks briskly out of the hut, holding the lamp out, swinging the beam from side to side. In the darkness, however, it is impossible to distinguish any movement, and the noise echoes off the cliff-like walls of the Farringdon Cut.

'What you doing in there?'

It is the voice of the watchman, returning to the platform, bearing a third lantern.

'Did you hear anything, just then?'

'I heard the pair of you making fools of yourselves.'

Cotton sighs with relief; there is something comforting in the presence of the man, curmudgeonly or not. Then he notices a flicker of light in the distance; past the entrance of the great tunnel further down the line. Webb sees it too.

'Are there men working at this hour?'

'Where?' asks the old man, his bemused tone suggesting he suspects both Cotton and Webb of madness.

'In the tunnel?'

'No. They're running a couple of night trains tonight; deliveries for the works, but there ain't men, not at this hour, anyhow.'

Webb contemplates for a moment, then shakes Cotton by the arm.

'Come on, follow me!' he shouts, running along the track in the direction of the tunnel. The old man looks on incredulously as the blue-uniformed figure disappears into the blackness.

'You can't go down there!'

Henry Cotton looks at the old man, then the tunnel, takes a deep breath and runs after the policeman. He can hear Webb's footfalls on the dirt and, now and then, on the wooden sleepers; his light, moreover, stays visible ahead, swinging wildly as he runs. In consequence, Henry Cotton, with the advantage of youth, finds pursuit is possible, even in the pitch-darkness, and catches up with him a hundred yards or so inside the tunnel. Their twin lamps shed an eerie light on the smoke-black brickwork.

Webb takes the opportunity to catch his breath.

'Here,' he says, 'listen, I can hear him. He's not far.'

Cotton can hear nothing but the sound of his own heart-beat; it is the only sound of their pursuit that does not echo and magnify itself within the tunnel. Every other noise seems to go on for ever in the chill subterranean air. Then a single breathless word is spoken.

'Enough.'

Ten yards or so down the track, Bill Hunt stumbles from his hiding place.

CHAPTER FORTY-SEVEN

'YOU SEE, MR. Cotton?' says Webb, a note of triumph in his voice as he shines his light at the shabby figure before him. 'We have our man.'

Cotton nods, but looks nervously at the man in front of them.

'I ain't done nothing wrong,' says Bill Hunt, squinting into the light, his face black with dirt from the tunnel.

'I think you have, my good man, haven't you? Otherwise you would not be skulking here, hiding from an officer of the law.'

'I ain't hiding from no-one. I was just having a quiet drink,' he says sarcastically.

'Murder is not a laughing matter, my friend. Will you give yourself up and come peaceably?'

'It ain't murder, I reckon. He deserved it.'

Webb frowns.

'He?' says Cotton, unsure if he heard the man correctly.

'The old bastard. You'd think butter wouldn't melt, to look at him. You wouldn't know his game, not to look at him. He didn't even fight it, you know? He just let me . . .'

Hunt's voice trails off as he peers at the two men. Even in the semi-darkness, with only their lamps to illuminate them, he can see the confusion on both their faces.

'You don't even know about him, do you?' says Hunt, incredulously. 'God Almighty.' He looks anxiously over his shoulder as if estimating his chances of running once more.

'Don't think of it,' says Webb, observing his glance. 'I've got men all along the way. You'd better just come with us, eh?'

'I don't hear no-one else.'

'There is nowhere to go, my good fellow,' says Webb, ignoring Hunt's comment, though there is a hint of nerves in his voice. Hunt backs away slightly, still facing the two men.

'What about the girl? The dead girl?' asks Cotton. He says it hurriedly, and the words seem to him to escape his mouth too quickly and echo back down the vast tunnel.

'I never touched her. Leastways, only to shift her.'

'Shift her?'

'I put her on the train, but what's the crime in that? I had to put her somewhere, out of the way.'

'Who killed her then?' asks Webb, stepping closer, mirroring Hunt's movements as he steps backwards.

Hunt scowls. 'No-one.'

'She was strangled.'

'It weren't me, I tell you.'

'Who then? Someone's for the gallows, think on it. Must it be you?'

Hunt shakes his head. He suddenly seems less calm; perhaps the word 'gallows' strikes some chord in him, some forgotten visit to Newgate Gaol on a Monday morning, standing in the crowd, watching a hooded man fall through the trap-door, "stretched". His face creases, tears welling in his eyes.

'I've bloody told you about the old man, ain't I?' he says pleadingly. 'I'm already dead.'

His breathing is still fast, almost panting; with a shout, he turns and runs once more.

'Damn it,' mutters Decimus Webb. He looks at Henry Cotton, and once more the two men reluctantly give chase. But there is something different this time. It begins just as a sound; a distant heralding thunder, very distant at first, that seems behind them, then in front, then a constant accompaniment to their breathless progress through the darkness. There is something so strange about their situation that it takes a moment to register that it is there; but it is unmistakable, as it comes closer. The ground vibrates with the motion; the twin metal rails hum with anticipation. A ball of light appears down the track, growing steadily larger, and the figure of Bill Hunt flits before it, like a silhouette in a lantern-show. It is a familiar spectacle to him, the approach of this iron monster. But he still runs, towards the burning light and clattering wheels of the engine as it flies along the track.

It is far too late for it to stop.

'For God's sake get clear!' shouts Cotton, pushing Webb flat against the wall of the tunnel. As he does so, however, Cotton stumbles against the damp brickwork; his head makes contact with the cold surface, and his body folds away beneath him. If he hears anything, as consciousness slips away, it is not the shout of the train driver, nor the anxious voice of Decimus Webb, holding him against the brick; it is the endless angry squeal of the brakes.

It is as if the machine thoroughly resents the man crushed beneath its wheels.

Chapter Forty-eight

'You awake, sir?'

Henry Cotton is awake, albeit with a headache, and alive to the unpleasant sensation of someone lightly slapping his face. He opens his eyes; around him is the familiar structure of Farringdon station, though now with all its gas-lights illuminated. For a moment, in half-conscious confusion, looking up at the flickering lamps, he fancies the place is on fire, and sits up with a start. The policeman standing over him, sergeant Watkins, bends down and looks closely into his eyes.

'Seems all right, sir,' he shouts to the figure of Decimus Webb, who stands a little way down the station platform, supervising the efforts of a dozen police constables, each with his own lantern, who are exploring every quarter of the station and, tentatively, the building works behind it.

'Ah,' replies Webb, walking over to him. 'Mr. Cotton is awake! Did I not tell you, sir, not to come running after me like that?'

Cotton tries, feebly, to protest.

'No, no need to apologise,' continues Webb.

'How long have I been . . . ?'

'Unconscious? A good ten minutes. I rather feared the worst.'

'I thought we were dead,' says Cotton.

'No,' says Webb, his face becoming a little more grave. 'Just that wretch in the tunnel.'

'Who was he?'

'One of the navvies here, nothing more. His name was Bill Hunt.'

'Hunt?'

'Come, come. You know the name at least. I believe he is related to your partner-in-crime, a cousin or some such. The same officer has identified him.'

'I have never met him in my life.'

Webb looks at him quizzically, Watkins with unconcealed suspicion. 'You have a talent, at the very least,' says Webb, 'for picking unfortunate acquaintances.'

Cotton frowns, recalling the moments in the tunnel.

'You are sure he is your man?' he says, rubbing the lump on his head. 'That he killed the girl?'

'I think so,' says Webb.

'But he denied it.'

'Bluster, that is all. A morbid attempt at justification.'

'But what he said about an old man . . .'

Cotton's voice trails off as a shout goes up from one of the uniformed men, a dozen yards or so from the wooden tool shed, his bull's-eye lantern swinging above his head. He calls the other men over. Webb turns and runs immediately along the platform, jumping down on to the track. Watkins, on the other hand, keeps a wary eye on Henry Cotton who, though a little unsure of his feet, gets up and attempts to follow. Doubtless the sergeant should, in his turn, attempt to stop him, but he is equally curious to know the cause of the commotion. In consequence, the two men eventually join the little group of police that are gathered around a spoil heap of rubble. At first, it appears that a piece of old black sacking is being tugged from beneath the stones; then the beam of a lantern reveals that it is, rather, the body of a man.

'It was the rats that give it away,' says one of the constables, knowingly. 'Saw one scurrying over here. Can always smell blood, they can.'

'Here,' says Webb impatiently to the nearest man, 'give me that light.' He bends down, rubbing the dirt from the man's face. 'I know this man,' he adds, shaking his head in defeat.

'Lord!' says Henry Cotton, catching sight of the mortal remains of Dr. Arthur Harris. 'So do I.'

Sergeant Watkins turns and stares amazed at the man beside him. In his mind, he can already picture him climbing the steps to Newgate's scaffold.

'I think,' says Webb, looking up at Henry Cotton, 'we need to have a few more words.'

———

In the clutter of Decimus Webb's office at Marylebone Lane station house, Henry Cotton sits alone, meekly sipping a cup of tea. After a few minutes of silence, Webb himself enters the room and sits down at his desk. It is seven o'clock in the morning and neither man has slept since the discovery at Farringdon station. In the interim, amongst other things, Cotton has narrated all his movements since the night of the murder to the inspector and the disbelieving sergeant Watkins.

'Mr. Thomas Hunt is, shall we say, not a co-operative man by nature.'

'That is where you have been? Well, that does not surprise me,' replies Cotton.

'He says he hardly knew his cousin, and cannot account for anything he may have done.'

'I see.'

'And he says we are all a pack of lying hounds, and we should rot in hell.'

Cotton raises his eyebrows.

'I have left Watkins with him, who, for your information, Mr. Cotton, believes we should take *you* as the cousin's accomplice.'

Cotton shakes his head; he has spent several hours denying any connection with Bill Hunt, and he is tired of it.

'It cannot be a coincidence,' says Webb.

Cotton shrugs.

'Well, you must wait here, all the same. I am going to see Mrs. Harris, and perhaps that will shine some light on all of it, eh? A pleasant meeting that will be, mind you. And we'll see what your Miss White has to say about your little affair.'

'Please believe me, Inspector. There was no "affair".'

'It is difficult to believe most of your story, Mr. Cotton, but so far I have given you the benefit of the doubt. Remember that.'

'I explained, Inspector, I met Miss White by chance.'

'Outside the refuge?'

'I had read about the Bowker girl in the press that morning. I was merely curious to see where she lived. I had an interest, after all. And there I chanced upon Clara White. I told you, Inspector.'

'Hmm.'

Cotton sighs. 'So you have not told Mrs. Harris yet about her husband?'

'I thought she deserved her night's sleep,' says Webb, getting up from his desk once more.

Cotton looks up at him. 'I would like to go with you.'

'What purpose would that serve?'

'I might speak to Clara; encourage her to speak with you. She has no love for the police.'

'That is my experience. But you might just arrange to tell the same story.'

'I did not mean speak in private. Beside, I believe you owe me something, Inspector. One might say I saved your life.'

Webb sighs. 'You might say that, sir. I did not.'

Cotton takes another sip of tea.

'You may come,' says Webb, 'and stay in the carriage with Watkins, in case you can help with the girl.'

'Thank you, Inspector.'

'Do not thank me, Mr. Cotton. I merely think I had better keep a close eye on you. You seem to be a veritable magnet for trouble.'

CHAPTER FORTY-NINE

Decimus Webb rings the doorbell at the house in Doughty Street. He can hear it echoing in the kitchen and hallway, but there is no sound of footsteps on the stairs, no servant to greet him. He steps back and looks up at the front of the house; all of the curtains are drawn.

He tries the bell again. But there is no reply.

He walks back down to the cab, which sits waiting by the kerb, and beckons both Watkins and Cotton to step out.

'Sergeant, you ask next door, see if there's been any trouble, or if she's gone off somewhere. You, Mr. Cotton, come with me.'

'Should I stay?' mutters the driver of the cab, looking down at the trio, conscious he has not been paid.

'If you would,' replies Webb.

The cabman takes out his pipe, and lights it.

'Do you suspect some mischief?' asks Cotton.

'I do not know, sir. I don't suppose there is something you are not telling me?' says Webb.

Henry Cotton does not have time to refute this suggestion, as both men notice the front door of the house being abruptly opened. Behind it is Mrs. Harris, dressed in a smart mourning dress of black velveteen;

her hair is tied back in a black silk band, and jet earrings compliment her face. She looks more composed than on Webb's previous visit, and the calmness with which she addresses them is almost peculiar in itself.

'Ah, Inspector. And, why, it is Mr. Phibbs, is it not?'

Henry Cotton nods a little nervously. Webb gives him a sideways look.

'Would you like to come in?' asks Mrs. Harris.

The inspector nods, advancing back up the steps, and, uncertain what to do with Henry Cotton, beckons him to follow.

Mrs. Harris leads the pair of them into the downstairs parlour, and bids them to sit down, arranging her crinoline over the chaise longue as she seats herself.

'I'd rather stand, if you don't mind, ma'am,' replies Webb. 'I have some news for you.'

'It concerns my husband, does it not? He is dead, then?'

Webb looks a little taken aback. 'How did you know, ma'am? Did someone speak to you last night?'

'I had hoped he might be, that is all.'

'Hoped?' says Cotton, involuntarily blurting out the question.

'You heard me correctly, sir. In any case, I am afraid, if you wished to see my husband, you are clearly too late.'

Cotton can think of no appropriate words to answer her.

'Mr. Phibbs is here with me, ma'am,' interjects Webb, 'and I will explain the reason later, if I may? Indeed, I am sorry, ma'am, but I share his sentiment. You wished your husband dead?'

'You are married, I believe, Inspector?'

'No, ma'am.'

'Well, then you cannot imagine what sacrifices I

284

made for that man, Inspector. That worthless, rotten imitation of a man.'

Webb frowns, but continues, 'You are upset, ma'am. There is no pleasant way to say this, but your husband was killed, by a man named Hunt. Do you know anyone of that name?'

'Not as far as I am aware.'

'Forgive me, but you are remarkably composed.'

'I have finished grieving, Inspector.'

Webb exchanges a nervous glance with Cotton. The conversation is not proceeding as he had expected.

'Can you tell me, then, why you yourself just said you wished him dead?'

'I . . .' Here, she hesitates. The look of steely composure that marks her appearance almost falters, her hand trembling as she touches her face. But only for a moment. 'I cannot say it.'

'I fear you must, ma'am.'

'Come,' she says, getting up, walking briskly out of the room.

Mystified, the two men follow her into the hall, and upstairs; she leads them into her husband's study; its customary order is marred by the disarray of numerous notebooks and papers heaped upon his writing desk.

'I was going to take them out and burn them, but I suppose you shall want them now. I'd be grateful if you would take it all away. You are an antiquarian, are you not, Mr. Phibbs?'

Cotton nods.

'The books – the published books, I mean – ' she says, gesturing to the bookshelves, 'they are yours if you like. I should like to be rid of them.'

Webb walks over to the writing desk, and picks up one of the notebooks, left lying open at a particular page.

'Read it, if you have the stomach for such stuff, Inspector.'

Webb casts his eyes over Harris's neat script.

July 31 1863. Pleasant girl; ripe and unplucked; not as fresh as I would like, but Mrs. F. had primed her well. Conducted a <u>full</u> examination; fatter than I had expected, and her physiognomy not as pleasing as the last girl; unremarkable, excepting that she did <u>scream</u> awfully when I had her; told Mrs. F. I prefer the quiet ones, even if no-one may hear us; still, gave the girl five bob.

Henry Cotton does likewise; the two men read several similar entries, and can both see a dozen or more of such books set out upon the desk. Webb shuffles his feet, uncertain quite how to proceed with Mrs. Harris, who seems more anxious than before.

'This is why . . . ?' he says, his sentence deliberately not finished.

'You don't see, Inspector, do you? You don't see the worst of it? That man has made a fool of me for thirty years. Look,' she says, taking a particular book, showing him the open page, 'look at the names by the entries, here. Look!'

Webb looks in the margin and reads the names of Meynell and, a few weeks later, White.

'He had the pick of these soiled creatures come live in my house, Inspector. *My* house! My servants – these were the women he chose for me! What do you think of my blessed husband now?'

'Well, I am rather afraid,' says Webb, 'that I must speak to them both, ma'am, the White girl in particular.'

'You cannot, I am afraid.'

'I cannot? And why is that?'

'I dismissed them last night. Do you think I would keep them here for a moment longer, for my own amusement?'

Mrs. Harris looks a little flushed. 'Will you take it away, all of it?' she says.

Webb nods. 'We will, ma'am. Perhaps you should rest yourself.'

———

It is only when Mrs. Harris has left the room that Webb addresses Henry Cotton.

'An awful business.'

'I would never have thought it of him,' replies Cotton, still reading, incredulously, the contents of one of Harris's books.

'Hmm. You think, perhaps, Mr. Bill Hunt had the right idea?'

'I do not say that, but at least it explains what he meant, does it not? Some girl, a sister, cousin, or what-have-you, was one of these girls; he came across Harris, wanted revenge of some kind.'

'Some girl? You need to look at all the facts, my good man. It is plain who is behind this whole wretched business, from Sally Bowker onwards.'

'It is? You have the better of me, Inspector.'

'Well,' says Webb, 'rather, I should say, I have narrowed it down to one of a pair. But it is rather hard to say which one.'

CHAPTER FIFTY

CLARA WHITE WALKS along Wapping High Street. The smoke stacks of the London Docks are belching sulphurous spirals of soot-black cloud into the sky, and the heavens themselves are dark and pregnant with rain. She looks down at the small carpet-bag containing her few belongings, and cannot help but picture her mother walking the same dirty street, with two bedraggled little girls trailing behind. Indeed, the relics of her childhood are all around her, the same frowsy public houses; the slopsellers who specialise in 'souwesters' or 'norwesters', as the fancy takes them; whole fronts of buildings taken up with dirty-looking oilskins and draped lines of canvas trousers; the pawn-broker's shop by Red Lion Street, where the sign is not the three balls, but an iron globe and mariner's compasses. Even the air is familiar, spiced by the presence of the docks, a faint foreign aroma, the dust of oriental cargoes dragged into the great warehouses behind the walls; and then there is the ever-present smell of tobacco and, passing by the Black Boy, of rum and cheap gin.

She is not fond, she decides, of any of her memories; and yet somehow her feet have conspired to drag her back to the wretched place where she began.

Gravehunger Court.

She hesitates by the alley; she has not been down the muddy passage since the night her mother was found. She looks over her shoulder and walks hesitantly down it, towards the courtyard. When she was a girl, she thinks to herself, the yard seemed such a large playground; now it makes her feel hemmed in, and her very lungs feel constricted by the rank and foetid air that lingers in the place. She does not look overly long at the well; rather, she stares at her grandmother's house, the wretched pile of crumbling bricks and stucco that was once something resembling a home. As she glances upwards, it begins to rain, and, for a moment, she fancies she see someone moving by a window upon the second floor; or, at least, by the empty frame, since there is no glass to be seen there.

She hurries under the porch, and pushes against the front door, which hangs only loosely on rusting hinges.

'Halloa?'

Her voice reverberates about the house; the building seems in such disrepair that she fancies the very sound of it will shake free another piece of the plaster from the walls. She looks in the downstairs rooms; they are quite empty, stripped long ago of anything of value, down to the water-logged bare boards of the floor, the only thing that remains. It is peculiar, she thinks, how loud the river sounds in these rooms now, when there is nothing else to be heard.

Wait.

The sound of footsteps. She retraces her steps into the hallway, and shouts once more, but there is no reply. She knows the stairs are not to be trusted; she can see two or three are splintered in half, bent nails projecting from the wood where someone has attempted to prise a few loose for the timber.

But there it is again.

She tries the first step, then the second; gradually she makes her way upwards, to the first-floor landing, gingerly testing every board before she puts her full weight upon it. The wind bellows in through another of the empty casements, behind her this time, at the rear of the house, carrying the rain with it. From the landing she can look down on the black river; the boats at anchor seem to her to huddle together, tall masts nodding in silent communication. In a moment, as the breeze dies down a little, she can hear it again.

'I know you're there,' she says, shouting upwards.

She ascends the second flight more confidently; the boards are not quite so dilapidated. She looks hesitantly into each of the rooms, until she comes to what, at one time in the distant past, might have been the drawing-room of some long-forgotten merchant, overlooking the courtyard. Now it is simply an empty box, lined with peeling wall-paper, the air carrying the earthy smell of damp plaster and decay. A solitary figure is inside, standing by the window.

'Lizzie?'

'I knew it would be you,' says Lizzie Hunt, not turning to face her sister.

'Lizzie? What are you doing here? Look at me.'

Lizzie inclines her head to the doorway; even in the dim light of the room, as the rain thunders outside, Clara can see her face is wan, her eyes bloodshot, the skin around them puffed and swollen.

'What do you want?' says Lizzie. 'Come to put things right? Too late for that.'

'I didn't know you would be here. I've . . . well, I've lost my place.'

Lizzie laughs, a blurted, hysterical laugh. '"Lost your place?" A fine place it was, weren't it?'

'Lizzie, I swear, I didn't know about him, not until

yesterday when I found out . . . about what he did to you.'

'Oh, so you do now, though? Know it all, do you?'

'Alice told me something. And he kept books. His missus found 'em; they had names and everything. I saw yours.'

'My name?'

Clara nods.

'And yours?'

'No, he never touched me. Alice, though. It don't matter. His missus gave us both the push, straight off. Lizzie, why did you go with him? Was it the money?'

'Why did I go with him? Ask our blessed mother, ask her.'

'She's dead, Lizzie.'

'I know that, don't I? Why do you think he never touched you, eh? Like you was such a good little girl.'

'I don't know.'

'Because that was the arrangement.'

'I don't understand.'

'She sold me, Clarrie. Our ma, the old whore. For a home in that damn refuge and your blessed place. Took me to some damn house. They locked me up, did you know that?'

Clara White shakes her head in disbelief. 'You're raving.'

'I ain't. My own bleedin' mother served me up on a plate, like a piece of meat, to that butcher. He kept his word too, didn't he? Proper gentleman. Why do you think I went and did it?'

'What?'

'You don't understand, do you? It was me who killed her, our sainted mother.'

Clara flinches. There is such a note of satisfaction in her sister's voice.

'You can't have.'

'Well, I pushed her, anyhow,' she replies. 'That was enough.'

Clara leans against the doorway. 'I don't believe you,' she says, though the tremor in her voice belies her words.

'I thought that stuff she was taking would do it, if she had enough of it, but it didn't.'

'What stuff? The mixture, at the refuge?'

'I gave her a good bottleful. Told her what I thought of her too, then that girl came in and spoilt it.'

'Sally Bowker.'

The voice is not that of Clara, but rather Decimus Webb, who stands behind her on the landing.

'You come for me, have you?' says Lizzie, with no defiance in her voice, but rather as if the policeman were some cabman or delivery boy. 'How did you know I was here?'

'I took advice from an acquaintance,' replies the inspector, cautiously. 'You killed the Bowker girl, you admit it? Or was it Bill Hunt?'

'Bill? He wouldn't hurt a fly, not unless you got him riled. No, I told her I'd see her right if she didn't blab.'

'You gave her drinks, and the opium.'

'She was quite merry. Said she'd never seen the railway, see? It was a little jaunt, Bill's little secret place. Then I told Bill she was ill, so he went off to see if he could get her something.'

'And you strangled her?'

Lizzie Hunt shrugs.

'She couldn't hardly stand up straight, weren't hard.'

'And Arthur Harris?'

She shrugs.

'Hunt admitted it,' says Webb. 'You may as well tell the truth.'

'I told Bill what he did to me,' she says, a tear falling down her face. 'I made out it was him who'd smacked me, too. Bill went straight off and did for him. He came back all proud of himself.'

'Bill Hunt is dead.'

Lizzie Hunt does not flinch. If there is a look of regret in her eyes it does not linger too long.

'It don't matter,' she continues, looking out of the window, 'it's all ruined, ain't it? I ain't even got the babby no more.'

Webb looks puzzled, but Clara steps forward a little; she notices a streak of dark blood on the back of her sister's skirts.

'You lost it?' she asks. There is, strange to say, a hint of tenderness in her voice. For the second time, her sister brushes aside a tear.

'When Tom hit me. He didn't mean it . . .'

Her words stop as the inspector steps forward, perhaps to take hold of her; behind him she makes out the figure of Henry Cotton.

'You!' she exclaims in surprise and indignation. 'You brought him here! You nosed on Tom, didn't you, you bastard? I knew you was with 'em.'

The lassitude that previously marked Lizzie Hunt's demeanour abruptly vanishes, and, with a shout, she launches herself at Cotton as if reaching him were the object of every nerve in her body. She darts past the policeman and her sister like some vengeful Fury, her arms outstretched as if to claw at his face. Cotton, in turn, tries to step backwards, only to realise, too late, that the mouldering boards will not quite take his weight.

The rest happens so quickly, it is impossible to take it in. There is a crack of splintering wood as Cotton falls backwards, his body flying through the floor. It is not a graceful fall, however, but an explosion of dust and shattering timbers, and, in the confusion, Lizzie Hunt trips, and, in trying to right herself, is sent tumbling down the stairs, cracking the remains of the banisters like a row of matchsticks, falling twenty feet or more down the open stairwell.

And when she lands, she does not move.

EPILOGUE

Henry Cotton shifts uneasily in the chair provided for him at the back of the court-room. The pain in his leg, though bearable, is amplified by the stuffiness in the packed room. In consequence, he cannot help but wish the coroner might draw matters to a swift conclusion, so that he might finish taking his shorthand account of the proceedings. It takes, however, a good ten minutes or more for the facts of Lizzie Hunt's demise to be recounted for the last time, and for the verdict of 'accidental death' to be pronounced.

When at last the full ritual of the inquest is completed, Cotton is ushered into an ante-room by Decimus Webb. It is a slow business, since Cotton is relying upon a crutch for his broken leg. They find that Clara White is already seated there. She wears a plain black dress, and a black ribbon in her hair.

'I think,' says the inspector, 'that you might wait here for the gentlemen of the press to depart. I said as much to Miss White.'

'I intend to write my own account of the whole business,' says Cotton, *sotto voce.*

Webb smiles. 'I do not doubt it for a moment, sir. I will be back shortly.'

With this, Webb departs the room, leaving Cotton and Clara alone.

'Today has been an awful trial for you, I should imagine,' says Cotton after a long interval.

'Yes.'

'I have reached a *rapprochement* – an agreement, I should say – with my family.'

'I am happy for you.'

'It is a smaller annuity, but sufficient to live upon. You have a new position to go to?'

Clara shakes her head.

'I shall, of course,' continues Cotton, 'be taking new rooms.'

'Under your own name?'

Cotton smiles. 'Indeed. I was thinking, Clara, I have need of a reliable servant.'

Clara looks at him, startled. She says nothing, but walks to the far side of the room, her movements hurried and anxious, her body turned away from him.

'You are as bad as him,' she says, amazement in her voice.

'Who?' replies Cotton, mildly indignant at such an ungrateful response.

'Harris.'

'Come now, I meant nothing wrong.'

'Did you not?'

'No.'

Cotton stands up, and walks unsteadily to stand behind her. He puts his hand lightly on her shoulders, and gently pressures her to turn to face him.

'I would treat you,' says Cotton, leaning closer to her so that their bodies almost touch, 'as well as any man would. Better.'

She looks at him uncertainly.

'Besides,' he continues, 'who else will take you after this wretched business? It would be a fresh start, for us both.'

Clara turns away and picks up her hand-bag from the table.

'I believe the newspaper men may be gone by now,' she says.

'I doubt it,' replies Cotton.

'I need some fresh air, in any case.'

'I will come with you.'

'There is no need. I believe I can make my own way.'

'Will you think on what I said?' he asks.

'I will,' she replies, as she opens the door.

Cotton watches her step outside. The little room is, in its own way, as oppressive as the court, and he fidgets restlessly until, some quarter of an hour later, when Decimus Webb returns. It is only then that he realises Clara White is unlikely to reappear.

'I think she has gone,' remarks the Inspector, drily.

Cotton says nothing. But if he harbours any doubts on the matter, they are swiftly dispelled; for he finds, reaching inside his jacket pocket, that he is suddenly missing his wallet.

Clara White steps cautiously out on to Wapping High Street. Her exit goes quite unnoticed. She is soon in the back-alleys that lead to Ratcliffe Highway.

A half-mile further on, she examines the contents of a leather wallet, extracting a pound note and sundry pieces of change, before tossing it into the gutter.

AUTHOR'S NOTE

The Metropolitan Railway

THE WORLD'S FIRST underground railway opened on the 10th January 1863, between Farringdon Street and Paddington. *The Times* newspaper had described the scheme in 1861 as 'Utopian', comparing it to proposals for 'flying machines, warfare by balloons, tunnels under the Channel and other bold but hazardous propositions'. On the opening day, however, the newspapers were full of praise. *The Times*, in particular, stated 'the novel introduction of gas into the carriages is calculated to dispel any unpleasant feelings which passengers, especially ladies, might entertain against riding for so long a distance through a tunnel.' The gas supply was actually stored in canvas bags on the roofs of the carriages, and regularly refilled at the stations.

The Times had only one complaint: the amount of steam and smoke to which passengers were exposed whilst travelling through the tunnels. Indeed, such conditions would remain a perennial hazard for underground travellers in the age of steam, until trains were powered by electricity (beginning with the City and South London Railway in the 1890s). Nonetheless, the Metropolitan Railway proved a roaring success, extending north to Swiss Cottage, south to south Kensington, west to Hammersmith, and east to

Moorgate – all during the 1860s – then to Liverpool Street in the 1870s, and Tower Hill by 1882. The modern 'Circle Line' was created when the rival Metropolitan District Railway, forerunner of the modern District Line, also extended to Tower Hill in 1884. Other Victorian underground lines followed: the East London Railway (now the East London Line) was opened in 1876; the City and South London Railway (now the Northern Line) opened in 1890; the Waterloo and City in 1898; and the Central London Railway (Central Line) in 1900.

A Metropolitan Murder is, however, firmly set in 1864 – just twelve months after the opening of the Metropolitan Line. I must confess that this period particularly fascinated me, because the new railway was in a rather chaotic state. In 1864, Farringdon Station was still a temporary wooden structure; the tunnels had not yet been lit by gas; frantic work was taking place to extend the line to Moorgate, and to construct a new permanent station at Farringdon (the one we still use today). Also, 1864 was the year of the country's first actual 'railway murder' – on the North London Line, approaching Highbury – which had passengers entering a blood-soaked carriage, and the discovery of a comatose body discovered by the railway line.

But that, of course, is an entirely different story.

Buy *Arrow*

Order further Arrow titles from your local bookshop, or have them delivered direct to your door by Bookpost

☐ **London Dust** Lee Jackson	0 09 943999 9	£6.99
☐ **The Patient's Eyes** David Pirie	0 09 941658 1	£5.99
☐ **The Night Calls** David Pirie	0 09 941659 X	£6.99
☐ **The Fiend in Human** John MacLaughlan Gray	0 09 942145 3	£6.99
☐ **The Music of the Spheres** Elizabeth Redfern	0 09 940637 3	£6.99
☐ **Auriel Rising** Elizabeth Redfern	0 09 944322 8	£6.99
☐ **Quicksilver** Neal Stephenson	0 09 941068 0	£8.99
☐ **Q** Luther Blisset	0 09 943983 2	£7.99

Free post and packing
Overseas customers allow £2 per paperback

Phone: 01624 677237

Post: Random House Books
c/o Bookpost, PO Box 29, Douglas, Isle of Man IM99 1BQ

Fax: 01624 670923

email: bookshop@enterprise.net

Cheques (payable to Bookpost) and credit cards accepted

Prices and availability subject to change without notice.
Allow 28 days for delivery.
When placing your order, please state if you do not wish to receive any
additional information.

www.randomhouse.co.uk/arrowbooks